Fatal Frost

Center Point
Large Print

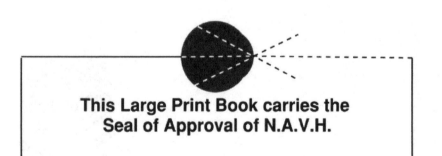
Also by Karen MacInerney and available from Center Point Large Print:

Killer Jam

Fatal Frost

A Dewberry Farm Mystery

Karen MacInerney

CENTER POINT LARGE PRINT
THORNDIKE, MAINE

ISBN: 978-1-68324-553-7

Library of Congress Cataloging-in-Publication Data

Names: MacInerney, Karen, 1970– author.
Title: Fatal frost : a Dewberry Farm mystery / Karen MacInerney.
Description: Center Point large print edition. |
    Thorndike, Maine : Center Point Large Print, 2017.
Identifiers: LCCN 2017028897 | ISBN 9781683245537
    (hardcover : alk. paper)
Subjects: LCSH: Large type books. | GSAFD: Mystery fiction.
Classification: LCC PS3613.A27254 F38 2017 | DDC 813/.6—dc23
LC record available at https://lccn.loc.gov/2017028897

Dedicated to my amazing editors:
JoVon Sotak, who gave me
the time and support I needed
(not to mention great suggestions),
and Charlotte Herscher, whose terrific
editorial eye and expert guidance
helped me bring it all together.
Thank you!

Chapter 1

When you move from the big city to the country, you don't expect crime to follow you—but sometimes, you can be wrong.

It was mid-December, and I was dreaming of being clamped into a milking machine by my mother when Chuck, my apricot rescue poodle, woke me up with a low, menacing growl. I sat up and squinted at the clock: two thirty in the morning.

"What's up, buddy?" I asked.

Instead of settling down, he waddled down the steps from the bed and stood at the bedroom door, growling like a fluffy version of Cujo.

Goose bumps rose on my arms. I listened, but didn't hear anything. Still, I had a bad feeling. Chuck didn't usually growl at nothing.

I pulled on my robe and walked through the dark farmhouse behind Chuck, who led me to the back door. I could see why he was growling: there was a light down by the creek, right by my burgeoning peach orchard. I opened the door a crack, letting a cold winter breeze swirl into the kitchen. There was the sound of metal scraping against soil. Chuck's growl intensified, and I closed the door, adrenaline pumping.

Unlike a good number of my neighbors, I didn't own a gun. Should I just let whomever it was be? On the other hand, I didn't like the idea of someone messing around in my peach orchard . . . and I didn't want someone letting my escape-artist cow, Blossom, free.

Besides, my land was my livelihood.

Chuck's growling started to swell into barking, and I hushed him, my eyes on the light. It had stopped bobbing; now it seemed to be fixed in one spot.

I could call the police, but Sheriff Rooster Kocurek and I weren't exactly on what you'd call good terms; odds of him coming out were slim to none. I could wait until morning to see what the damage was—but as I heard the sound of metal hitting wood, I worried that might be too late for my peach trees. I could practically hear my friend Quinn in my head, shouting, *"Lucy Resnick! Be sensible!"*

But "sensible" was never one of my favorite words. If it were, I never would have quit my investigative reporting job in Houston to move to Buttercup, Texas, and buy a farm.

A farm that was currently being ravaged by some unknown intruder.

I didn't have a gun, but there was a hoe just

outside the back door. Shooing Chuck away, I slipped through the door and slid into my rubber boots, then felt around until I located the hoe. I wasn't going to announce my presence, but I was going to see if I could find out what was going on in my pasture.

The chilly wind nipped at my bare knees as I padded across the yard to the gate. I unlatched it quietly, my eyes still on the light, which was moving again. My heart pounded in my chest as I stepped through the gate and closed it behind me. I was just going to find out what was up, I told myself. I wasn't going to get involved.

As I got closer, I could hear a beeping sound. I paused; a moment later, there was another scraping sound, and a thunk. After a moment, there was another one.

Someone was digging down by the creek.

On my property.

I quickened my pace, feeling violated. In addition to my peach trees, there were dewberry vines down there and all kinds of vegetation that I didn't want disturbed. Who had the nerve to dig up my creek bed?

Sure enough, the light of a flashlight showed the shadowy outline of a person with a shovel. As I hurried toward the creek, there was a clinking sound, and the person with the shovel bent down to investigate. I was close now. I held the hoe in front of me and was steps away from confronting the intruder when my boot snagged on a tree root.

I yelped and stumbled forward, dropping the hoe.

Before I could get up, the light had snapped off, leaving me in darkness. Fear and anger flooded me as I fumbled for the handle of the hoe. There was a crashing sound somewhere to my left. "Hey!" I yelled. "You're trespassing!"

The crashing stopped for a moment as I desperately felt the ground for the hoe. My arm scraped against something sharp—probably a dewberry branch—and I muttered a curse.

Chuck barked from the house, sounding distant and anxious. I scrabbled backward, still searching for the hoe.

Something exploded out of the bushes in front of me, and the glare of a flashlight blinded me. My hand closed on the hoe and I raised it to shield my head, but I wasn't fast enough. There was a searing pain in my skull, and everything went black.

It was still dark when I woke up. Chuck was snuffling at my face, whining with worry.

"How did you get out here?" I asked as I sat up, my head throbbing. The wind ripped over the pasture, slicing through my bathrobe. I was chilled to the bone.

I didn't bother with the hoe—whoever had hit me seemed to be long gone anyway—and stumbled back toward the house, shaking with cold.

The screen door had a new hole in it where Chuck had burst through—yet another thing to add to my list of repairs—but despite the door being ajar, the kitchen felt relatively warm and cozy, thanks to the wood stove.

I closed the door behind me and glanced at the clock: it was 4:00 a.m. I'd been out there for almost two hours. I stumbled to the bathroom, where I examined myself in the mirror. My long, slightly gray-streaked hair was a messy halo around my face, and there was a huge purple bump on my left temple. Very attractive. I swallowed two ibuprofen and considered getting ice, but decided I was already cold enough.

"Great way to start the Christmas season," I said to Chuck, who was sitting at my feet. Together we adjourned to the bedroom and I burrowed under the covers, trying to get warm, wondering who in the heck was digging on my land—and even more, who had hit me over the head.

I felt as if I hadn't slept at all when the alarm went off at six. I reluctantly left Chuck behind and crawled out of bed and into the kitchen to fix myself a pot of coffee.

My head was still throbbing, but when I touched the bump, it didn't seem to have gotten any bigger. As the coffee brewed, I pulled on my boots and headed out to milk Blossom. It was too dark to see what had happened down by the creek yet, but I planned to investigate as soon as it was light.

The coffee was ready by the time I got back to the farmhouse kitchen with a few eggs and two buckets of milk. I poured the milk into mason jars and tucked them into the refrigerator, then poured myself a cup of coffee and sat down by the stove with Chuck at my feet—he had finally deigned to get up—to wait for the sun to rise.

"It's an ill wind that blows nobody good," my Grandma Vogel used to say when I visited her at Dewberry Farm as a young girl. I wondered what she would think of the blue norther that had blown in with a fury just two days ago, requiring me to cover all the cold-season crops and put two extra quilts on the bed. Even after I weighed down the row covers, the wind had torn several of them up, and I still wasn't sure how many of my lettuce seedlings had frozen.

It had blown in an intruder, too, I thought grimly. Who had been digging down by the creek? And why?

I'd have to ask around at the Christmas Market tonight, I decided as I poured myself a second cup, doctoring it with a dollop of fresh cow's milk and a spoonful of vanilla sugar. Somebody would know. In the meantime, I hoped they hadn't done too much damage to my dewberry vines.

When it was bright enough to see, I tramped out the back door again, leaving Chuck curled up in front of the stove in a red-and-white argyle sweater and grumbling about the cold weather. He attracted burrs like Velcro in the summer, so I had to keep him trimmed, but now that the weather had turned chilly, I was experimenting with letting his fur grow out a bit. Unfortunately, it just made him look more sausage-like. It didn't help that his apricot fur was the color of a hot dog bun.

"Wanna go?" I asked, and he just looked at me before putting his head back down on the rug. Evidently he felt he'd already done his duty for the day. Whoever had been out last night was long gone.

As I traipsed out over the frost-rimed fields toward the creek, I felt my anger rising. Unfortunately my fears of the previous night were justified. Where my dewberry patch had thrived, there was now a field of holes, and several of the canes were pulled up or broken off. Worse yet, two of my young peach trees had been torn out by the roots, leaving gaping holes beneath them.

I kicked the trunk of a cypress tree in frustration, then wished I hadn't. I righted the peach trees the best I could, piling dirt on the roots, but they just fell over again. I'd have to come out and stake them down later. They probably wouldn't survive, but I was going to try. And whoever had done this was going to pay for it.

After leaning the hoe up against one of the saplings, I hurried back to the farmhouse and filled my mug with coffee again. The warm ceramic felt good against my icy hands. For breakfast, there was bread from the Blue Onion Tea Shop and Cafe, along with butter I'd churned myself and the spiced pear preserves I'd put up last month. And eggs, of course—not quite so many from the chickens now that it was winter, but enough for scrambled eggs a couple of times a week.

My life in the small town of Buttercup was simple, and money was tight, but I wouldn't trade it for anything. I just hoped I'd be able to make it through the year. I'd had to replace a water heater recently, and my truck had started making ominous clunking sounds. I'd drained my reserves getting the farm going, and even though I made a bit of extra income helping out at the Blue Onion cafe in town, I wasn't sure how I was going to be able to afford to fix it. And now I had two upended peach trees, a mess in the dewberry patch, and a broken screen door to add to my list. I pushed that uncomfortable thought aside and grabbed a couple of eggs from the basket in the refrigerator.

I had just poured two whisked eggs into a hot skillet when the phone rang. It was Quinn, one of my closest friends and the proprietor of the Blue Onion cafe.

"Hey, Lucy!" she said. "What are you up to this morning?"

"Well, someone dug up the creek last night. Took out most of my dewberry patch and two peach trees. Hit me over the head when I went down to investigate."

"Oh, no," she said. "Are you okay?"

"I think so," I said. "I have a goose egg, but I'm more worried about the trees."

"I hope you can save them. Were they the big ones?"

"No, I just put them in last year, but still . . ."

"I get it. You're not the only one that's happened to recently."

"No?"

"Somebody snipped the fence at the Kramers' the other day and left the pasture looking like it was hit by meteors. The cows were all over the highway; it's a miracle none of them got hit. Apparently the Bacas have had trouble, too."

"Why?"

"Some idiot looking for treasure, probably," she said. "Lots of old lore about buried gold around Buttercup. Of course, no one's ever found any, but it doesn't keep them from trying."

"Any idea who?"

"Krystal's uncle's hunted on and off for years," she said. "I guess it could be him. Speaking of

15

Krystal, she didn't show up for work again."

A cold breeze stirred in the kitchen, and I felt goose bumps on my arms. "Did you call her?" I asked.

"Yes, but her phone went straight to voice mail." She sighed. "Maybe she ran off and eloped with her mystery boyfriend."

"Maybe," I said, stirring the eggs in the pan. Like me, Krystal Jenkins had moved to town from Houston about six months ago. "Or maybe we should swing by and check on her."

"I was thinking that myself."

"Do you have enough coverage at the cafe?"

"Actually, I was hoping you could spare a few hours to help me out. I have to make about four hundred Christmas cakes by this weekend," she told me. "I've got more orders than I know what to do with, and I still need to have some for the market."

"I'd love to, but I'm scheduled to pick up goats from Peter this morning. Maybe I can drop by after I get back."

"Are you going to get your head checked out?"

"I'm going to see how it does for a day or two," I said.

"If you have any trouble at all, you get to a doctor immediately, okay?"

"Got it," I said.

"Oh—I've got some other news, too," she said. "And I don't think you'll like it."

I glanced out the window. I knew it wasn't that Blossom had escaped the pasture and headed down to eat the ornaments off the Christmas tree in the town square; after all, I'd milked her in the barn only twenty minutes ago, and it took her at least an hour to make it to town.

"Tobias's ex-wife is in town," she said.

I felt my stomach churn. Tobias was Buttercup's handsome resident vet; he and I had been dating for about six months. We hadn't seen each other as much lately. Not only was he covering for a nearby vet who was on vacation, but his practice had been expanding, and he'd been short on free time. I missed him. From what Quinn had told me, Mindy Flynn was gorgeous, successful, and charming. I wasn't sure why she and Tobias had divorced, but I knew it was still a sore spot. Could he still be carrying a torch for her?

"She got in yesterday; apparently she's here looking for a weekend home."

"Entertainment law must be lucrative," I said, looking down at the eggs in the pan. They suddenly seemed much less appealing. Tobias hadn't said anything about his ex-wife coming into town. Did he know?

"I saw her coming out of the vet hospital yesterday," Quinn added, answering my unspoken question. "I don't want to upset you, but I thought you should know."

"Thanks," I said, and we hung up, my stomach

17

feeling a bit queasy. A moment later, I dished a bit of scrambled egg into Chuck's bowl. It was a good thing I'd already taken him out, or he might have had an accident out of excitement. I put the rest of the cooked eggs in a bowl and stuck them in the fridge; after the conversation with Quinn, I'd lost my appetite.

Chapter 2

It was a short, picturesque drive to Peter Swenson's organic farm, Green Haven. His hobbit-like rammed-earth house was decorated for the season, looking warm and welcoming with red candles in the windows and a homemade cedar wreath adorning the wooden door.

Peter was out tending to his goats when I pulled up next to his fry-oil-powered truck, whose sides had been painted with a beautiful mural of his farm. He ambled over as I got out of the pickup, greeting me with a smile.

"Hey there, Lucy!"

"Hi, Peter!" I said, smiling at the lanky, bearded young man. He wore what appeared to be a hand-knitted hat and a tie-dyed sweatshirt, and his rubber boots were caked with mud.

"Hey, Lucy. What happened to you?" he asked, squinting at the lump on my temple.

"Someone was digging down by my creek last night. I interrupted him—or her—before they pulled up my whole peach orchard, but they messed up my dewberry patch and uprooted two trees."

"Messed up your head, too, it looks like," he

said, walking over and peering into my eyes. "Any headaches? Dizziness?"

"I'm fine," I said. "And don't worry; my pupils are the same size." I'd checked for the obvious signs of concussion before leaving the house.

"I'd take it easy, if I were you," he said.

"I will," I said. "As soon as I find out who did it."

"It's a small town," Peter said. "I'm sure it won't be a secret for long."

"It won't be—not if I have anything to do with it," I said. "Quinn said there are treasure hunters in Buttercup. Know any?"

"Just ask Bubba Allen, and he'll talk your ear off about the old treasure legends," he said.

"I'll ask him at the market tonight," I said.

"Will Quinn be there?"

"Of course," I said, grinning. That meant Peter would be there, too; they were smitten with each other.

"Anyway," he said, blushing, "you're here for goats, aren't you?"

"That's the theory."

"Follow me," he said.

Together, we walked over to the enclosure where the two floppy-eared goats were housed. As we approached, they poked their noses through the fence. "Hi, girls," I said in a soft voice. One was brown, and the other was mottled with a pattern of white, brown, and black patches that reminded me of a calico cat. To my delight, they came over and nuzzled my hand; one of them even licked me, then sampled the sleeve of my jacket.

"How are you going to get them home?" Peter asked, glancing back at my pickup truck.

"I was hoping you could help me figure it out." I'd been meaning to come up with a plan but had spent so much time preparing for the cold front that I hadn't gotten around to it.

"I have a few crates you can borrow," he told me.

"That would be great. They're so sweet!" I said, reaching out to touch a velvet nose. I was rewarded with a warm lick.

"This one's Hot Lips," Peter said, stroking the goat who had licked me; she was the one with the mottled coat. "The smaller brown one is Gidget."

I laughed. "Terrific names. You must have watched a lot of reruns as a kid."

"I did," he confessed, looking a bit sheepish. "Did you put extra fencing on the pasture like we talked about?"

"Just finished it last week," I said.

"If you thought Blossom was bad about getting out, wait till you see what these gals can do," he warned me. "They go through fences like water, and they *love* fresh salad. I lost two rows of lettuce last spring when they learned how to unlatch the gate."

I blinked at him. "They what?"

"They're smart," he said. "They figure things out."

"Good to know," I said, wondering what exactly I'd gotten myself into. Running Dewberry Farm was rewarding, but the learning curve was steep, and I was only just keeping up with the mortgage payments.

"It's worth it, though," he said. "By the way, I ran into Mary Jane Heimer the other day and told her you were thinking of making goat milk soap. She offered to let you come make some with her, if you're interested."

"That would be terrific," I said, "but I won't have milk for a few months!" Both goats had been bred; I wouldn't be milking them until they had their kids, in February.

"I've got some frozen—you can use that. In fact, I think it needs to be frozen if you're making soap. If you'll wait here, I'll toss it in a cooler and bring it out to you."

"Thank you so much!" As he disappeared into his house, I patted the goats some more, getting to know them. They were sweet—and from what Peter said, their kids would be even more affectionate after I bottle raised them.

Peter reappeared a few minutes later with a battered cooler. "Here you go," he said. "Say hi to Mary Jane for me." Mary Jane had lived in Buttercup her whole life and ran her farm pretty much single-handedly. If you wanted to know anything about the old way of doing things, Mary Jane was the woman to call.

"I will," I said.

"And tell her thanks for the tip on the spider mites last summer," he said.

"What did she tell you?"

"Liquid seaweed," he said. "It's weird, but it worked."

"I'll have to remember that."

"They love tomatoes," he warned me.

"How do the goats feel about tomatoes?" I asked.

"They're not as crazy about them as the mites are," he said. "But they love lettuce, so keep an eye on them."

"I've been warned."

Peter helped me get two crates and secure them in the bed of my truck. Then he propped up some plywood to make a ramp and led the goats into the crates. Gidget walked up easily, but Hot Lips seemed reluctant. "She's always been attached to me," Peter said. "I gave both of them some probiotics to help them get through the transition, but if you have trouble, give me a call. Better get her home before she hurts herself," he said, looking worried.

"Any special instructions?" I asked.

"Just follow the directions I e-mailed you," he said, "and if you have any questions, you can call me anytime. I might come out and visit them sometime, if that's okay."

I smiled. "Of course; please come out anytime. I'd love to show you what I've been doing—and get your advice on a few things, to be honest."

"Happy to help," he said, flashing me the smile that had caused many of Buttercup's teenage girls to swoon.

"I know you and Quinn have been spending a lot of time together, but how are things going out here?" I asked as I headed to the front of the truck.

"The farm's doing great," he said, surveying his domain. "I'm thinking of expanding operations."

"How so?"

"Flora Kocurek's offered to sell me some acreage. It's pretty beaten up, but I think I can rehabilitate it."

"That's terrific! Sounds like neighborly relations are improving."

"They are," he said. "Ever since her mother died, she's been starting to step out a little bit—trying to do things differently. I shared some of Molly's friendship bread with her and gave her the starter; I don't usually eat sugar, and I didn't want it to go to waste."

My friend Molly Kramer had been giving out friendship bread and starter as Christmas gifts this year, and from what I'd heard, it was a popular gift. "I haven't gotten mine yet," I said,

24

"but I'm looking forward to it. I'm glad you mentioned Flora. We had lunch together a few times in the fall." I glanced at the goats, making sure they weren't getting too anxious. "I should probably ring her again sometime soon. I know it was a tough year for her, and the holidays can be difficult sometimes." Flora's overbearing mother, Nettie Kocurek, had been murdered over the summer, and it had been a tough adjustment. Now, for the first time in her life, at the age of fifty, she was in charge of a large estate—and having to make decisions by herself.

"She seems to be doing okay," Peter said, and then his nose twitched. "Do you smell smoke?"

I sniffed. "I do," I said, turning to look for the source. "Think someone's burning a brush pile?"

"It smells too much like plastic for that," he said. "And it's close." He pointed to a billowing plume of black smoke that looked to be right on the other side of a nearby hill.

"What do you think it is?"

"A house or a car would be my guess," he said.

"I'll call the fire department," I said.

"I'm *on* the fire department," he said, sprinting toward his truck. "Call and tell them it's near Skalicky Road," he called over his shoulder. "And tell them I'm on my way."

I notified the fire department, then hesitated as Hot Lips bleated from the back of my truck. Even though the goats needed to get home, I didn't feel comfortable leaving without making sure Peter didn't need help, so after a moment's indecision, Hot Lips, Gidget, and I followed his truck up the gravel driveway and turned left onto Skalicky Road.

Within two minutes, we had arrived at the source of the black smoke.

It was a small white frame house about a hundred yards off the road. Half of it was engulfed in flames, and the fire was spreading fast. As I put the pickup in park, the gingham curtains in one of the windows began to smoke, then burst into flame.

Peter jerked the truck to a stop about thirty yards away and hurled himself out of the cab, racing to the front door of the little house. I parked and leaped out of my own truck, running in the direction of the fire. I could hear the goats bleating anxiously behind me.

"I'm going in!" he yelled. He tried the doorknob, but either the door was locked or the doorknob was too hot. He hurled a kick at the door, but it didn't open. He kicked it again harder, leaving a dent in the red-painted wood. It buckled and sprang open on the third blow, and a cloud of black smoke issued from the doorway.

"Peter!" I called as he disappeared into the billowing cloud.

There were sirens by now, but they were still in the distance. I approached the little house, frantic for something to do to help, and spotted a faucet attached to a hose. I turned the spigot and pointed the end of the hose at the doorway. A thin stream of water emerged; it sizzled and steamed as it hit the hot interior.

"Peter! Are you okay?"

There was no answer. The flames had now engulfed three-quarters of the wooden house. Should I go in after him? I stepped closer to the doorway with the hose, hoping the water would buy him at least a few extra seconds. "Peter!" I yelled.

I was about to follow him in when he appeared in the doorway, clutching a woman's body in his arms. He stumbled down the steps and laid her on the ground, then turned back.

"Peter! No!"

"There's a dog," he told me, and ran back in. He emerged just as the roof caved in, a small black puppy limp in his arms.

"Is there anyone else?" I asked as I helped him away from the fire. The woman he had rescued lay prone on the bleached winter grass, unmoving. My stomach lurched with recognition; it was Krystal, the missing waitress from the Blue Onion.

"I was too late," he said as I reached to take her pulse. Her skin was waxy and stiff under my fingers. "If I'd only come a bit earlier . . ." he said, his voice filled with guilt.

"It wouldn't have helped," I told him, feeling my skin prickle.

"What do you mean?"

"She's cold," I told him. "It wasn't the fire that killed her."

Chapter 3

"Take her to the vet," Peter said, thrusting the unconscious dog into my arms. "We can't do anything for Krystal, but this puppy's still alive."

"What about the goats?"

"They'll be okay," he said, "but this one needs medical attention. I'll stay here until help comes."

"You won't try to go in again?" I asked as another part of the roof fell in with a shower of sparks.

He shook his head grimly. "I'm just going to try to make sure it doesn't spread," he said, stamping out a coal smoldering in the tall grass.

"Be careful," I said, and hurried to the truck, where I laid the limp puppy on the front seat as Gidget and Hot Lips pounded their hooves in the crates behind me.

Tobias met me on the stone walkway in front of the Buttercup Veterinary Hospital. His face filled with concern at the sight of the little black puppy.

"Poor thing. Bring her back," he said, and I followed him inside to the exam room.

"What happened?" he asked as he took the puppy from me and laid her on the exam table, then pressed a stethoscope to the little dog's chest.

"Fire on Skalicky Road," I said. "We found Krystal Jenkins dead."

He looked up at me, startled. "That's awful. Was anyone else there?"

"I think she was alone. I mean, I hope there wasn't anyone else in there."

Tobias grimaced as he pulled back one of the puppy's eyelids. "I'm glad you got this little girl out, at least. She's pretty wheezy, though. Keep an eye on her; I'll be right back."

I kept both hands on the little body as he hurried out of the room and returned a moment later with an oxygen canister; I could feel her young lungs laboring for breath beneath my hand, and watched with trepidation as Tobias fitted a mask over her small muzzle.

"You think she'll make it?"

"I hope so," he said. "There are only a few surface burns"—he pointed out raw spots on her paws and muzzle—"but I'm guessing her airways and lungs are pretty damaged from smoke inhalation." He grimaced. "I don't like that she's unconscious, but I'm glad you brought her to me right away."

I winced.

He put an arm around my shoulder and gave me a squeeze. "I'll do what I can for her; it'll be a watch-and-wait kind of thing, I'm afraid."

"Poor baby," I said, touching her silky ear.

"She looks a little dehydrated, too; I'll set her up with some IV fluids."

"What kind of puppy is she?" I asked.

"Looks like a Lab mix," he said, stroking her head. The tenderness in his strong, calloused hands tugged at my heart.

"What can I do to help?" I asked.

"I've got appointments here for the rest of the afternoon," he said, "so I can keep an eye on her, and I'll take her home tonight and watch her there. Once she's ready to go, though, she'll probably need a lot of care."

"I'm happy to do it," I said. "I hope she'll pull through."

"It's still early to say," he said, "but I like to be optimistic." He glanced at me as he reached for a bag of saline solution. "So you were the one who found poor Krystal. She was young . . . what, twenty-five or so?"

"I think so," I said.

"So sad. I hope she didn't suffer too terribly."

"The thing is," I said, "she was already dead when the fire started, I think. She was . . . cold."

"Did you tell Rooster that?"

"I'll tell him when I see him," I said, "but you know how he is."

Tobias sighed. Neither of us had high opinions of Sheriff Rooster Kocurek.

Tobias hooked up the tubing and reached for a razor. "Watch out, Lucy."

"There's no possible way Rooster could connect me to what happened," I said. "I was at Peter's when the fire broke out, and besides, she was already long gone when we got there."

"If there's any hint of foul play, I'll bet he swings by to 'talk' to you," Tobias predicted. "Hold on to her paw for me, will you?" he asked as he deftly shaved the little puppy's front leg, then swabbed it with antiseptic before inserting the IV. I kept both hands firmly on the puppy's body, but she didn't even twitch.

"Now what?" I asked.

"I'll give her some bronchodilators; that'll help the wheezing."

"Is there anything I can do to help?"

"Let me get her through the critical time first," he said. As he examined the burns on her paws, there was a thudding sound from outside.

"One of the goats doesn't seem too happy," I said.

"You should get them home before one of them breaks a leg."

"That's all I need," I said, glancing out the window at the crates tied to the back of the truck. "I probably should drop off the goats and go back to where Krystal was found in case there are any questions."

"Be careful," Tobias warned. "And as for the

goats . . . I hope you added some new fencing."

"The guy who sold the fence to me told me water couldn't get through it," I told him, feeling confident.

"We'll see," he said, giving me a quick, distracted kiss on the forehead. "Call me when you've got them settled."

"I will," I promised, then hesitated. "The Christmas Market is tonight. Are you going?"

"Afraid not," he said. "Sorry . . . it's been so busy lately that I need to catch up on paperwork."

"I'm sorry to add to your burden with the dog," I said. It was on the tip of my tongue to ask about Mindy, but before I could speak, one of the goats started making noise. Instead, I said, "I should go."

Then I turned and walked out to the parking lot and the two bleating goats in my truck, feeling somehow deflated.

I didn't call Quinn until I'd gotten home, maneuvered the goats out of their crates, and managed to persuade them to investigate the enclosure I'd made them. Gidget went willingly, but Hot Lips was reluctant to leave the crate without Peter to encourage her. I ended up luring her out with apple chunks, a process that took a half hour and five McIntosh apples, then dialed Quinn's number.

"What do you mean, she's dead?" Quinn asked when I told her what had happened.

"I was over picking up the goats," I told her as I cradled the phone against my ear and closed the gate of the goats' new enclosure. My cow, Blossom—Tobias had told me that now that she was pregnant with her second calf, I couldn't call her a heifer, or even a first-calf heifer, anymore—had sauntered over and was watching the new arrivals with interest. "Peter smelled smoke and could tell it wasn't an agricultural fire. He took off in the truck and I followed; it turns out Krystal's house was on fire."

I heard the intake of breath. "She burned in it? What a horrible way to go!"

"No," I said. "Peter got her out before the fire got to her, but she was . . . already cold. There was a puppy in the house, too; I took her to Tobias."

"He went into the burning house?" Quinn asked. "I mean, that's totally heroic, but he's going to get himself killed!"

"He's a member of the fire department," I reminded her. "He knows what he's doing."

"Even so," she said. "I'll bet he didn't have protective gear on, or his equipment, and I just worry. I know we haven't been together long, but if something happened to him . . ."

"I know," I told her. "I feel the same way about Tobias."

"It's amazing how quickly you can fall for someone, isn't it?"

"It is," I agreed, wondering with a little twist in my stomach if perhaps I'd fallen prematurely. "But you picked a good one this time." She'd spent years fearing her abusive ex; now, Peter's kindness and gentle nature were wonderful for Quinn.

"Poor Krystal," she said. "Molly will be glad she's not influencing Brittany anymore, but I'm sure this isn't the way she would have wanted it to happen."

"What do you mean?" Brittany was Molly's oldest child, a bright teenager in high school.

"Didn't you hear?" she asked. "Molly and Krystal had a run-in at the Blue Onion the other day. She told her to keep away from Brittany, or else."

"Or else what?"

"I don't think she went into specifics. Unfortunately, half the town heard."

I groaned. "Molly never does have much restraint when she gets into mother-bear mode."

"The thing is, Krystal was young," Quinn said. "What if she didn't die of natural causes?"

"Are you thinking Rooster might try to pin it on Molly?" I shivered. "But who would have wanted Krystal dead?"

"I don't know," she said. "It's weird, though. She never said anything about a puppy."

"Unfortunately, the puppy's in pretty bad shape. She's got smoke inhalation damage and was unconscious when I left."

"That's awful," Quinn breathed. "And I still can't believe Krystal is dead. Were there any marks or anything on her?"

"No," I said, trying not to remember the young woman's pale, waxy face. "You really do think it was foul play, don't you?"

"Just a hunch," Quinn said. "She was such a nice person . . . I never would have wished anything like this on her." My friend was silent for a moment, and I watched as Hot Lips and Gidget nosed the perimeter. Already looking for weak spots.

A cold breeze swept the pasture, chilling me to the bone. "Well," I said, "I'm sure we'll know what happened soon enough. I just stopped by the farm to drop off the goats; I'm on my way back to her house now."

"You know what really makes me think it was something fishy?" Quinn asked. "If she was . . . already cold, then how did the fire start?"

"I don't know. An electrical short?" I suggested.

"Or arson," Quinn said.

"You think?"

"If you murdered someone and wanted to cover your tracks, how better than to burn the place down?"

The skin on my arms prickled. "Why wait, then?" I asked. "Wouldn't you burn the house down right away?"

"True," Quinn conceded.

"Hopefully it was a freak thing," I said, not wanting to think about the alternative. "I'd better get back there," I said, checking to make sure the gate was securely locked. Blossom was nosing the fence, and Gidget had trotted over to touch noses with her through the hog wire. I hoped they got along.

"Let me know what you find out," Quinn told me as I turned away from the goats and headed back to the truck.

"Will do."

By the time I got back to the scene of the fire, they had whisked Krystal away, but the fire truck was still parked in the driveway. Rooster was standing near the smoking remains of the wood house, an annoyed look on his fleshy face, while Peter directed a stream of water into the structure, making blackish plumes of smoke and steam. The air smelled of burning plastic. As I hopped out of the truck, the sheriff adjusted his too-tight collar, his reddish wattle jiggling.

"How's the dog?" Peter asked, almost yelling to be heard over the hose.

"Not great," I called back. "Smoke inhalation—she's unconscious—but Tobias has her on an IV and oxygen. We're keeping our fingers crossed."

Rooster swaggered over toward me, squinting at me suspiciously. "Peter says you were over in this neck of the woods when the fire started."

"I was at Peter's place, picking up some goats," I said, taking a small step back from the sheriff. He was clad, as usual, in his favorite brand of polyester pants—size 42, with extra room in the seat, which I knew from having to buy him a pair after Chuck put a hole in the sheriff's trousers last spring. "We both saw the smoke, and I followed Peter over here."

"How do you know Miz Jenkins?" he asked me.

"I've met her," I said, "but I don't—didn't—know her very well." Krystal had only worked for Quinn for a few months. The few times we'd talked, she'd been pleasant enough, but we hadn't really gotten to know each other.

"Mmm," Rooster said.

"You might want to talk to Quinn, though," I suggested, intentionally leaving out any mention of Molly. "Krystal worked at the Blue Onion. Quinn was a little worried about her when she didn't come into work."

"How many days did she miss work?"

"I don't know," I said. "Quinn would be able to tell you."

"I hear your friend Molly had a spat with

this young lady the other day," Rooster said. "Something about leaving her daughter alone or she'd do her in."

My stomach lurched. "I didn't hear that," I said, and glanced at the charred remains of the small white house. A few flames were still licking at the siding, though Peter and another firefighter were attempting to quell them. The cheerful gingham curtains had gone up in flames, and the white siding—what was left of it—was blackened. The gray-green rosemary on the front stoop, fresh and unscathed, looked incongruous next to the destruction behind it. "But I'm sure that doesn't have anything to do with this. Any idea what started the fire?" I asked Rooster.

"Can't get in to see yet," he told me. "Still on fire."

It was a valid point. The wind kicked up a little bit, cutting through my jacket, and I hugged myself. "Anything else I can help you with?" I asked Rooster.

"Not at the moment, but tell Molly I'll be wanting to talk to her," he said in a warning voice before swaggering back toward the smoldering house, where he stood looking officious in his polyester pants.

It took another fifteen minutes to fully extinguish the flames. Peter's face was grim as he and another firefighter returned the hose to the truck.

"What do you think?" I asked, glancing over toward the sheriff. Rooster was out of earshot; he had ambled over to his Crown Victoria and was making notes on a yellow pad. "Arson?"

"Hard to tell," Peter said. There was a smudge of soot on his cheek, and one cuff of his sweatshirt looked a little bit charred, but other than that, he appeared unscathed. "But I have to say it looks awfully suspicious."

"Rooster suggested Molly might be involved," I said.

"You're kidding me, right?"

"I wish I were." I eyed the burned-out house. "I guess nobody uses crime scene tape in Buttercup."

"I hadn't thought of that." He turned toward the Crown Victoria. "What should we do to close off the scene?" he called to Rooster.

"We'll just lock the gate," the sheriff responded in a surly tone.

"You're right," Peter told me. "This isn't like the city; no crime scene tape. Probably invite more interest than not, now that I think of it."

"True," I said, "although I'm sure the news is halfway across town already." I surveyed the house and the field behind it. Several little hillocks of fresh dirt were scattered around, as if there were a family of giant moles living in the pasture. "Think she was digging for buried treasure?"

"It sure doesn't look agricultural," he said.

"Is this her property?"

Peter shrugged. "I don't know who owns it. Why?"

"Just wondering," I said. "We were supposed to come and check on her tonight, you know; Quinn was worried."

He looked back at the house. "It's too bad what happened. She was awfully young."

"She was," I said, feeling my stomach wrench. If it turned out that somebody did kill Krystal, I was guessing Rooster wouldn't look any further for a suspect than he had to. "Did you know her at all?"

"We were friendly, but not close. I've heard that she and her sister lived with her uncle, Buster Jenkins, for a few years when they were teenagers."

"I knew Buster was a local, but I never knew Krystal lived with him," I said. "What happened to her parents?"

"Mom disappeared early and dad died young, from what I hear. Krystal moved back to town six months ago, and I gather she spent most of her time at that new church out on 71. The one that's picketing the Christmas Market tonight. Word of the Lord, I think it's called."

"Why on earth would a church be picketing the Christmas Market?"

"Didn't you hear? The pastor says it's too commercial."

"Isn't he the one who's going to sign a TV contract soon?"

"Ironic, isn't it?"

"It sure is. Particularly since the market's proceeds are going toward a new roof on the town hall—and to fix up Bessie Mae's house." The whole town looked after Bessie Mae, who was, as Bubba Allen once put it, a few sandwiches short of a picnic, but a lovely person nevertheless. She'd spent her life in a little house by the old train station—until recently, when she broke her hip. The hope was that the market would make enough to retrofit her little house to be wheelchair friendly.

"I know," he said. "You're preaching to the choir." He sighed and shoved his hands in the pockets of his sweatshirt, and I noticed his collar was singed. "Well, we can't do anything to help Krystal, but I hope the puppy's okay."

"I hope so, too," I said, hugging myself as a gust of wind swept over us, carrying the acrid scent of smoke with it. "I told Tobias I'd help him out as much as I could."

"Keep me posted on how she's doing," he told me. "And let me know if you have trouble with the goats."

"Will do," I said, taking a last glance at the house before retreating.

Chapter 4

I was still feeling shaken up about Krystal, but the Buttercup Christmas Market was in full swing when I arrived at seven that night. The Christmas tree in the town square sparkled with white lights, the smell of spices and candied nuts was in the air, and the Brethren choir was singing a rousing rendition of "Hark! the Herald Angels Sing." I grabbed a box of mistletoe from the back of my truck and headed into the bustling square, which was filled with shoppers from Houston and Austin, their chattering adding to the market's festive feeling.

The only blight on an otherwise perfect scene was a small but loud group of people with handmade signs who had taken up a position in front of the Buttercup Bank and were chanting, "Put Christ back in Christmas," and, "More praying, less shopping." Pastor Matheson and mayoral wannabe Ben O'Neill were at the center of the throng. Most of the picketers, I noticed, were wearing "Ben for Buttercup" buttons. Ben, a hobby rancher who had moved from Houston not long ago, had his eye on longtime mayor Rose Niederberger's seat. I wasn't quite sure what he wanted out of it—maybe he was bored in his retirement—but something about it made me nervous. I had the feeling he didn't have Buttercup's best interests at heart.

Rooster was on the scene, at least; he was decked out in his polyester uniform and stood about ten feet away from the picketers, eating a sausage sandwich. It wasn't exactly the kind of imposing police presence I had seen in Houston, but it was something. Fortunately, the sound of the Brethren choir issuing from the speakers outside the courthouse drowned out most of the noise, but I was chagrined to see Molly's daughter Brittany in the crowd of picketers, clinging to the arm of her boyfriend. As I walked through the throng, I waved to Molly; she was wheeling Bessie Mae around the market with a grim look on her face. Had Rooster talked to her already?

I said hello to Bessie Mae, who was fingering a pair of hand-knitted socks, then looked up at Molly.

"I heard you found Krystal Jenkins," she said.

"I did," I said, and she grimaced.

"It's such a tragedy, and right before Christmas. I just keep thinking of her poor mother . . ." She glanced over at the picketers, and her face hardened.

"What's wrong?" I asked.

"That," she said, stabbing her index finger

toward Brittany and her boyfriend, Bryce Matheson.

I grimaced. "Yeah, I saw."

"I wish she'd never met him," she said, her normally cheerful voice bitter. Brittany and Krystal had met working together at the Blue Onion; Krystal had brought her to Word of the Lord one Sunday, and she and the pastor's son had been inseparable ever since.

"And now there's poor Krystal. Rooster already came by to talk to me. Apparently he heard the dustup we had the other day, and thinks I might have done her in. Utter nonsense, of course."

She didn't look concerned, but I wasn't comforted by this news.

"Krystal and I had our differences," she continued, "but it's really a tragedy. She was so young! Brittany was beside herself when I told her."

"She seems to have recovered," I said, glancing at Molly's daughter.

Molly frowned as we strolled through the market together. "I know. I can't believe she's picketing the market. She's been coming to this market since she was a baby!" Molly said as Bessie Mae admired a bright-green knit cap at one of the booths. "And Flora Kocurek, too."

Toward the back of the group, Flora was standing next to a slightly hunched man in his forties: Dougie Metzger from the gas station.

I was surprised to see them; from what I remembered, Flora had been a lifelong member of Brethren Church. "When did Flora switch churches?" I asked.

"When Dougie Metzger moved over from the Lutheran church," she replied. "Her mother would be rolling over in her grave to think of her dating another German. Not that they're dating; from what I hear, he's interested in a younger woman." Nettie Kocurek had forbidden her daughter to marry her fiancé the year before because he was of German descent. It turned out he hadn't been marriage material after all, but it hadn't seemed to keep Flora from falling for another German. Even though Dougie, with his somewhat vacant eyes, wasn't exactly *GQ* material.

"I guess Brittany isn't the only one to be suckered in by a crush," Molly said.

"I'm sure what Brittany's going through is just a phase," I said. Brittany was a straight-A senior with a bright future ahead of her; she'd wanted to be a vet since she was old enough to talk. "She's a smart girl."

"I wish Krystal—and the Mathesons—had never moved to town," Molly said with feeling. "Ever since Halloween, that church—and Bryce—is all she ever talks about."

"He's the pastor's son, isn't he?" I asked.

She nodded, and her hands tightened on the

handle of the wheelchair; I could see her knuckles whiten. "This isn't how I raised her!"

"Can't you talk to her about it?" I asked.

She looked at me with an expression of helplessness. "She's threatened to leave home and move in with him."

"I thought the Word of the Lord Church frowned upon that."

"You'd think, wouldn't you?" She sighed. "Alfie and I are hoping if we just ride it out, she'll forget about him when she goes to college."

"That's still several months away," I mused.

"I know," she said, looking pained. "And she's got to graduate from high school to be able to go to college."

I glanced over at the group of picketers again. Brittany was in the front row, pink cheeked and beautiful, clutching the hand of a tall, slim boy with a shock of blond hair.

"I just can't believe my own daughter is standing in that line," Molly hissed through gritted teeth. She seemed more concerned with her daughter than with the fact that Rooster was eyeing her suspiciously from his position next to the picketers. I didn't want to mention it, though.

"She'll get past it."

"Let's hope she figures it out before it's too late," Molly said as Bessie Mae put down the hat and smiled up at her. "First Brittany gets hung up on this church boy, and now Krystal . . . it's not shaping up to be a great Christmas." Molly sighed and looked at Bessie Mae. "Ready to move on?" she asked.

The older woman nodded, blue eyes merry. It was good to see Bessie Mae; I missed seeing her at her usual post watching the trains go by at the old depot. She'd been living at a nursing home in La Grange for the last few months; I hoped the market would raise enough money to make her house accessible enough for her to move back in. I was more worried about Molly, though.

"Are you coming for dinner tomorrow night?" Molly asked me as she wheeled Bessie Mae toward the candied-nut stall. I walked beside her.

"Are you sure it wouldn't be too much?"

"To be honest, I'm hoping you can talk to Brittany. Ask Tobias, too; maybe talking to a veterinarian will re-inspire her."

"I'll check with Tobias, although you may be stuck with just me; he's covering for another vet over the holidays, so I hardly ever see him." I thought of Mindy, but didn't bring it up; Molly had enough to worry about without listening to me.

"Let's shoot for tomorrow night," she said. "If Tobias can't come, then come by yourself. I need help!"

"Tell me what to bring and I'll be there," I said, and gave her a hug. She wheeled Bessie Mae off as I turned and headed toward the Blue Onion's holiday booth, savoring the festive scent of mulled wine and candied almonds as I made my way through the crowd.

Despite the news about Krystal, Quinn was smiling as she sold another loaf of her famous Czech Christmas bread, *vánočka*, from the Blue Onion's stall, her cheeks pink under her bright-red wool hat, a few red curls framing her face. The white tent was adorned with a lit garland and red bows, and the rows of baked goods with their red ribbons and glistening packaging looked irresistible.

"How's it going?" I asked.

"I've sold thirty loaves of vánočka, and I'm going to have to restock the Christmas cakes." She nodded toward the display of candles near the register. "Your candles are a big hit, too. Putting raffia and a sprig of holly on the jars was a great idea!"

"I'm glad they're selling," I said. "Not much mistletoe left, either!" I noted. Since Thanksgiving, I'd been harvesting bunches from the oaks at Dewberry Farm and tying the sprigs with red ribbon. Quinn had hung them from a cord stretched across the front of the stall, and a good number had sold. I set the box I'd brought on top of the skirted table at the front of the stall and busied myself hanging fresh bunches.

"It's a romantic time of year," Quinn grinned,

but then the smile faded. "Except for Krystal. I keep thinking about her."

"Me too," I said. "And I'm worried about Molly."

"The whole town heard them arguing," she said, grimacing.

I told Quinn what Molly had said about her daughter and Bryce.

"Love is blind," Quinn said grimly. "I know that better than anyone. Look at the jerk I married."

"We all make mistakes when we're young. I spent three years with a starving drummer from a band called The Cream Pies."

"The Cream Pies?"

"Should have hit him with one at the first show and skipped the next three years," I said. My drummer boyfriend had been a big fan of one of the band's groupies, as it turned out. Unfortunately, I had been the last to know. "You made a good choice this time, though," I said. "Peter is amazing."

"I know." A dreamy smile drifted across her face for a moment. "But I still regret getting together with Jed. I just hope Brittany doesn't make a mistake like I did."

"Hopefully it'll pass soon," I told her as I attached another bunch of mistletoe to the cord. "Good thing I've got a lot of oak trees out at the farm. If this mistletoe keeps selling so well, maybe I'll be able to afford a Christmas bone for Chuck!"

"Don't tell Tobias," Quinn warned me, grinning.

"One bone won't kill him," I said.

"Speaking of Tobias, have you talked to him?"

"Not really," I said. "I saw him, but we were worried about the puppy. Are you and Peter spending Christmas together?" I asked, hoping to change the subject.

She blushed. "We've only been going out for a little while," she reminded me.

"It's quality, not quantity."

"Yes, but it makes Christmas kind of weird. You don't want to do too little, but also not too much." As she rearranged a stack of vánočka, Fannie Pfeffer of Fannie's Antiques came by.

"I heard you found Krystal Jenkins," she said, looking at me.

"I did," I said.

"Any word on what happened to her?" she asked.

"Not yet," I said. "Why?"

"It's funny . . . I haven't heard anything about the Jenkins family in months, and now they've come up twice in one week."

"What do you mean?"

"Her uncle called the other day and said he wanted to get a couple of coins looked at," she said.

"Has he brought them in for you to look at?"

"Not yet," she said.

"When did he call?" I asked, thinking of the digger in my backyard from the night before.

"Two days ago," she said. "Why?"

"There were holes all around Krystal's house. Plus, someone was out digging behind my house last night," I said. "Hit me over the head with something I'm guessing was a shovel."

She winced as I showed her the goose egg on my temple. "Could be Buster," she said. "Or Clyde Swartz," she said, scanning the crowd and pointing out a short, thin man with nervous eyes. "He and Buster have been competing to find Confederate gold for years." She shrugged. "He probably got lucky and turned two coins up while he was cleaning the junk pile in his backyard." She shrugged. "It takes all kinds," she said. "At any rate, I just wanted to stop by and say hello. Hope to see you in the shop!"

"I'm sure you will," I said. "I'm behind on my shopping."

Quinn looked at me as Fannie drifted away. "What are you giving Tobias for Christmas, anyway?"

"I still haven't decided," I said. "I considered knitting him a scarf, but I'd like to get him something he can use for more than a month a year. Plus, I should have started in July."

"So no plans?"

"None that we've talked about. It looks like Chuck and I will be on our own."

Quinn gave me a sympathetic look. "I'm sure things will be fine with Tobias. I know you're worried about Mindy, but there's a reason they divorced, Lucy."

"I hope so," I said, not feeling convinced. I popped a sample of bread into my mouth and turned my thoughts to my mental Christmas list.

Money was tight since I'd moved to the farm, so I'd been making gifts by hand for the last month. I'd finished knitting a soft green tea cozy for Quinn just last week, and had been making special candles and batches of fudge for my friends and neighbors. I was hoping to get a small package out to my parents tomorrow; I just had to put the finishing touches on the scarf I'd made for my mother. One thing I loved about Buttercup was that people were more likely to gift others with things they'd made than things they'd bought. Molly had promised me a loaf of friendship bread and some starter, and there were a lot of talented people in town making all kinds of wonderful crafts—many of which were on display at the market, and very tempting. Local artist Martin Shaw had made an enormous robin's-egg-blue bowl I'd had my eye on—it would make a wonderful pasta bowl—and although it was expensive, I would have bought it if my truck hadn't started making strange thumping noises. It wasn't time to treat myself, though, unfortunately. And speaking of treats . . .

"Want some *Glühwein*?" I asked Quinn.

Quinn's eyes widened. "I'd love a cup," she said.

"I'll go get us some," I said, tucking the box of mistletoe under the table. As Quinn sold another loaf of vánočka to a family from Austin, I headed over to Bubba Allen's delicious-smelling stall, watching as he ladled out cups of hot liquid.

"What can I do for you?" Bubba said, smiling at me. He usually made the best barbecue in Buttercup, but he'd traded in the smoker for a big pot of mulled wine—known as "Glühwein"—for the holiday season.

"Two Glühweins, please," I said.

"For you and Quinn?"

I smiled. "You guessed it."

"With that rabble over there, you'll need it," he said, nodding toward the picket line. He looked back at me and peered at my temple. "That's a nasty lump. What happened?"

"Someone was digging down by the creek at my place last night. I interrupted them, and they knocked me over the head."

"They attacked you on your own property?" he asked. "They're lucky you weren't carrying."

"Quinn told me the Kramers and the Bacas have had trouble, too," I said. I'd forgotten to ask Molly about that, I realized. "I heard you know

54

all about the treasure legends here—and who might be looking for it."

"Probably Buster Jenkins or Clyde Swartz."

"That's what Fannie said," I told him. "Buster called about a couple of coins the other day."

"He finally found something? I never thought I'd see the day."

"I've heard they're looking for Confederate gold, but is there a story they're working off of?"

"There is," he said, stirring the pot of mulled wine. "Apparently when the South was losing the war, General Beauregard gave a chest of gold to a trusted friend, Lieutenant Morgan, to hide away until the Confederacy rose again. Morgan was heading to Mexico with it when he was ambushed by Indians. The story is, he escaped long enough to bury the gold before he was captured."

"And this was in Buttercup?"

"That's what the story says. He buried it by Dewberry Creek and marked a tree so he could find it again."

"Then what happened?" I asked.

"He was taken captive, and escaped about six months later. But when he came back, he never could find the gold." Bubba shrugged. "Maybe someone dug it up while he was gone—or maybe it's just a story."

"Either that, or he took the cash and hightailed it to Mexico," I said.

"It was a long time ago," he said, "and as far as I know, nobody's ever found anything. But it doesn't stop them from looking."

"Maybe Buster found something after all," I mused. At least it wasn't in my backyard—or not that I knew of. Just because I'd found someone digging the night before didn't mean they hadn't been there already; I hadn't been down to the creek in a week or two. Whoever it was might have found something—without me knowing—and was now looking for more.

"Buster's my guess," he said. "A shame about his niece, Krystal. I heard you found her."

"I did," I said. "There were holes all around her house, too, like someone had been digging."

"Maybe her uncle gave her gold fever," he said.

Or maybe her uncle found something—and knocked Krystal off so he wouldn't have to share, I thought.

The Brethren Church's choir launched into "Holly Jolly Christmas" just then. As they did, the chanting from the Word of the Lord contingent grew louder.

"Look at that," Bubba said with chagrin. "And that Houston hobby rancher is smack-dab in the middle of them."

"Ben O'Neill?" I asked.

He nodded. "That O'Neill ordered so many campaign buttons you could pave the square with them. I'm wondering what's in it for him," he said. "I've seen him huddled with Faith Zapalac a few times, and that can't be good."

I felt a twinge of misgiving. Faith Zapalac was Buttercup's rather crooked real estate agent. I'd blown up a shady deal she'd been trying to make last year. Were she and O'Neill trying to put together something else?

"I have seen a lot of buttons," I said. Mostly in trash cans, but there was no denying he'd spent heavily. "Have you heard why he wants to win so badly?"

"He wants to leave his mark, I heard him say the other day."

"What kind of mark?"

"Wants to make Buttercup a tourist destination or something, I'm guessing. Probably change the name to O'Neillville while he's at it."

"Any idea what property he was thinking of buying?"

"No, and Faith ain't sayin'. I've got a bad feeling about it."

I looked over at the picketers, picking out Ben O'Neill's ruddy face. "He sounds a little like Nettie Kocurek." Before her untimely demise, Nettie had considered herself the town's aristocracy, and had treated everyone accordingly.

"At least Nettie was from here. He never set foot in this town before last year."

I wasn't strictly from here, either—then again,

I wasn't running for mayor. "He seems to be popular with the church members."

"Give enough money, and anyone is popular in that church," Bubba grumbled. "They're starting a big-bucks TV show, and they've got the nerve to come call the Christmas Market too commercial."

"I know. Kind of ironic."

He shook his head in disgust as he handed me two warm, full cups. "Gonna be broadcasting all over the country, and raking in the cash, I'm sure. I'm sorry to gripe at you; I didn't mean to go on. It just chaps me, is all."

"I get it," I said.

"Speaking of cheerful topics, I feel real bad about that young lady you found. That must have been terrible for you."

I shuddered, trying not to think of her pale, waxy face. "It was."

"Talk around town is, someone did her in and then burned the place down."

"She was definitely gone when the fire started," I said, "but I think the jury's still out on what happened."

He cut a glance at the portly sheriff. "I saw Opal a few minutes ago; she told me Rooster got an anonymous tip."

Opal womanned the front desk at the sheriff's office. "What kind of tip?"

"The caller said Molly poisoned Krystal with

friendship bread, and then torched the place to cover her tracks."

I felt my blood turn to ice. "Poisoned her with friendship bread? The autopsy isn't even done!"

"I don't think Rooster cares much about that," he said darkly. "If something did happen to that girl, I'll bet you dollars to doughnuts Molly Kramer's on the hook for it."

"I'm getting that impression, too . . . but why would she kill Krystal?"

"Bad influence on her daughter, to hear Rooster talk," he said.

"That's ridiculous," I said.

"I'm just telling you what's going around town." He shrugged. "Hopefully nothing will come of it. Now, not to change the subject, but how's farm life treating you?"

"We're still in business," I said, but my thoughts were on Krystal—and Molly, who was still wheeling Bessie Mae around the market.

"I'm glad," Bubba said. "It's good to see a Vogel back on Dewberry Farm."

"It's good to be back, even if it hasn't been the best week." I set the cups down and pulled out a ten, but he waved it away.

"Nah. This is on me; I know what it's like just getting started."

"Are you sure?"

"Of course," he said. "Tell Quinn to save me one of those vánočka breads!"

"Thanks, Bubba," I said. "Need some mistletoe?"

He grinned. "My wife might like it!"

"Come get a sprig at the Blue Onion stall and surprise her!"

"I just might do that," he said with a twinkle in his eye as I headed back to the booth with two warm cups of the spicy-smelling wine and a feeling of foreboding.

Chapter 5

"Yum," Quinn said, sipping the hot wine. "Just what I needed; it's kind of cold out here!"

"I got more than wine from Bubba's booth," I said, and relayed what he'd told me. "I have a feeling if someone doesn't come up with an alternate suspect, it's going to be tough sledding for the Kramers soon."

"Maybe her uncle did find treasure and killed her so he could keep it," she said.

"At least it's something to go on."

"And then there's her mystery boyfriend . . ."

I sighed. "We're looking for murder suspects, and we're not even sure she was murdered."

"Better safe than sorry," Quinn said. "Unless you want to count on Buttercup's finest."

I glanced over at Rooster. "You're right," I said.

"I'll ask around," she said.

"I'm supposed to have dinner at the Kramers' tomorrow," I said. "Maybe Brittany will know something."

"And I'll keep an ear out at the cafe," she said with a sigh. "I just hate all this."

"Me too," I said. We paused for a moment

as another group of shoppers eddied up to the booth. By the time they'd drifted away, we'd sold a Christmas cake and three candles.

"On another note, how are the goats?" Quinn asked.

"I've barely seen them, to be honest," I told her, taking a sip of the mulled wine. The flavor was complex: fruity, spicy, and a little bit citrusy. It warmed me from the inside out. "Ooh. This is delicious."

"Have a bite of bread to go with it," Quinn said, offering me a piece from the sample basket.

"Don't mind if I do." I bit into the vánočka. The dried fruit was a wonderful counterpart to the sweet, moist bread, and went beautifully with the Glühwein. "I think I've died and gone to heaven," I moaned.

"Just like Krystal," Quinn said in a mournful voice.

I shivered and took another sip of mulled wine. Quinn scanned the market, her eyes drifting to the pottery stall, which was doing a brisk trade.

"Do you want me to cover for a bit so you can shop?" I asked.

"Would you mind?" she asked. "I was hoping to buy my mother one of those pretty blue salt pigs, and I'm afraid Martin will sell out."

"Go for it," I said. "Browse the whole market while you're at it. Take all the time you need."

"Thanks, Lucy," Quinn said, and untied her apron. "The price list is right there. You remember how to run the register, right?"

"I've got it," I said, sitting down on the stool behind the register. "Have fun!"

No sooner had Quinn drifted into the crowd than Peter Swenson walked up to the booth, his hands in the pockets of his brown field jacket. It was the first time I'd seen him since the fire. "Quinn around?"

"She just headed out to do some shopping; she'll be back in a bit."

"Shoot . . . I was hoping to see her."

"Have you heard anything more about the fire? Or Krystal?"

His smile faded. "It looks like arson," he told me.

I felt a coldness that had nothing to do with the crisp December evening. "I was afraid of that."

"Someone emptied a gallon of gasoline inside and set it on fire."

Which meant that whatever happened to Krystal wasn't an accident. I searched the crowd for Molly. I needed to warn her. "Heard any rumors yet?" I asked.

"I have," he said. "Molly's going to be in the hot seat soon, I think."

"That's what I'm afraid of," I said. Unless I managed to find the killer, I thought.

"I've been thinking about the puppy. Who's going to take her if she makes it, do you think?" he asked.

"We'll figure that out when we get there, I guess." To be honest, I wasn't sure Chuck was up for a canine companion, and with my truck's ominous clunking getting louder by the day, I knew I couldn't afford two dogs anyway.

But Krystal—and Molly—were my main concerns right now. "I heard Krystal had a boyfriend, but no one seems to know who it is." Something told me the mystery boyfriend had a lot more to do with Krystal's death than Molly did. I was determined to find out who it was.

"I never saw anyone," he told me, "but I did see a beat-up truck in her driveway from time to time."

"What kind?"

"An old Chevy," he said. "Half blue, half rust."

"That shouldn't be too hard to find," I said.

At that moment, the sound of a "put Christ back in Christmas" chant intensified, overtaking the sweet sound of "Silent Night." Peter glanced over toward the group. "At least Mayor Niederberger put some limits on their float in the parade."

"I just hope she doesn't get ousted by O'Neill. He and the pastor seem pretty buddy-buddy."

"Maybe we should take up a collection for her campaign," he suggested. "The last thing we need is a Houston business tycoon in charge of Buttercup."

We both lapsed into silence for a moment, watching the picket line. Was one of the men Krystal's mystery boyfriend? And if so, what did he know about Krystal's death? "I keep thinking about what happened at Krystal's today," I said. "The whole thing doesn't seem right."

"The fire?"

"Yes. If it was murder, and someone was trying to cover the evidence, why wait to burn the place?" I asked.

"It's a good question," he said. "Hopefully someone in the sheriff's office will be asking the same thing."

Before I could respond, a large family drifted up to the stall, eyeing the loaves of vánočka. I handed out samples of Quinn's traditional Czech bread. The two young boys in the family were immediately hooked, and their parents bought two loaves—"One for us, and one for Grandma." Peter waited while they bought a couple of candles and a sprig of mistletoe for their front hall.

"By the way," Peter said once they'd drifted away, "how are the girls doing?"

"I've hardly had a chance to see them, to be honest. It's been a crazy day."

"Hot Lips is a sweetheart," he said with a smile.

"But she'll give you a run for your money if she ever slips out."

"Thanks for letting me have them; I know they're like your children."

"It makes it easier when I know they're going to a good home," he said. "Besides, Hot Lips and Murphy Brown didn't get along very well; I figured they'd be happier if I separated them." He sampled a bit of the vánočka Quinn had put out. "This stuff is addictive," he said when he'd swallowed it.

"I know. I'm going to need to buy elastic-waist pants if I keep eating it."

At that moment, there was a voice raised from near the picketers. I looked over; Molly and her daughter were toe-to-toe.

"Uh oh," I said. "Can you watch this for a second?"

Peter had barely agreed before I was hurrying through the crowd toward my friend and her daughter.

"This is to benefit Bessie Mae!" Molly said, pointing to the woman in the wheelchair. "What about her? That's the whole point of this market—to help her!"

"I am doing what my morals tell me to do." Brittany gripped the sign in her hand hard, her cheeks flushed. Behind her, Flora edged closer to Dougie, but Dougie didn't seem to notice.

"*Your* morals? Or your boyfriend's?" Molly

shot back. "I wish Krystal had never talked you into going to that wackadoodle church."

Shut up, Molly, I thought.

But she continued. "It's like you're . . . brain-washed. What about your future? What about college?"

"My future is my business," Brittany said, taking a step back and grabbing her boyfriend's hand. Rooster had edged closer and was looking at Molly with an expression I didn't like. "You're glad Krystal's gone, aren't you?"

"This has nothing to do with Krystal. I just want you to come to your senses," she said.

"Molly," I said, coming up behind my friend and touching her on the shoulder. "The whole town is watching."

She started, then turned and blinked at me. Then she surveyed the audience that had gathered to watch the drama. She took a deep breath, her cheeks flushed, and gave me a thin smile. "Thanks," she said, and turned to her daughter. "I'll see you at home, Brittany." She grabbed the wheelchair and swung it around so fast she almost ran over young Teena Marburger.

"Look under the flowers," Teena blurted, staring at me.

"What?" I asked.

"I don't know," she said. "I just need to tell you to look under the flowers."

The skin prickled on my arms. Teena Marburger

was known as something of a psychic around town. The last time Teena told me something, it had figured into a murder investigation. But what could flowers have to do with Krystal's death? And why tell me instead of Molly?

Speaking of Molly, she was still pushing her way through the crowd ahead of me.

"Molly," I said, jogging after her to catch up. "Are you okay?"

"I need to be alone," was all she said, but I could see the tears welling up in her eyes as she hurried away. I looked back at Brittany; Bryce's arm was around her possessively, and she was leaning into him, but her face was troubled as she darted a glance at her mother's retreating back.

Chapter 6

By the time Quinn returned to the booth, a wrapped package in one hand and a paper cone of candied almonds in the other, I had taken over the register and Peter had moved on.

"How's it going?" my friend asked as she tucked her package under the front table.

"You missed Peter," I told her. "And did you see the showdown between Molly and Brittany?"

"I ran into the shop for a few moments; I must have missed it. What happened?"

I told her about the words they had exchanged. "And the whole town—including Rooster—was right there watching."

Quinn winced. "That's all Molly needs," she said. "I'm surprised Rooster hasn't arrested her yet."

"I know," I said. "On the plus side, Peter said he'd come back in a little bit. And your Christmas cakes are selling so fast, you might have to bake another hundred this week."

"Good news and bad news, I guess. Try a few of these," she said, offering me the cone of nuts. I took two and popped them into my mouth. They were still warm, and the spicy, slightly salty sugar crust was a wonderful foil to the almonds inside.

"These are amazing," I said.

"Aren't they? It's a good thing they're only here in December."

"No kidding," I said, popping another few in my mouth. "By the way, Peter told me he saw a rusty Chevy out at Krystal's a few times."

"A rusty old Chevy truck?" Quinn asked. "Sounds like Buster Jenkins."

"It was Buster Jenkins," said a wiry man who had walked up to the booth. I recognized him as Clyde Swartz.

"How do you know that?" I asked.

"He's been digging things up all over town. Convinced he's onto Beauregard's cache."

"Isn't that illegal?" Quinn asked.

" 'Not if they don't find out' is his motto. I keep reminding him that people around these parts carry guns, but it don't stop him."

"Do you know if he had any luck?" I asked. "I heard he called Fannie's Antiques about a couple of coins he found."

"He claims to have struck gold so many times there's no telling," he said. "But if he did find any, you can be sure it wasn't on his land."

"But he didn't say anything about a recent find?"

"Not to me," he said. "I saw him day before yesterday, and he didn't breathe a word. He's been over at Krystal's place a lot, though. Poor thing."

"Were they on good terms?" I asked.

"Good as they ever were," he said. "Not a lot of family affection. He was trying to talk her into helping him out with something, I heard . . . don't know what that was all about. But if Krystal's place was on Dewberry Creek, you can bet he was out there with a shovel."

"That explains the holes dug up around her place," I said.

"At any rate, I'm just here for a sample of that famous bread of yours," he said. Quinn offered him a sample, and he took three, then kept ambling on.

"Well, we know Buster was over there, at least. Did Peter say he saw any other cars?" Quinn asked.

"He didn't mention any," I said.

"Shoot. I was hoping if he did, it might help us figure out who Krystal's boyfriend was. He gave her a necklace as a birthday present," she told me. "The day after he gave it to her, she walked into the Blue Onion looking like Cinderella after she'd met her prince."

"What kind of necklace was it?"

"It was a small blue-sapphire cross on a gold chain, and she was over the moon about it. She polished it with her shirt collar all the time."

I wished we had a jewelry store in Buttercup.

There was one in La Grange, though; it was worth seeing if anyone remembered selling a sapphire cross.

"Did she say anything that might help us figure out who he was?"

"Only that he had a hard time getting away from work. I got the impression she didn't see him as often as she liked."

"Not much to go on."

"She talked with Brittany a lot; she'd be a good person to ask. And Dougie Metzger down at the gas station—he was incredibly jealous. If anyone would know who she was seeing, it would be him."

"He was jealous of Krystal's boyfriend?" I asked, looking over at the picketers again. "I wonder what Flora thought of that."

Quinn blinked at me. "I hadn't considered that," she said. "Krystal did turn Dougie down several times—the last time just a few weeks ago. And I have heard that Flora had a crush on him."

"People do funny things around the holidays," I said. I took a sip of my Glühwein and looked out at the festive tree in the square and the cheery lights, trying to recapture the Christmas spirit. But the image of the burning house—and the look on Rooster's face when Molly was arguing with Brittany—kept swimming back into my thoughts.

• • •

The lights were still on at the Buttercup Veterinary Hospital as I drove home to Dewberry Farm an hour later. Peter had come back and kept us company during the rest of the market; he couldn't stay away from Quinn, and despite the day's tragic events, I'd never seen her so happy.

I still had to milk Blossom, but I couldn't resist stopping by to visit the puppy.

And Tobias.

I knocked lightly at the door, feeling butterflies in my stomach despite the fact that we'd been seeing each other since June.

He opened the door and gave me a weary smile.

"How is she?" I asked as I walked into the warm, antiseptic-scented hospital.

He gave me a brief kiss on the top of my head. "About the same. It'll take time."

I followed him through the waiting room to the back of the hospital, where the puppy was lying in a crate, covered in a red fleece blanket. I could hear her wheezing. Tobias opened the door to the crate, and I reached in to touch her silky head, avoiding the sores where the skin had burned.

"She's so small. You really think she's a Lab mix?"

"I do, but her paws aren't huge; I doubt she'll get too big."

The future tense was encouraging. "Is there anything I can do to help you out?"

"I'm keeping her with me until the critical period is over," he said. "After that, though, if you'd like, you could take her home in the evenings—provided Chuck doesn't object."

"He's pretty easygoing. Unless you're Rooster Kocurek." The sheriff was the only person Chuck had ever taken issue with. "By the way, I hear your ex is in town," I said in a breezy tone. At least I hoped it was breezy.

He took a deep breath. "Yes," he said. "She is."

"You didn't mention it to me," I pointed out.

"I'm sorry, Lucy. It's just . . . she just turned up two days ago. There's nothing still between us. I promise."

"She's looking for a house," I said, unable to help myself. "I thought she didn't like the country."

"She's . . . I think she's here for more reasons than one," he said.

"Oh?"

"I'm not supposed to say anything. I promise it has nothing to do with me. Or us," he said, looking at me from clear blue eyes.

I wanted to believe him. But I also knew that old passions sometimes die hard, and Mindy was nothing if not beautiful. "Okay," I said. "Sorry . . . it's just a little weird."

"I've hardly seen her since she got here,

anyway," he said with a shrug. "I spend half my time in barns and the other half chasing cows down in pastures." There was a mischievous glint in his eyes. "You've started calling Blossom a cow now, haven't you?"

"Yes, yes," I said. "Although I still think she's young enough to be a heifer."

"Greenhorn," he teased.

I grinned and stroked the puppy again, feeling slightly better—about Tobias, anyway. "She's so sweet," I said, playing with a floppy ear.

"If you do take her home, it might be best to introduce the two dogs slowly. Chuck's used to having you all to himself." He gave me a look that made my insides quiver. "Well, almost all to himself . . ."

"Lately there hasn't been a lot of competition," I reminded him.

"It's been busy," Tobias said shortly, the teasing look gone.

"Covering two practices is a challenge . . . I know." I looked down at the puppy and tried to put the whole Mindy thing aside. It was hard. And it was hard to watch the puppy laboring for breath. I looked up at Tobias. "You think she's going to get better, then?"

"I hope so," he said. "I'm doing everything I can."

I fumbled with the puppy's ear for another

moment, then stood up. "I'd better get home and check on the goats," I said.

"Thanks for stopping by," he said, his voice softer now.

"Let me know if there's any change," I told him as he followed me to the front door of the practice. I gave him a smile and pushed through the door. "Thanks for taking care of her."

"Anytime," he said, following me out. "Let me know what you find out about Krystal; I'll ask around and let you know if I hear anything."

"Thanks," I said. "See you tomorrow." He gave me a quick kiss good-bye and turned to go back inside.

The truck gave an ominous clunk as I backed out of my spot. Despite Tobias's assurances, I realized I still wasn't feeling good about Mindy.

And how, I reflected as I pulled out of the hospital parking lot, was I going to find out what happened to Krystal before Rooster clapped Molly in irons?

The lights were on in the farmhouse when I pulled up in the truck a few minutes later. There was a silver Accord parked near the fence, and I headed up to the door, confused. No one in Buttercup locked their doors, and people often just stopped by for a visit, but I didn't recognize the car, and no one had said they would be stopping by.

"Hello?" I called when I opened the door.

"Lucy!" My mother and father sat at the kitchen table, smiling at me. "Merry Christmas!"

I blinked, feeling something between surprise and shock. I couldn't imagine my mother ever coming back to Dewberry Farm. It was a Christmas miracle. At least I hoped it was a miracle; it depended on whether or not my mother behaved. "Mom! Dad! What are you doing here?"

"We thought we'd surprise you," my mother said, beaming. Chuck, who had been lounging at her feet, got up and trotted to greet me.

"You certainly succeeded," I said as my mother pulled me into a hug. She smelled like Halston, and in her tailored slacks and colorful jacket, she looked like she was ready for a board meeting at the museum where she worked as the head of fundraising. Although I was happy to see her, I felt a twinge of misgiving; she had told me I was crazy to buy the farm, and things between us were still awkward.

My mother stepped back and took a look at me. "What happened to your head?"

"I fell," I said. No need to tell her I'd been attacked, I decided. It would only make her double down on her campaign to get me to move back to Houston.

"It looks terrible. Have you had it checked?"

"It looks worse than it is. So," I said, changing

the subject, "what made you decide to come down?"

"We missed our girl," my dad said. He gave me a hug that smelled like Old Spice and wintergreen. He was in slacks and a button-down shirt as usual, and his brown eyes twinkled. "Plus, your mom was homesick for farm life."

"Ronald," my mother chided him as I bent down to rub Chuck's ears.

"Did you hear? Lucy's got a cow, Linda. You could go visit the old stalls. It'll be just like old times."

My mother gave him a playful swat, then looked around the kitchen. "I already did the rounds of the place—I hope you don't mind," she said. "It does bring back memories." She walked over to my grandmother's pie safe. "You still have this, even," she said, her hand stroking the tin panel. Although she'd grown up in Buttercup, after twenty years in Washington, DC, my mother had lost almost all trace of her Texas accent. "How's farm life treating you?"

"It's been a challenge—there's a lot to learn—but I love being here," I told her.

"The place looks terrific," my dad said. "You must have put a lot of work into it."

"There's still a lot to do, I'm afraid," I told him, thinking of the newly replaced water heater, the gardens around the house, and the fields I still hadn't reclaimed.

"There always is," my mother said. "It's a farm."

I grinned at her. "True. I'm so glad you're here. How long are you staying?"

"We were hoping to stay for Christmas," my dad said. "I hope you don't mind . . . we just missed you."

"Mind? I'm thrilled!" I was, too; particularly with things going as they were with Tobias, I hadn't been sure if I was going to have to spend Christmas alone. "I hope you'll come with me to the Christmas Market this week. I'll bet everyone would love to see you."

"I wonder how much it's changed?" my mother mused.

"We could head back tonight, if you want; it's open for another hour or so. Did you eat?" I asked.

"We stopped for dinner in La Grange," my dad said.

"Good," I said. "Can I get you guys something to drink while I take care of a few chores? I've got to go milk Blossom and check on the goats."

"When did you get goats?" my mother asked.

"Just this morning," I said. "We haven't had time to get acquainted yet, really."

"Watch out for those," my mother warned me. "They get through fences like water."

"So I've heard," I said, heading for the back door.

"I'll go with you," my mother volunteered.

"What about your shoes?" I asked, looking at her kitten heels.

"I'll go change," she told me. "We put our stuff in my old room; hope you don't mind. Got a spare pair of boots?"

"Uh . . . by the back door," I said.

"Be back in a moment," she said, leaving me in the kitchen with my dad, who was looking amused.

"Maybe she misses it more than she thinks," he suggested.

"Maybe," I said. "Has she gotten over the fact that I've left my job and moved to the country?" The news had not been received well by my mother, who had always had great aspirations for me.

"She'll come around," he said.

I hoped he was right, but I wasn't optimistic.

"Something got into your broccoli," my mother mentioned as she followed me to the barn. She'd changed into jeans and a tailored flannel shirt: the fashionable farm girl.

"I'll check it in the morning," I told her.

"Are you checking for cabbage looper and cabbage worms, too?"

I looked back at her, surprised. I knew she'd grown up here, when my grandparents owned the place, but she never talked about it; most of her life had been spent distancing herself from her childhood. I had no idea my mother had even heard of a cabbage worm. "Yes," I said. "Since when do you know about cabbage worms?"

"I know about lots of stuff," she said, squinting at the fence. "You might want to shore that up. Goats lean against everything and knock it down."

"I thought you didn't want me buying the farm," I said lightly.

"What's done is done," she said. "And you can always change your mind. Right?"

"The way the newspaper industry is going, I'm not so sure. Besides, things are really coming together here."

"Mmm," she said in a tone that indicated just the opposite. "It's hard keeping things going by yourself. What if you get sick?"

"I've got lots of friends," I replied. Of course, one of them was likely to be behind bars soon, but I decided not to mention that. "So, want to do some milking, for old time's sake?" I asked.

My mother shocked me by saying, "Why not?"

I watched in awe as she expertly chivvied Blossom into the milking parlor, swabbed down her teats, and filled a bucket. It took her half the time it took me.

"Have you bred her yet?" she asked.

"She's due in a few months," I told her. She'd spent a bit of time with the Kramers' bull at the end of the summer. I was hoping for a girl calf.

"Are you still calling her a heifer?" she asked as I strained the milk into mason jars—it cooled faster that way.

I sighed. "No, Mom." I rinsed the strainer and petted Blossom's nose affectionately.

"You know to stop milking her two months before she's due," my mother advised as Blossom stepped out of the milking parlor.

"I've been told," I said, still marveling at the font of information my mother had suddenly become. "Maybe you should have bought the farm instead of me," I joked.

"Not on your life," she said. "I worry about you, Lucy. Farming is hard work, and it's so . . . unreliable. And you're not married, so you don't have a second income."

I was starting to remember why I didn't visit home more often. "Thanks for reminding me."

"Do you have a backup plan?"

I hoped this wasn't going to be the topic of conversation till Christmas. "I'll be fine, Mom," I said. "I'm a lot happier here than in Houston."

"I hope you're right," she said darkly.

Chapter 7

My dad was in the kitchen when I got back from milking Blossom the next morning. The goats seemed to be settling in, thankfully, and Blossom seemed happy for the company. I just hoped she didn't encourage them to make a break for it.

"Did you sleep okay?" I asked as I set the milk jars down on the counter.

"Like a baby," he said. "Your mom's still down for the count."

"I'm glad," I said.

"So, are you going to tell me what happened to your head?" he asked.

"What do you mean?"

"I can always tell when you're lying," he said. "Your left eye twitches."

"It does?"

"Always has. So, what happened?"

I relayed what had happened two nights ago, and he shook his head. "Where was Chuck?"

"I left him inside."

"Lucy, next time, don't leave him inside when you go down to check on strange lights in the middle of the night. Or better yet, stay inside and call the cops."

"But they were digging up my peach trees!

83

Besides, clearly you haven't met our sheriff," I said.

"One of the Kocureks, right?"

"Just like always," I said.

He poured himself a cup of coffee and added a spoonful of sugar. "Your mom's told me about them."

"Also, I didn't want to freak Mom out when I got home, but I found a young woman dead yesterday morning. I think she was murdered, and I think the sheriff is going to pin it on a friend of mine."

"Did you tell him about the assault on your property?"

"No. It's most likely pointless, but I probably should."

He cocked an eyebrow. "You think? Why didn't you just leave the trespasser be and wait until morning to investigate?"

"I was worried about Blossom," I said. Plus, I wanted to know who it was.

"Lucy, be careful. And next time, call the cops—or someone—okay?"

"I will, Dad," I told him, and took a big sip of my coffee. Although to be honest, I didn't know what good calling the cops would do. Rooster wouldn't even answer the phone.

After we finished a big breakfast, my mother insisted on doing the dishes, so my dad and I walked down to the creek to stake the peach trees, a reluctant Chuck trotting along behind us.

Frost sparkled on the grass, and the morning was crisp and quiet. "I love the silence out here," my dad said. "Nothing but the leaves rustling."

"I know," I said. "I feel such a sense of peace out here."

"Except for two nights ago," my dad said as we got closer to the creek. "I haven't told your mom what happened. I figured I'd leave that up to you. I know she's already giving you a hard time about moving out here."

"I'll tell her," I said. "I don't want to keep secrets. She certainly doesn't keep her opinions secret from me."

"No, she doesn't," he said. "But I'm proud of you."

I looked over at him. "Really?"

"It takes a lot of guts to give up a job and follow your dream," he said.

"Thanks," I told him, feeling a flicker of pride. "I just hope I can make it work."

"That bad?"

"I had to replace the water heater last month, and now the truck's making weird noises. I should have more income from the goats in a few months, but money's pretty tight right now."

"It's hard starting a business," my dad said.

Chuck growled beside us as we got close to the place where I'd been hit. He sniffed the ground

85

intently and trotted ahead. The grass was still flattened from where I'd fallen.

"It looks like an army of moles moved in," my dad remarked.

"Large moles. With shovels." I kicked at a pile of dirt. "They really messed things up down here; with the next big rainstorm, all this will just wash into the creek."

"The holes seem to be clustered near these trees," my dad said as he plunged a stake into the ground next to one of the fallen peach trees.

"Oaks," I said.

"And one of them has a mark on it," he commented, pointing to an "X" carved into the bark. "Not recent, though. It looks like an old tree."

"Bubba Allen told me that at the end of the civil war, some lieutenant supposedly got attacked by Indians and buried a hoard of Confederate gold by Dewberry Creek," I said. "Maybe that's what whoever was down here was looking for. I thought I heard a metal detector."

"But if they found it here, it would be yours, wouldn't it?"

"Not if I didn't know they found it," I pointed out.

"Looks like they got into your pasture, too," my dad said, pointing to where the fence came down to the creek; someone had snipped through the barbed wire.

"I didn't see that," I said. "I'd better get that fixed before Blossom finds it. Thank goodness she's in the other pasture right now."

"Do you have any wire in the barn?" he asked. "I can get that taken care of for you."

"You sure?" I asked. "I thought you and Mom were going to walk down memory lane."

"We've got all the time in the world," he told me. "Don't worry about it."

Chuck sniffed around a little bit more, still growling, as we staked down the second peach tree. I used my phone to take a picture of a boot print. "Looks like a size eleven, like mine," my dad said, then followed me as I walked through the rest of the farm. Together, we adjusted the row cover and checked on the sugar snap peas. They had suffered some frost damage but looked like they'd survive. The rows of turnips and radishes were thriving, as were the pale spears of green garlic I had planted around my beds as a natural pest repellent. After harvesting some lettuce, radishes, and a stalk of green garlic for a lunchtime salad, I watered everything, checked to make sure the row cover was holding—another freeze was expected tonight—and cut a few more sprigs of mistletoe to take to the Christmas Market.

"Are the older peach trees still producing?" my dad asked, looking back at the small orchard.

"So far, so good," I said. "And hopefully the

new trees will survive now that we've staked them down. I'll have to send some of last year's peach jam home with you."

"That sounds terrific," he said. "We're supposed to have dinner with one of your mom's old high school friends in La Grange tonight. Do you want to come with us?"

"I'm supposed to go to the Kramers' for dinner, actually," I told him.

"Well, then, that works out just fine," he told me.

"And today's kind of a mess, too. I've got to go learn how to make goat milk soap, and then I'm supposed to stop by the Blue Onion and help out this afternoon."

"No worries," he told me. "I'll take care of the fence while you're gone. We don't want you to put your life on hold for us; we're going to be here for a while. Like I said, your mom wants to poke around some of her old haunts, anyway."

My mother was sitting at the table with a cup of coffee when we got back to the farmhouse. "How is everything?" she asked.

"We were just staking down some uprooted peach trees," I told her. "Someone was out digging by the creek the other night and pulled up a couple of them."

"Looking for gold, still, I'll bet."

"You know about that?" I asked.

"Oh, yes," she said. "Everyone knows about the

missing gold of the lieutenant who was heading to Mexico."

"Well, I just heard it yesterday."

"I can't believe they're still looking for it. Some things never change."

"Speaking of things never changing, I told Lucy we're going to go out and poke around today," my dad said. "She's got a full plate—and a dinner invitation tonight."

"We'll catch up tomorrow, then," she said, patting me on the arm. The smell of my mother's Halston in my grandmother's kitchen was strangely disconcerting; I was more used to the lavender scent of my grandmother. My mother looked out the window. "I still can't believe we're here. When I left, I never dreamed my daughter would move back someday."

"Circle of life, eh?" my dad said.

My mother gave him a strained smile and said nothing.

Chapter 8

Mary Jane called while I was on the way out the door; I'd decided to visit the jewelry store in La Grange and see what I could find out.

"I hear you're ready to try out soap making," she said. "You free this morning?"

"I've got a quick errand to run," I said, "but how about eleven?"

"Works for me," she said. "You have frozen milk?"

"And a bunch of oils, too," I said. I'd done my research. "I'm prepared."

"Good for you," she said. "See you then!"

I hung up the phone and climbed into the truck, hoping it would make it to La Grange and back. I was dying to know who had bought that necklace. After all, how many sapphire cross necklaces could be out there?

It was a short but noisy drive, and I said a small prayer of thanks that I made it to Jasper's Jewels intact.

The salesperson behind the counter was a thin woman in a short black dress, with dark hair swept up into a chignon, and something about the dusty red carpet and small glass cases made the store feel like it was trapped in the past. "Can I help you?" she asked.

"Yes," I said, scanning the jewelry in the cases. "I think someone bought a sapphire cross here recently. I was wondering if you could look it up and let me know who that might have been."

"We have one sapphire cross model," she said, pointing me to a case near the back, "but our clientele list is private. I'm sure you'll understand."

"But someone bought one?"

"Yes," she said. "But I'm not at liberty to divulge his name."

At least I knew it was a man. "How old was he?" I asked.

"I'm sorry, ma'am," she said. "I couldn't say."

"It may be part of a murder investigation," I said.

Her eyes widened. "I'm sorry. Unless you're here with the police," she said, casting an eye over my rather unofficial ensemble, "I'm afraid I can't help you."

I sighed. "Can you at least tell me when was it bought?"

"A few months ago, I believe," she said.

Without asking, I whipped out my phone and snapped a photo of the cross.

"What are you doing?"

"Just making sure it's the right one," I said. "Thanks . . . what was your name again?"

"Eleanor," she said.

"Eleanor," I repeated. "If you change your mind, give me a call," I said, fishing a card out of my back pocket.

"You're a farmer?" she said, peering at the card.

"I used to be an investigative reporter," I said, then waved and headed back into the cold morning. Quinn would at least be able to tell me if it was the same one, and then perhaps we could persuade Rooster to get a warrant. Or convince a pig to fly. I wasn't sure which would be easier.

I was still thinking about the sapphire cross when I pulled up to the Heimers' farm at eleven o'clock that morning, with frozen goat milk from Peter in a cooler in the back of the truck and some palm and coconut oils on the seat beside me. I felt a little guilty about spending the morning making soap when I could be looking into Krystal's death—or visiting Buster Jenkins and asking him a few pointed questions—but on the other hand, Mary Jane might know something helpful. Information sometimes came from the unlikeliest places, and Mary Jane had been in Buttercup a long time. I parked next to a sculpture of a cow that had been made out of what seemed to be a barrel, not far from the wooden farmhouse she had painted a rosy peach color.

Mary Jane and her husband had started out with

the farm as a weekend place but fully migrated to town thirty years ago, and they embraced the old ways of doing things. Mary Jane grew and canned her own produce, did most of her own repairs in and around the old outbuildings, and even smoked her own sausages in the little red smokehouse just down the hill from her old well.

As I got out of the truck, I saw Mary Jane nailing a board to the bottom of the barn. "What happened?"

"There's a rabbit family living under the barn, and Brooks keeps ripping off the boards trying to get to them," she said, hammering in a last nail and standing up. Brooks, the dog in question, came to nuzzle my knees, then sat with his head cocked, observing the proceedings.

Mary Jane wore her long gray hair in two barrettes on either side of her head, and her blue eyes were bright under wire-rimmed glasses. "I'm just about finished up out here," she said. "Will you grab that board for me? I'll just put this up, and then we'll head into the house."

I helped her put the wood and tools up in the dusty barn, then retrieved the cooler from the back of the truck and followed her into her house.

Mary Jane and her husband were both artists, which was immediately apparent when I stepped inside. Mary Jane's beautiful stained glass adorned the kitchen windows, glowing in the frosty light, and the walls were covered in oil paintings her husband, Clyde, had painted of the Buttercup landscape.

"Can I get you a cup of coffee?" Mary Jane asked as she washed her hands at the sink.

"That would be great. Thanks," I said, putting the cooler down on the floor next to the kitchen table. Mary Jane had laid out a number of wooden soap molds on the table. "These are beautiful," I said, inspecting the antique molds. "Where did you get them?"

"I picked them up for next to nothing the last day of the antique fair," she said. "I always get the best deals when the dealers are about to pack up and go home. I have a few more in the barn if you're interested."

"I might be . . . thank you!" I said as she handed me a cup of coffee.

She sat down across from me with her own cup and surveyed what I'd brought. "Looks like you've got everything," she said, nodding with approval. "Ever worked with lye before?"

"No," I said.

"I've got goggles, gloves, and an extra apron," she said.

"That bad?"

"It's not terrific," she said. "But the final product is well worth it." She grinned at me. "Let's finish up our coffee, and then we'll get started. I need to sit down for a few minutes, anyway."

As I sat in her cozy kitchen, watching a cardinal visit the bird feeder outside the window, I felt peace steal over me, despite the turmoil I'd experienced the last few days. The open shelves were colorfully painted and lined with Mexican plates and glass, and the wind battered against the greenhouse Mary Jane had appended to the kitchen. It was filled with red geraniums and poinsettias, which were blooming brightly.

"I heard you discovered Krystal Jenkins," she said.

"It was Peter, actually. I was picking up the goats when we smelled smoke," I told her. "We got to the house before it was totally gone, but Krystal was already dead."

"She was renting the place from me," Mary Jane said with a grimace. "I hate that someone doused it with gasoline, but I'm glad it wasn't something wrong with the electricity; I'd feel awful about it."

"I think someone was covering their tracks," I said.

She nodded. "I got the impression Rooster thinks Molly did her in," she said.

"I think someone did, but I'm sure it wasn't Molly. I didn't know you owned that house; have you always had it?"

"I bought it about ten years ago, hoping my daughter would move back, but she decided to go to Austin, instead. I kept it as a weekend house for a while, but she was too busy with kids to come out—and when she does, she usually comes here." She took a sip of her coffee. "Ben O'Neill actually asked about buying it about a month ago. Faith Zapalac stopped by to say he was interested."

"Did she say why he wanted it?"

"She said he thought it was a pretty piece of property, and he liked the creek access."

"But his house is miles away," I said. "Why buy acreage on Skalicky Road?"

"Who knows?" She shrugged. "Anyway, now that the house is gone, I'm thinking about giving Faith a call. I can't lease the house out anymore, and I hate thinking of what happened there, so I might as well get rid of the place."

"Was the house insured?"

"It was. It wasn't worth much, but I was fond of it. I don't really care about the house, though; I'm more upset about Krystal. She was so young."

"I know," I said. "There was a puppy in the house when we found her. Did you know she had a dog?"

She shook her head. "Poor thing. Did it die, too?"

"No, Peter got her out in time, and she's at the vet hospital. Dr. Brandt thinks she'll pull through."

"Krystal never said anything about a dog," Mary Jane said, looking perplexed. "She would have had to have a pet deposit." She sighed. "Stupid thing to think about. It doesn't matter now, does it? She's gone . . . and so's the house."

"Did you get over there much?" I asked.

"Last time I was there was a couple of weeks ago; there was a problem with the sink," she said. "She did seem jumpy, though."

"Jumpy?"

"When I knocked on the door, she only opened it a crack; she was relieved when it was me."

"Why?"

"She told me someone had been outside her window at night, and had been leaving things on the front porch in the middle of the night. She was nervous about it."

I felt my hopes rise; this was the first real lead I had. "Who was it?"

"She didn't know," she said. "But whoever it was had been leaving flowers on her doorstep at night and love notes on her car, but without a signature. If you could find out who was leaving gifts, it might be a good place to start."

"Maybe that's why she got a dog," I suggested.

"Maybe," she said.

"She had no idea who the admirer was?"

"When she dropped off the rent, she mentioned it might be Dougie Metzger, but she wasn't sure."

"Maybe Brittany Kramer knows more. They were pretty close." I'd ask tonight, when I was at the Kramers' for dinner.

"I can't believe the sheriff thinks Molly did in that young woman. Rooster doesn't know his back end from his front," Mary Jane said, getting up and reaching for the cooler I'd brought in. "But I guess it will all work out."

I wasn't so sure, so I wasn't going to leave it to chance.

"How are you doing with the goats?" she asked.

"We're getting to know each other," I said. "I'm a little worried about keeping them in, though."

"Better double-check your fence," she warned me, just like everyone else had. "I ended up electrifying mine. I swear they can chew through wire."

"The last thing I need is to have to chase down goats," I said. "This week's been tough enough."

"Sounds like it. And just before Christmas, too." She sighed. "Ah, well. Ready to make some soap?"

"I think so," I said, reaching for the goggles and gloves and giving the lye a sideways look. "Should I be scared?"

"You'll be fine," she said, tying on her old apron. "Now, let's get those oils melting, shall we?" she said.

After we weighed and measured all of our ingredients, Mary Jane dumped the oils into a pot on the stove and directed me to break the frozen goat milk into chunks with a mallet.

"Why does it have to be frozen?" I asked.

"It keeps it from heating too fast and scorching," she said. "If that happens, the batch is ruined, and you have to start over."

"Got it," I said. Once the frozen milk was in chunks, she directed me to pour it into a bowl in the sink that she'd filled halfway with ice and water. "Now," she said, "put on your goggles, let's trade places, and I'll add the lye."

I switched with her and watched as she poured in the caustic substance. We stirred our respective mixtures, waiting until they both reached the magic temperature.

As we stood together in the kitchen, I thought of the holes I'd seen outside Krystal's house.

"I noticed a bunch of holes in the ground when we found Krystal," I told Mary Jane as I stirred. "And someone was digging by my house two nights ago, too. Bubba Allen said it might be Buster Jenkins or Clyde Swartz. Do you know anything about buried treasure?"

"Bubba's right; it was more than likely Krystal's uncle," she said. "He's been digging up Buttercup for twenty years, on and off."

"Treasure hunting, I've heard. Confederate gold?"

"Oh, that old story about a Confederate lieutenant who got caught hightailing it to Mexico. Supposed to be waiting for a second uprising of the South . . . only it never came to pass." She shook her head. "There's another story, too, though."

"I haven't heard it," I said.

"Well, it's not a story everyone tells," she said. "One of the Kocureks told me once, when we were at a party, but not too many people know it. There was a man named William Keene who came to Buttercup from New Orleans. He made his fortune in shipping . . . or pirating. Whatever it was, he made enough enemies that he decided it was better for his health to retire."

"To Buttercup?" I asked.

"Yes . . . I guess it was far enough inland that he thought he'd be safe. He'd fallen in love with a woman in New Orleans, though—her name was Violette, and apparently she was known as a great beauty."

"Sounds Creole."

"I think she was a mix—quadroon, or whatever it was they called it back then. He talked her into moving with him, then came to Buttercup to get things ready. He built a house and then went back to get her, but fell ill along the way—it was winter, and there was some kind of nasty sickness going around. Anyway, before he died, he sent a letter telling her that if he didn't make it to New Orleans, she should come to Buttercup and look for a tree marked with a fleur-de-lis. He'd buried the gold he had left from his exploits under it."

"Did she come to town?"

"She did, of course, but she never found it, and left heartbroken and disappointed."

"Sad," I said. "Do you think it's true?"

"There's a copy of the letter at the library, if I recall."

"Did anyone ever find the gold?"

"No. Even though there have been crazies tramping around in the woods with metal detectors for as long as I've been here."

"Good way to get bitten by a snake," I said.

She grinned. "That's the truth. Thing is," she said, "most of the property here is owned by other folks; it's not public land. So the treasure hunters are trespassing; whatever they find generally belongs to the landowners."

"Does anyone know where he lived when he was in Buttercup?" I asked.

"He had a house somewhere along Dewberry Creek, but it's not in the records, and no one knows where he supposedly hid the gold. The house probably fell in years ago, or was moved, though; there's no telling. There are lots of old foundations around town, so it could be any one of them; there's the remains of an old homestead out behind Krystal's house, in fact. It probably got washed away during a flash flood; it was awfully close to the water."

"Do you think Krystal might have been involved in the treasure hunting?"

"I didn't check up on her," she said. "Maybe I

should have, though. She probably let Buster dig on my land."

"And if they found something, he'd have a motive for getting rid of her," I mused. "In case you can't tell, I'm looking for any suspect I can find. Any suspect other than Molly, that is."

"I'm with you on that," she told me, then bent down and peered at the soap mixture. "Looks like it's about done. You have the essential oils ready?" she asked.

I pointed to the vial of lavender oil I'd gotten from the Hill Country Lavender Farm that summer.

"Let's mix them, then," she said. Mary Jane poured the milk and lye mixture into the oils. "Stir it with a spoon," she instructed me, and after I'd worn out my arm for a few minutes, Mary Jane told me I could stop and switched to a stick blender. "This is the tricky part," she told me as the blender whirred. "You have to reach what's called 'trace'—when everything is emulsified, and there aren't any streaks. The consistency should be something like cake batter, and it should be easy to pour."

"I'm glad you're here to help me figure it out," I said, watching as she pulsed the blender. Finally, she judged the time was right.

She nodded to me. "Add in your lavender oil, Lucy."

I poured in the essential oil, filling the kitchen with the wonderful scent of lavender, and we filled the prepared molds on the kitchen table. "Now we cover them with plastic wrap and a few towels to keep them from cooling too quickly," she said. "In twenty-four hours, you can cut them into bars; then let them sit somewhere dry for about a month."

"No soap for the Christmas Market, eh?"

"Not this year," she said smiling. "But now you know what to do. Easy, right?"

"Except for that whole trace thing," I said.

"You'll learn it with time," she told me. "We can do another couple of batches together if you want, until you get the hang of it," she said. "Your grandma taught me a few things when I first moved here; I'm happy to return the favor. I know she'd be thrilled you're living at Dewberry Farm again."

"How well did you know her?" I asked as we laid towels over the molds.

"I moved back here after a long time in Houston," she said, taking off her gloves, "and it was tough finding my place, but your grandmother just opened her heart to me. She taught me what she knew, too, which was quite a lot."

"Soap making?"

"That I picked up later," Mary Jane admitted. "But I learned the planting cycles, and how to make cottage cheese . . . your grandma's cottage cheese was the best. Really good in her kolaches, too."

"I remember," I said. "Sometimes, when I'm in my kitchen," I told her as I peeled off my gloves, "I almost feel like she's there with me."

"I've had that feeling a couple of times, too," she admitted, replacing her goggles with her glasses. "She was always such a warm, nurturing presence. Sometimes I feel like if I said something, she'd answer."

I smiled at her. "Me too."

The sun streaked through the stained glass windows above the kitchen sink. Although there was still a hint of lye in the air, the smell of lavender filled Mary Jane's warm kitchen, combining with a loamy scent from the greenhouse and the spicy scent of oranges and cloves from a bowl of pomanders on the window sill.

"What else did she teach you?" I asked.

She laughed. "How to cut the head off a chicken, for starters. And pluck it."

I shivered. "Haven't had to do that yet."

"Wait till you have a few chicks grow up to be roosters," she grinned. "She also taught me how to use the smokehouse."

"I haven't tried," I confessed. Although I'd hung up onions and garlic to dry in the little wooden building next to the shed, I hadn't actually attempted to use it. The walls and roof were blackened from years of use, though; I needed to give it a shot eventually.

"Tell you what," she said. "Next time we have a pig, you can come over and help me make sausages."

"Doesn't that involve . . . intestines, and stuff?"

"My dear," she grinned, "if you're going to run a farm, you're going to have to get used to things like that."

"I guess," I said, although I mentally resolved not to add pigs to the mix. I liked bacon, and I tried to get my meat from other farmers, but I wasn't sure I could bring myself to slaughter an animal I'd raised. Besides, goats were proving to be challenging enough.

"Now," she said, rubbing her hands together. "I've got chores to do this afternoon, so let's get cleaned up. I'll send the soap molds home with you."

"I'll return them after I cut the soap, tomorrow," she said.

"Don't worry about it," she told me, waving me away. "You can have these; I've got another dozen in the barn."

"Let me buy them from you, at least," I said as I helped wash out the pots.

"Consider it payback for all the wonderful things your grandma did for me," Mary Jane said with a smile. "You'll do the same for someone else one day, I'm sure."

"I hope so," I said, thinking about Krystal. She hadn't had a chance to pass anything on to anyone. Would I be able to make the farm survive long enough to pass on what I'd learned? And more importantly, I thought, would I be able to save Molly from going to jail for Krystal's death?

Chapter 9

I got to Molly's at six, with one of Quinn's Christmas cakes in hand.

My friend met me at the door, a smile on her tired-looking face. "Thanks so much for coming!" she said, pulling me into a warm hug as the family's Lab, Barkley, sniffed at my shoes. "I feel like it's been ages."

"Thanks for having me," I said. "I keep wanting to have you guys over to dinner!"

"With all the kids, it's easier if you come here," she said. "I hear your parents are in town; you should have brought them!"

"They already had plans," I told her.

"Well, come on in and have a glass of wine," she said, inviting me into her warm kitchen. Fiestaware in a rainbow of colors filled the open shelves, and the lace curtains at the window gave the room a homey feel. Homemade cedar wreaths decorated the farmhouse windows, and a red pillar candle surrounded by greenery burned in the center of the table, adding a spicy scent to the already delicious aromas wafting through the kitchen.

"It smells heavenly," I said, trying to sound

cheerful, even though I was worried sick about Molly. "What did you make?"

"King Ranch Casserole," she said.

"My favorite," I said. "Can I help with anything?"

"You can convince my daughter to dump her boyfriend," Molly joked, but there were worry lines around her eyes. She poured two glasses of red wine and sat down across the table from me.

"Still going strong?"

She nodded. "Her grades are dropping, just when she needs them the most. She's always been so driven," Molly said. "I don't know what to do." She took a big swig of wine. "I was hoping Tobias could talk to her."

"I'm sure he needs help down at the hospital," I said. "It might inspire her to work on her studies again."

"I heard his ex is in town," Molly said, raising an eyebrow. "She's pretty, too, unfortunately."

"I've heard, but I haven't met her yet."

"I hate to pile on, but Alfie saw him in the backseat of Faith Zapalac's SUV the other day. Mindy was in the front."

"So they're looking for property together," I said, feeling glum. I sighed. "Well, if I ever get around to talking to him, I'll see if he's got time for Brittany."

"I'll call him," she said. "Unless you want an excuse . . ."

"No," I said. "I'll call."

"My only worry is that Quinn needs the help. I don't want to leave her shorthanded."

"I think Quinn would understand. Plus, I could use the extra hours."

"Poor Krystal." Molly shook her head. "I feel terrible about what happened to her."

"Molly, be careful," I said. "I'm worried Rooster might try to finger you."

"I don't see how he can possibly think I murdered her just because she was friends with my daughter," she said. "I didn't like her, but I'd never kill her. I'd never kill anyone." She grimaced. "I have to admit, though . . . on some level, I'm glad she won't be in Brittany's life anymore. I just wish she'd never introduced her to that church—and Bryce Matheson."

I was about to respond when Brittany walked into the kitchen. How much had she heard? I wondered.

"Hi, Brittany," I said, putting on a smile.

"Hi," she said, shooting a frosty look in Molly's direction and walking over to the refrigerator.

"Dinner's in about twenty minutes," Molly said, "so no snacking."

"I'm just getting a drink," she said without looking at her mother.

"I'm so sorry about Krystal," I said to Brittany. She plucked a can of Diet Coke out of the refrigerator door. She was a beautiful girl, with shiny brown hair like her mom's, a slighter version of Molly's frame—and the same feisty personality. "Mom's not," she said tartly.

"That's not true," Molly said, and folded her mouth into a thin line.

Brittany didn't respond. I glanced at Molly, who suddenly announced she'd left something in the car and vacated the kitchen with a meaningful look in my direction.

"I wanted to ask you a few questions about Krystal," I told Brittany when we were alone. "If you don't mind."

She shrugged. "Like what?"

"I understand she had a boyfriend, but she never told anyone who it was."

Brittany's eyes flicked away from me for a moment; she looked uncomfortable. "She didn't tell me, either," she answered, but busied herself playing with the tab of the can.

Somehow I didn't believe that. "Are you sure?" I asked. "It could be important."

"Important? How?"

"I think someone killed her," I said quietly. "I'm trying to figure out who it was." I decided not to tell her the sheriff suspected her mother; she'd find that out soon enough.

Her eyes got big. "You mean she didn't die in the fire?"

I shook my head, then pulled the picture of the

sapphire cross up on my phone and showed it to Krystal.

"That's her necklace!" she said. "Why do you have a picture of it?"

"Her boyfriend bought it in La Grange," I said. "Are you sure she never told you his name?"

Her eyes cut away. "She didn't."

I knew she was lying. After a long moment, I said, "There was a dog there, too. Did she say anything to you about it?"

"A dog?" She looked perplexed. "She never told me she got a dog."

Strange, I thought. "Can you think of anyone who might have wanted to harm her?" I asked.

"No," she said. "I mean, I think some of the church ladies were jealous of her, but that's because she was such a free spirit. Wanda Karp couldn't stand her. Then again, she doesn't like anyone other than her best friend, Ethel. They sit around and gossip about everyone."

"Christian of them," I said dryly.

"I know, right?" she said, and for a moment I saw a spark of the old Brittany.

"Mary Jane told me someone was leaving gifts outsider her house at night. Any idea who?"

"Probably Dougie Metzger. He was ancient— almost twice her age—and I know he made her kind of nervous, hanging out at the cafe all the time."

"Did he ever threaten her?"

111

"Of course not! Flora Kocurek was jealous, of course; she kept flouncing by in poofy skirts, trying to get him to notice, but he wasn't interested in anyone but Krystal. He proposed to her one day at the cash register. She laughed it off, but I think he was serious."

"Do you think he might have hurt her when she turned him down?" I asked.

"I can't imagine him doing anything to her. I think he just thought he was going to wear her down."

I hoped she was right.

"I just don't know what happened, Ms. Resnick," Brittany said. "I wish I did. I miss her." Her eyes filled with tears.

"Oh, honey," I said, and held out my arms. I was still holding her as she wept into my shoulder when Molly came back into the kitchen.

Molly hurried over to her daughter. "Brittany. Sweetheart." I stepped back, and Brittany hesitated, then let her mother wrap her arms around her. "I'm so sorry, darling. If there's anything I can do . . ."

"It's just . . . she was my friend!" Brittany sobbed.

"I know," Molly crooned, stroking her daughter's hair.

"It's not fair." Brittany buried her head in her mother's chest. "She had her whole life in front of her."

I sat while the two embraced, feeling tears well in my own eyes. I hadn't known Krystal well, but she had seemed like a nice young woman—and Brittany was right. She'd been robbed of her life.

But—assuming she was killed, which my gut told me was the case—who had done it? A jealous Dougie Metzger? Krystal's Uncle Buster? Or her mystery boyfriend?

If only Brittany would tell me who Krystal's boyfriend was. Deny it she might, but I was almost sure that she knew.

Dinner was delicious, but uneventful. I made a suggestion that Brittany talk to Tobias about helping out at the vet hospital, but was rebuffed. Molly's four kids had homework or finals to study for, so they ate quickly and headed to their rooms, and Molly's husband, Alfie, was having trouble moving a few cows to a new pasture, so he headed out right after dinner.

As I helped Molly clean up, I noticed she still looked troubled. "You're really worried about Brittany, aren't you?" I asked.

She nodded. "I'm glad we finally connected a bit, but she seems to be completely under the sway of that boy, Bryce. She spends more time with him than with us."

"Young love," I said with a grimace.

She sighed. "I think he inherited his father's charisma, unfortunately." She handed me a bowl, and I dried it. "I also can't get Krystal out of my head. She wasn't that much older than Brittany." My friend shivered. "Her poor mother."

"I don't even know if her mother knows—or if she's alive," I said. "From what I hear, she disappeared when Brittany and her sister were little. Do you know what happened to her sister?"

"She left town years ago," Molly said. "I don't even remember her name, to be honest. You talked with Brittany?"

"Yes, for all the good it did," I said. "She didn't have much to tell me."

"She never does these days," Molly said darkly as we finished the last of the dishes.

"I'm worried about you," I told her. "Are you getting any sleep?"

"Some," she said. "But you know Christmas: it's a madhouse. Speaking of which, did I ever give you your friendship bread?"

"Half the town seems to have gotten bread from you," I said, thinking of the anonymous tip Rooster had gotten. If the bread was poisoned, just about anyone could have done it—but I knew that Rooster wouldn't bother to follow up on that. "How much did you make?" I asked.

"A dozen loaves," she said. "I've given out about ten, and I'm not done yet."

"No wonder you're tired!" I said.

She disappeared into the pantry, returning to hand me a loaf of golden bread, then dug in the fridge and gave me a Tupperware full of starter. "There's a card on the bottom with instructions," she said. "I made it with poppy seeds and a bit of lemon, but you can do all kinds of things with it."

"Thanks!" I said, lifting the loaf to my nose and taking a whiff of lemony sweetness. "I can't wait to try it. Who all did you give them to?" I asked.

"Oh, all kinds of people," she said.

"Apparently someone called Rooster and said you gave Krystal poisoned friendship bread."

"What? There was no way I'd give that girl bread," she said. "They'll figure that out soon enough."

"Unless someone doctored a loaf you gave them . . ."

"No one I gave bread to would do something like that," she said, dismissing the idea. "So, do you think Brittany will change her mind about going to work with Tobias?"

"I don't know," I said. "But I'll keep working on it."

"I'm sure it will all get worked out," Molly said.

It hadn't worked out well for Krystal, though, I thought as I headed out to my truck a few minutes later.

Chapter 10

I woke up the next morning and made a pot of coffee quietly, trying not to wake up my parents. As I sat down at the little kitchen table and watched a finch peck at the bird feeder, I reflected that although I was glad they were here, my mother was starting to get on my nerves. I knew I had disappointed her when I bought the farm, and I shared her worries about being able to make a go of it. For the most part, though, I'd made my peace with my fears and embraced my new life—and had managed to stop staying up nights wondering what I'd do if the peach crop failed, or locusts hit, or the well dried up . . .

Chuck, on the other hand, was unconcerned. Now, he relaxed on his bed in front of the wood stove as I sipped my coffee, nibbled at a piece of Quinn's vánočka, and mentally prepared myself to take care of the morning chores. The thermometer outside the window read forty-two—chilly for Texas, and cold enough that I was planning on wearing gloves. I had just grabbed the egg basket when the phone rang.

"Hello?"

"She's gone, Lucy. She left last night."

"Molly, what are you talking about?"

"Brittany," she sobbed. "She left a note on the table. I think she's eloped!"

Molly answered the door before I knocked, eyes red, face pale. She wore a fluffy bathrobe and slippers, but looked haggard. "I can't believe she's gone," she said. "She packed her clothes, took her cell phone . . ."

I followed her into the house to the kitchen, where Brittany had drunk a Diet Coke just the night before. "Can you track her on her phone?"

"She turned that function off," she said. "Too smart for her own good."

"Did you call her boyfriend's parents?"

"Of course," she said. "No one answered. I'm going to go over there. Alfie got up early and went into Houston . . . he must not have seen the note."

"I'll go with you."

"Let me talk to Ethan," she said. He was Molly's oldest boy, and only a year younger than Brittany. "He can make sure everyone gets to the bus stop. Then I'll get dressed and we can go." She reached out and grabbed my hand. "Thank you so much for coming."

"Let me look at the note while you go talk with Ethan," I said.

"It's there," she said, jabbing at a piece of loose-leaf paper on the kitchen table.

Dear Mom and Dad,
    I love you, but it's time for me to follow my own life. I'm going away with Bryce, and we're going to get married. I know you don't approve, but God tells me it's the right thing for me. I'll be in touch when I can. Don't worry about me; I'm in Jesus's hands.
Brittany.

"Jesus's hands?" I asked Molly when she came back in wearing jeans and a big sweatshirt.

"More like the devil's hands," she replied. "I can't believe she's going to marry that kid. Is it even legal? I've got to find her."

"Pastor Matheson's house first?" I asked.

"I should probably leave the shotgun at home," Molly said grimly.

"Might be a good idea," I said, as she followed me outside, the note in her hand.

The Mathesons lived in a sprawling new ranch-style house that was anything but modest.

"The rectory is nicer than the church," Molly noted as we pulled up into the driveway behind a brand-new white Ford truck. "Even if it does look like it belongs in a Houston subdivision rather than the outskirts of Buttercup."

"He does seem to be doing pretty well for himself," I agreed.

"God, I hope she's here," she said, opening her door almost before I stopped the truck.

She marched up to the front door with me in her wake and stabbed the doorbell with a finger.

When no one answered in the first five seconds, she jammed a finger into it again, then knocked. "Where are they?" she muttered.

"Probably still asleep. It's not even seven yet," I pointed out, taking in the attractive landscaping and the new limestone exterior of the builder house. Molly was right; it looked like someone had taken a house out of a ritzy Houston subdivision and plopped it down in the country. Not exactly in keeping with its quaint neighbors.

As I watched, Molly stabbed the doorbell again. I prayed Brittany was inside, but was guessing my prayers weren't going to be answered. My instinct told me she and her boyfriend were long gone.

Maybe a minute passed before I heard the thunk of a dead bolt snicking back. A sleepy-looking Phoebe Matheson peered out, looking confused.

"Can I help you?" she asked in a small, thin voice.

"I sure hope so," Molly said. "Your son ran

off with my daughter this morning. Brittany left this." She brandished the note.

The woman blinked at her. "He what?" She reached for the note and read it, then let out a sigh. "Oh, that silly boy. He is such a romantic."

"Is he here?" Molly asked in a tight voice.

"I'll go see," she said, and without inviting us in, she closed the door and locked it, leaving us marooned on the cold porch.

"Friendly," I noted, glancing at my friend. Her lips were a thin line, and her jaw was set, but what I saw more than anything was fear. "I'm sure she's fine, Molly," I said, touching her arm.

"I knew I never should have let her go to that church," she said, tears welling in her eyes. "She's throwing away her whole future."

"We'll find her. Let's take one thing at a time," I told her. "For all we know, she's here."

As I spoke, the dead bolt clicked, and the door opened. It was Phoebe again, looking remarkably placid. "He's not here, I'm afraid," she said.

Molly seemed to shrink next to me. "So they're gone."

I looked at the woman, who seemed strangely unconcerned about her son's disappearance. "Can we come in and talk about this?" I asked, a little put out she hadn't already invited us in.

"Sure," she said. "I should probably wake Pastor Matheson, too."

Pastor Matheson? My eyebrows started up

toward my hairline, but I reined them in as we followed her into the potpourri-scented front hall. "That would probably be a good idea," I said politely, running an eye over the house's interior. Crosses covered the wall of the front foyer, which featured a double-height ceiling and an enormous crystal chandelier that looked like it had been lifted from a hotel ballroom.

"Why don't you come into the kitchen while I go and wake him?" she asked, leading us through the cavernous front hall to a kitchen with a granite-topped island adrift in the middle of a sea of tile. We sat down at the pickled pine table as she disappeared into another hallway.

Molly's eyes darted around the room as if she thought Brittany might be hiding behind one of the enormous country-style platters displayed on the counter. The walls were covered with airbrushed portrait-style family photos: Pastor Matheson, Phoebe, and their two kids, Bryce and Andrew. One of those two kids had run off with my friend's daughter, though. Why did that not bother Phoebe as much as it bothered Molly? Was it the difference between having a son and a daughter? I wondered.

"Expensive house," I murmured, taking in the decorator-fresh surroundings. "I didn't know preaching paid so well."

Molly was on her phone again, sending texts to Brittany. "She's going to miss her finals," she fretted. I knew she was worried about a lot more than finals. "She's got such a bright future . . . I can't believe she's throwing it all away, and for a boy. Where can they be?"

"Molly Kramer, isn't it?"

I looked up to see Pastor Matheson, dressed in khakis and a button-down shirt, looking remarkably fresh for six forty-five in the morning. His wife trailed behind him, head slightly bowed.

"Your son ran away with my daughter," Molly announced without preamble. "I need your help finding them." She shoved the note at him.

He scanned it, then looked up at her. "You found the note this morning?"

"Yes," she said. "Does he have a cell phone you can track him on? We need to find them."

"Our children aren't allowed to have phones or computers," Phoebe said primly from behind her husband.

"Well, evidently your son has one anyway. My daughter's done nothing but text him for a month," Molly shot back.

If this was a surprise to the pastor, he didn't show it. "I'm sure they'll be back by dinner," he said, handing the note back to Molly.

"You're not worried?" Molly said. "They've eloped!"

"At least they're not intending to engage in sin," the pastor said. "And your daughter has been a very faithful member of our flock. I'm sure she'll make an excellent wife and mother."

"She'll make an excellent veterinarian," Molly spat. "She is way too young for marriage and motherhood. She's seventeen years old!"

I put my hand on her arm. "She can't get married until eighteen without your consent, Molly."

"Not in Texas, she can't," my friend said, twisting the hem of her jacket anxiously. "But I'll bet that's not the case in Arkansas or Oklahoma."

"Does he have a car?" I asked.

"No," Pastor Matheson said.

"Are both of your cars here?"

"I'm sure they are," Pastor Matheson said. "Honey, go look in the driveway, will you?"

"Of course," she said with a demure smile, and disappeared down a hallway.

"Where do you think they might go?" I asked the pastor as he pulled up a chair at the head of the table. "If they don't have a car, they can't have gone far."

Unfortunately that did not seem to be the case. "He took your Range Rover, honey," she said.

He sighed. "Young love. So impetuous."

"Impetuous? Your son kidnapped my daughter!"

"It looks like she went pretty willingly, to me," he said, glancing down at the note in Molly's hand. He turned to his wife. "How about some coffee, Phoebe?"

"Of course, Pastor," she said, and scurried to the coffeemaker. Was this the kind of marriage their son expected to have? I couldn't imagine bright, driven Brittany turning herself into a clone of Phoebe Matheson.

"So," the pastor said, leaning back in his chair. Behind him, his wife was scooping coffee into a filter, a placid smile on her face. I took a close look at her hands; they were shaking. Maybe she wasn't quite as unruffled as she seemed, I thought. "They've gone off to get married. At least they're both good Christians. They're welcome to live here when they get back," he told us. "We've got plenty of room, and I'm sure we can find Brittany some work in the church until she starts having babies."

Molly looked like he'd smacked her across the face. "You're kidding me, right? They are way too young to get married."

"We got married at seventeen, right, honey bunny?" he said, looking over his shoulder at Phoebe. "And everything worked out great."

She nodded, but I caught a flash of something like anger before her face assumed its bland expression again.

"Look," Molly said. "You may be okay with this, but I am not. As far as I'm concerned, your son has kidnapped my daughter."

"But she consented," the pastor repeated. "It's not a crime."

Molly looked like she was resisting the urge to strangle the man. "Let me put it to you plainly. You can either help me find them—pronto—or I'm going to the police."

"The police?" Phoebe put down the mug she was holding. "There's no need to involve the police."

"I'm sure we can figure this out on our own," the pastor said in a soothing voice. "Now, Mrs. Kramer . . . can I call you Molly?"

"Ms. Kramer will be fine, unless you want me calling you by your Christian name as well," my friend said in an acid voice.

He dropped the name thing. "Did your daughter say anything in the last few days about leaving?"

"Not a word," Molly said. "Did Bryce?"

"Nothing," he said, shaking his head. "He always did have an impetuous streak. But he's a good boy. I'm sure your daughter is in good hands."

Molly didn't look convinced. "Where would he go?" she asked. "Does he have a favorite place?"

He opened his hands. "He always enjoys our trips to Port Aransas," he said. "I suppose it would make a nice place for a honeymoon, even if it is a bit cold for the beach this time of year."

"At least it's in Texas," I said to Molly. "They can't get married there."

"As long as they're not living in sin!" Phoebe said as she brought a tray of coffee mugs to the table. She turned to us. "Cream or sugar?"

"Uh, yes, please," I said, still processing her last comment. What was wrong with these people? They seemed totally unconcerned that two teenagers had run off to elope.

Molly ignored the coffee offer; all she cared about was getting her daughter back. "Where did you used to go in Port Aransas?"

"We stayed in a condo down there. I doubt he'd be able to afford it, though."

"Does he have a credit card we can track?" Molly asked.

"We're a cash-only family, I'm afraid," the pastor said.

The better to embezzle church funds with? I found myself wondering. The money to afford this place must be coming from somewhere. Family money?

"Does he have cash?" Molly pressed.

"He has a savings account," he said. "And we always keep some cash on hand."

"No cell phone, no credit card . . ." Molly sighed. "No way to track them."

"Does Brittany have a card?" I asked.

"No," she said. "And she turned the tracking function off on her phone."

"She'll come back," I said. "I'm sure of it."

"I hope so," Molly said, looking defeated. She

looked up at the pastor. "You really have no idea where he might be?"

The pastor opened his hands and shrugged. "I promise, I'm as concerned as you are."

"Forgive me if I'm not convinced." Molly fished in her purse and pulled out a pen and an old receipt. She jotted her name and number down and slid it across the table to the pastor. "Call me if you hear anything—anything at all. I'm going to go talk to the police."

Phoebe drew in her breath. She looked pale.

"Do you really think that's necessary?" Pastor Matheson asked. "I'm sure they're just out on a lark."

"Yes, I think it's necessary," Molly said, pushing back her chair and standing up. "If you hear anything—anything at all—call me."

"Of course," the pastor said. "But don't you think we should . . . wait a little bit? They could be back any moment."

"No, I don't," Molly said, snatching the letter back from the table. "I'm sure we'll be in touch," she said, and marched to the door with me right behind her.

She didn't burst into tears until we'd pulled out of the driveway.

Rooster wasn't at the sheriff's office yet when we arrived. In fact, no one was at the sheriff's office yet. "What kind of police force is this?"

Molly asked, wiping her eyes. "I thought they were supposed to be on duty twenty-four seven?"

"I'm sure the phone is being forwarded," I said. "Why don't you call?"

She pulled out her cell phone and looked up the number for the sheriff's office, then dialed. It rang several times, and then I heard Rooster's faint, sleepy voice answering the phone.

"Rooster, is that you? It's Molly Kramer. I need to file a missing person report. My daughter has disappeared."

I heard his voice for a bit, then her answer.

"No, it hasn't been seventy-two hours. But she's a minor. Pastor Matheson's son has kidnapped her."

He said something indistinguishable.

"I have a note that says they've run off to elope," she said, clutching the paper in her lap.

He said something else.

"Yes, she's missing! Just because she went willingly doesn't mean this isn't a crisis. Brittany's my seventeen-year-old daughter!"

More noise from Rooster.

"I'm staying at the station until you get here, Rooster Kocurek. And if you don't help me find my daughter, I'm going to find out who your boss is and I'm going to keep calling until somebody does something."

Rooster sounded a little more agitated now, but

Molly didn't bother listening; she hung up on him and turned to me.

"Think I should call the FBI?" she asked.

"Let's deal with the locals first," I said. "Tell you what. Why don't we go get a coffee with Quinn at the Blue Onion while we wait? The office should be open by eight."

"I should go home," she said.

"Ethan's got things under control," I told her. "Besides, we'd have to turn around and come back to town as soon as you got there. Let's just go talk with Quinn. Maybe she'll have some ideas."

"You think?"

"I do," I said, and without waiting for her to respond, I started heading toward the Blue Onion.

Quinn was already in the kitchen, up to her elbows in dough, when I knocked on the back door.

"Come in!" she yelled, and we let ourselves in through the glass-paned door. Bing Crosby was crooning in the kitchen, which smelled like cinnamon and yeast.

"Brittany ran off with Bryce Matheson," Molly blurted before I closed the door behind us.

Quinn paled. "Oh, no. How do you know?"

"She left a note," Molly said, and told Quinn about our trip to the pastor's house—and Rooster's indifferent response.

"What a jerk," Quinn said. "Did she say any-thing about what she was planning to do, or where she was going?"

"They've eloped," Molly said, and burst into tears.

"Oh, Molly . . ." Quinn washed her hands, then came and gave Molly a big hug.

"We thought we'd come keep you company and have a cup of coffee until the sheriff's office opens," I said.

"You know you're welcome anytime," Quinn said as she stroked Molly's hair. "And I'm sure she's going to be fine," she told Molly. "She may be infatuated, but she still has a good head on her shoulders."

"I used to think so," Molly said, swiping at her eyes. "But now . . . I just wish she'd never met Krystal, or gone to that stupid church."

"There's got to be some way to track her down," Molly said. "Even though she's got the tracking function off, maybe there's some way the police can locate her with her cell phone."

"It's worth asking."

"But she hasn't read any of my texts," Molly said. "If she turned the phone off, they might not be able to do it."

"She's a teenager," Quinn reminded her. "She'll turn it on eventually."

"I hope you're right," Molly said as I handed her a cup of coffee and exchanged glances with

Quinn. I hoped she was right, too, and that Brittany hadn't lost all her common sense. But people in love make bad choices . . . and both Quinn and I knew from experience.

Rooster finally turned up at nine o'clock, looking like he'd spent too much time downing margaritas at Rosita's the night before.

"So, your daughter ran off with the preacher's son?" he asked as he unlocked the front door of the station. "Doesn't sound like a missing person to me."

"She's under eighteen," Molly said. We'd spent some time researching things at the Blue Onion. "We need to file a missing person report immediately and open an investigation."

He grunted and opened the door. He didn't hold it for us, which was no surprise.

"Where's Opal?" I asked.

"Called in sick," he said. "Cedar fever, she said . . . I'm guessing it's because her grandbaby's in town. Anyway, speaking of investigations, I'm glad you're here, Miz Kramer."

"Why?"

"Recognize this?" he asked, retrieving a plastic bag from his desk. Inside was a half-burned index card with a friendship bread recipe.

"Of course," she said. "That's one of my recipe cards; I gave a ton out for Christmas. Where did you get it?"

"Krystal Jenkins's house," he said, eyeing her with suspicion.

"But I never gave her a recipe card," she said.

"No? Then where'd she get it?"

"I don't know," Molly said. "What does this have to do with Brittany?"

"I figure she might be the reason you decided to do in Krystal Jenkins."

Molly blanched. "That's crazy," she said.

"There was a half-eaten loaf of poppy seed bread in what was left of the refrigerator. Only it didn't have poppy seeds in it."

"What are you saying?"

"It had some of those ground-up Jimsonweed seeds. Miz Jenkins was poisoned," he said.

"Poisoned?" Molly swallowed. "Wait. You think I poisoned Krystal Jenkins?"

Rooster fixed Molly with beady eyes. "I'll file a missing person report for your daughter," he said. "But in the meantime, I think you're going to be staying here for a while."

"What?"

"You're under arrest for the murder of Krystal Jenkins."

Chapter 11

It was almost noon by the time I walked through the door of the Blue Onion, still feeling like I'd been punched in the stomach. After Rooster arrested Molly, I'd called Alfie on his cell and headed back to the farm to do chores, hoping it would clear my head. It hadn't worked.

"Any word on Brittany?" Quinn asked.

"No," I said. "But Rooster arrested Molly."

She dropped the spoon she was holding. "No."

"Apparently the friendship bread was poisoned after all," I told her. I hung my coat up on a hook and inhaled the sweet smell of yeast and baked goods. This morning, it was little comfort.

"I can't believe it," my friend breathed, looking pale. "Why would Molly kill poor Krystal? Rooster is out of his mind."

"I know that and you know that, but I don't think it'll hold up in court," I said. "I plan to go visit that church. My parents dropped in for a surprise visit, but I'm afraid I'm not going to have much time to spend with them."

"Ouch. How are things with your mom?"

"Not too bad so far . . . but I'm more worried about the Kramers. Somebody at the church has got to know something—about Krystal, about Brittany . . . anything."

"I'll go with you," she said. "We've got to get Molly out of jail."

"We need to talk to Dougie Metzger," I said, tying on an apron.

"He's Opal's cousin, isn't he? I think he lives in a cottage behind her house."

"So odds are good the sheriff isn't going to take a close look at him," I said. I liked Opal, but I knew she'd balk at me asking questions about her cousin. "And I guess we need to go and see Buster; Mary Jane said he might have been treasure hunting. If he found something, that would give him a motive for killing Krystal." I sighed. Krystal Jenkins was turning out to be quite a cipher. If only Brittany were here, I thought, my heart twisting. Now that her mother was under arrest, there was a good chance she'd tell me what she was holding back yesterday. I prayed that she was okay. "But first we need to get through the lunch rush. What do you need help with?" I asked, trying to push my worries aside.

"Probably tables, if you don't mind." Quinn adjusted the green-and-red bandanna she'd used to corral her red curls, then lifted the lid of a pot on the stove; she'd made her famous baked potato soup. My stomach rumbled as I caught a whiff.

"Hear anything new?" I asked.

"I went out to the front this morning a few times to see if I could hear some gossip, but it's been too busy to spend much time chatting up customers," she said. "Maybe you'll have better luck."

"I'm on it," I said. I grabbed an order pad from the basket by the swinging door and was about to head to the front of the cafe when Tori pushed through the door and hustled into the kitchen.

"Oh, Lucy, thank goodness you're here," she said breathlessly, her round cheeks pink. "It's a mess out there! Everyone wants to know what happened to Krystal."

"Anyone have any ideas?" I asked.

"A faulty heater and the wages of sin are the theories I've heard so far," Tori said.

At least no one had heard about Molly's arrest. Although I knew it would be across town by dinnertime. "Wages of sin?" I asked. "What, did Krystal overcharge someone for a chicken salad sandwich?"

"Sounds biblical, doesn't it?" She sighed. "That came from one of the church ladies in the corner. Not Brethren or Lutheran. I think they go to that big old warehouse of a church where they do faith healings and stuff." Tori made a moue of distaste. "Wouldn't be surprised if they've got a snake pit in there," she said.

"Is that the table?" I asked, glancing over at

135

the corner she'd indicated. Two women in print dresses sat across from each other, backs ramrod straight, drinking tea.

"That's the one."

"Mind if I take over?"

"You're welcome to it," she said, handing me a slip of paper. "Why don't you take the rest of the tables on that side?"

"My pleasure!" After conferring with her for another moment, I stepped out to the front of the cafe.

Despite the recent tragedy, there was a happy bustle of pre-Christmas excitement in the Blue Onion. Quinn had placed a pine-wreathed candle on each of the antique tables, and garlands framed the front windows, which were filled with her Christmas cookie display. The cafe was packed with locals, most of them women, talking about holiday shopping, baking, travel plans—and, unless the Buttercup grapevine had dried up in the past twenty-four hours, the mysterious death of Krystal Jenkins.

Ben O'Neill was here this morning, I noticed, tucked into a corner table with Faith Zapalac, their heads bent over a pile of papers that looked like property listings. Why could he possibly want to buy more property? I wondered. He already owned over one hundred acres of the most beautiful land in Buttercup.

I headed over to the table with the church ladies

first. "Hello," I greeted them with a smile. "I'll be taking over as your server."

The two ladies turned to me, both with mouths that looked as if their primary hobby were sucking grapefruits. "We're waiting for our chicken salad," the shorter of the two said in a tart, prim voice.

"I'll get right on it," I told her. "I hear your church is about to be famous," I said.

The transformation was almost instantaneous; the taller woman's sour mouth turned into a dreamy smile. "Oh, yes," she said. "Pastor Matheson is going to spread the Word all through the country."

"That's terrific," I said. "When does the show start?"

"They're filming the pilot next Sunday."

"I understand you knew Krystal Jenkins from church," I said casually.

"Of course," the woman answered. "I'm the church secretary, Wanda Karp; I know everyone. This is my friend, Ethel, by the way. Ethel Froehlich."

"Nice to meet you," I said, smiling. Ethel looked as if she'd eaten something that disagreed with her; she gave me a wan smile. "Did you know Krystal well?" I asked. "We've been hoping to find her next of kin."

"She was not a godly woman," Wanda said before Ethel could answer. Although she wore a drab dress buttoned up to her chin, her highlighted hair was a spun-sugar confection she'd obviously spent quite some time creating, and she wore a heavy coat of foundation, topped off with pink lipstick. She had a 1950s mannequin-like feel to her, right down to the plasticized skin; it was a little bit disconcerting.

"It's not right to speak ill of the dead," Ethel said, looking upset. "She was a nice girl."

"You were just sweet on her," Wanda said. "You couldn't see her for what she really was."

"She was a good girl," Ethel said in a quiet voice. She looked like she was close to tears.

"Ethel had a soft spot for her," Wanda said. "Now, as Ethel said, I don't like to speak ill of the dead," she said in a tone of voice that made me suspect just the opposite, "but—"

Ethel shot her a look that made her snap her mouth shut. Before I could ask another question, the front door crashed open and a woman staggered into the Blue Onion.

"Where's Krystal?" she slurred, stumbling into a table full of ladies from the Brethren Church before falling face-first to the floor.

Chapter 12

Silence descended on the cafe. Except for Frank Sinatra, who continued crooning about angels from the little speaker by the cash register, nobody made a peep.

Wanda hissed, "I told you. She was trouble, that girl."

Her words galvanized me into action. I trotted across the cafe floor toward the fallen woman. She wore a tank top, tight jeans, and boots that were caked in mud. Her blonde hair was greasy, and she reeked of liquor. "Ma'am?" I asked, touching her shoulder.

She lifted her head. "Where is she?"

"If you're looking for Krystal," I said, "I'm afraid you won't find her here." How could I tell her Krystal was dead? I didn't know how she knew her—or what she might do if she found out Krystal had died. "Can I help you up?"

With my help, she staggered to her feet. "Where is she?" she repeated.

"How do you know Krystal?" I asked.

"She's my twin sister!" the woman announced.

Ethel let out a strangled sound behind me. I swallowed, wondering what to do. I didn't feel comfortable taking the woman outside into the cold, but I didn't want to seat her in the cafe, either; plus, she might be able to help us figure out what had happened to Krystal. After a moment's indecision, I said, "Come with me," and steered her toward the kitchen. The drunk woman leaned on me heavily as we navigated toward the swinging door. "Krystal," she moaned. "Gotta see Krystal."

We pushed into the kitchen as Quinn finished ladling baked potato soup into a bowl. She looked up, startled. "Who is that? What are you doing?"

"This is Krystal's sister," I told her as another wave of alcoholic breath broke over me. She appeared to have applied eyeliner at some point, but it had since migrated south; she looked as if she had two shiners.

"Brandi," the woman supplied.

She was appropriately named, I thought. Although the way she smelled, I thought "Whiskey" might have been closer to the mark.

"Oh," Quinn said, as the woman lurched toward the refrigerator. "Oh, my."

"She's looking for Krystal," I said.

Quinn's eyebrows rose as she figured out what I was saying. Then she leaped into action, grabbing a stool and hurrying over toward us. "Can you cover the tables again for a moment, Tori?"

"Of course," the young woman said, round eyed.

Quinn turned to Brandi. "Sit down, Brandi."

"Where is she?" she asked again when we had her sitting up, half-propped against a wall. "She said she worked here when she called. Don't know why she'd still be working as a waitress, though," she slurred, looking around the kitchen. "Said she hit the jackpot."

"Jackpot?" I asked.

"That's right," she said. "She told me she had enough to take care of both of us."

Quinn and I stared at each other. Had Krystal—maybe with the help of her uncle—found some kind of treasure after all?

Even if she had, we still had some awful news to deliver.

"She . . . your sister had an accident," Quinn said, touching her shoulder.

Brandi squinted, looking confused. "Accident?"

"Yes," Quinn said. "I'm sorry to have to be the one to tell you, but . . . your sister's passed."

The young woman blinked at her. "She what?"

"She died," Quinn said softly. "The police didn't know where to find you, or they would have notified you sooner. I'm so sorry."

"Died," she repeated. "Krystal." She blinked a few more times, and a tear rolled down her mascara-streaked cheek. "No," she said, trying to stand up. "That can't be right."

"Do you have someplace to stay in town?"

"She was my twin sister!" she said, her voice breaking. Tori pushed through the door and looked at Quinn; I knew the orders were piling up out there.

"Do you want me to take over?" I mouthed to Tori.

She shook her head and pointed to the weeping woman. "Stay with her," she whispered to me.

I turned back to Brandi, patting her shoulder as she cried.

"I can't believe she's gone," she said. "I just talked with her a few days ago . . . she can't be dead!"

"Were you and Krystal close?" I asked gently.

"Used to be," she said, wiping her smudgy tears away. "Back when we lived with Uncle Buster. Had to stick together with that one."

"Why?"

She snorted. "You think Buster was gonna take care of us? He was too busy cleanin' his guns and collectin' junk. We were lucky he remembered to go to the grocery store."

"I heard he's a treasure hunter, too."

"You got that right. All he ever talked about was that ol' Confederate general, and how there were millions right under our noses."

"Did he?" I asked. "Do you think that's what Krystal meant when she was talking about a jackpot?"

Brandi gave me a surprisingly shrewd look. "Why do you care so much about the money?"

I took a deep breath. "Because someone poisoned your sister," I told her.

She blinked. "Poisoned . . . what? Why? She was so nice . . . too nice, sometimes." Brandi burst into tears again. "We were gonna be together. Everything was finally gonna be all right. And now this . . ."

I pulled her into a hug, letting her sob in my arms. "I'm so sorry," I murmured as she cried.

Finally she pulled back and wiped at her eyes. "If I find out who did this to my sister . . ."

"Is there anything you can think of that might help us figure it out?" I asked.

"All I know is she said she came into some money," she told me. "And her boyfriend broke up with her."

Quinn and I exchanged looks. "We've been wondering about him . . . thinking maybe he had something to do with what happened to Krystal."

Brandi looked up at me. "You mean, you think he killed her?"

I shrugged. "Maybe. Did she mention his name?"

She shook her head slowly. "No. Only that he was the love of her life, except she said they met too late."

Met too late? Why? Because he was already involved with someone else? He wasn't around for Thanksgiving, and the relationship was hush-hush . . . I was starting to think Krystal's boyfriend—ex-boyfriend, that was—might be married. I didn't know of any divorces in progress . . . but it was always possible the mystery man was stringing Krystal along.

"Nothing else that might help us identify him?" I asked.

She shook her head. "We hadn't talked much until she called the other day. She told me she'd tell me more when I got here. And now . . ."

I squeezed her shoulder.

"Did she say anything about a secret admirer?" Quinn asked from where she was putting together a plate of chicken salad.

She shook her head. "Like I said, we were going to talk when I got here." A sob wracked her thin body.

"Do you need a place to stay while you're in town?" I asked.

"I don't know," she said miserably.

"Well, if you decide you do, I've got room," I said. "I'll give you my number."

"Thanks," she said. "What I really need is a drink."

I wasn't about to give her one of those.

"We should probably take her over to talk to Rooster," Quinn said.

"You think?" I asked.

"If Brandi can tell him about Krystal's boyfriend, he might take it seriously."

"Maybe," I said. "You're probably right." I turned back to Brandi. "Plus, he can tell you more about your sister."

"Poor Krystal." Brandi looked miserable, mascara streaking down her cheeks.

"Ready? It's not far. I'll give you my number; you can call when you're done."

"I guess," she said.

I levered the young woman up off the chair and toward the back door, thinking maybe if Brandi told Rooster about the "jackpot" Krystal had theoretically found, he'd be inclined to investigate further. I certainly was.

"Sorry to leave you in the lurch," I murmured to Quinn as she opened the glass door for me.

"Are you kidding me? Thanks for taking care of her," she said.

"Of course. I'll be back as soon as I can," I told her, and we stepped out into the wintry sun.

Rooster wasn't in the office when we arrived, so Opal made a pot of coffee and plied Brandi with it, hoping to sober her up. I sat next to Brandi on one of the plastic chairs in the front room of the station, which was situated in an old house. Opal had the station tuned to Christmas carols, so as I helped Brandi to a plastic chair in the front office, "Joy to the World" played softly in the background. Unfortunately, I thought as Brandi plunked herself down, almost missing the chair, this Christmas season had been anything but joyous.

"That one looks like she's been rode hard and put up wet," Opal murmured to me as she poured herself a mug of coffee.

I had to agree with her; Brandi might have been Krystal's twin sister, but she looked at least ten years older, with sunken eyes and lines around her thin, drooping mouth.

"Any word on Brittany?" I asked Opal in a quiet voice.

She shook her head, looking grim despite her reindeer sweater and candy-cane earrings. "Nothing yet. I've been on the phone with Dallas and Houston . . . they've got everyone out looking for the Mathesons' SUV."

"Thank you," I said. "Did Rooster talk with the Mathesons?"

"He did," she said. "They're not too het up about it, though. Although they might be trying to keep a low profile on account of the TV show they're tryin' to launch."

I sighed. I never would understand some folks' priorities. "Molly doing okay?"

"I gave her a stack of magazines a little while ago," she said. "Alfie's working on springing her as soon as they can get a bail hearing."

"Can I go back and see her in a minute?"

She glanced around. "As long as Rooster doesn't turn up."

"I hear your cousin was sweet on Krystal Jenkins," I said.

She shook her head. "Poor Dougie. I keep tellin' him to give Flora a spin—that woman is loaded—but he only had eyes for Krystal. He's barely eaten since she passed."

"Does he have any idea who might have killed her?"

"Not a bit," she said, and shivered. "I'm just glad she didn't give us that poison bread. Dougie and I ate the whole loaf last week."

So Dougie had access to Molly's friendship bread, I thought. Had he left some on Krystal's front porch? I wondered, but didn't say anything to Opal.

Opal adjusted a candy-cane earring and grimaced. "Not the best December for the Kramers, is it?"

"You can say that again," I said as she poured two cups of coffee, and we walked back to Brandi. I handed the young woman the fresh cup and sat down next to her. "When did Krystal call you?"

"Day before yesterday," she said.

"Did she tell you how she came by this . . . windfall?"

"Just that she'd hit the jackpot," she said. "Wouldn't tell me anything else. Wanted me to go to rehab."

Not a bad idea, I was thinking. "When was the last time you saw her?" I asked.

She squinted. "Must have been what . . . two years ago?" she said, swirling the coffee around in its Styrofoam cup and sloshing a good bit of it onto the hardwood floor. "Right around Christmas. We were at Uncle Buster's place. Got anything stronger than this?"

"No," Opal and I said in unison.

"Did you know much about your sister's life?" I asked.

"Like I told you, her boyfriend broke up with her," Brandi said, then slurped some coffee. "She was torn up about it. He turned out to be married." Ah; I was right. She took another swig of coffee, and tears welled in her eyes again. "I told her she'd find her a good guy someday. But now she never will."

At that moment, the door opened, and Rooster swaggered in. He took one look at me and his beady eyes narrowed, his wattle jiggling under his fleshy chin. So much for visiting Molly. "What are you doing here?"

"This is Krystal Jenkins's sister, Sheriff," Opal said. "Miz Resnick just walked her over from the Blue Onion. She's had a shock."

"I'll bet," the sheriff said, and gave me a hard look. "I can take it from here."

"I offered her a place to stay if she needs it," I told Opal.

As I finished speaking, Ethel came through the door, still looking stricken.

"Can I help you?" Opal asked.

"I just wanted to offer this young woman a place to stay," she said, staring at Brandi. It was almost as if she were seeing a ghost.

"That's kind of you," Opal said. "What do you think, young lady?"

Brandi gave a noncommittal shrug.

Rooster looked at me. "See? All taken care of. Now, why don't you run along?"

"Brandi said that Krystal's boyfriend had just broken up with her," I told him. I glanced at Opal and decided not to mention Dougie Metzger's crush. "It might be worth looking into. And she said something about Krystal 'hitting the jackpot' . . ."

The sheriff narrowed his eyes at me. "I said, I can take it from here."

"Of course," I said, trying to contain my irritation. Opal gave me a sympathetic look as I stood up and headed for the door.

By the time I made it back to the Blue Onion, the lunch rush was fading, and Quinn was cutting up potatoes for another pot of soup.

Quinn jumped, almost cutting herself with the knife as I shut the door behind me. Her years with Jed Stadtler had taken their toll on her; she was still easily startled.

"Sorry to scare you," I said.

"It's all right. I need to get better about that." She took a deep breath and pushed a reddish curl out of her eye with her sleeve.

"Can I give you a hand with anything?" I asked.

"Would you mind cooking up some bacon for me?" she asked. "I need a whole package; it's on the bottom shelf of the fridge."

"Got it," I said.

She picked up a knife and continued chopping up a potato. "Thanks. Now tell me what happened."

"Rooster didn't want to hear anything I said," I told her, and relayed what had happened.

"So Dougie could have poisoned the bread," Quinn said. "Interesting."

"He's definitely on the list of people I want to talk to," I said. "I offered Brandi a place to stay, but Ethel walked in and offered to take her in."

"That was nice of her. No word on Brittany?"

I shook my head. "I didn't get a chance to see Molly, either. Opal's on the Brittany thing, but no leads yet."

"I hope Brittany's okay," she worried. "I'm sure it's just a romantic fling."

"I just hope she and Bryce don't do anything stupid," I said. "I found out Krystal's boyfriend was married, by the way. And I visited the jeweler in La Grange; somebody bought a sapphire cross like the one Krystal wore within the last few months, but the saleswoman wouldn't tell me who." I'd forgotten to mention that to Opal, I realized; I'd have to tell her next time I saw her.

"Really? Now that's a motive for murder," she said. "Particularly if his wife found out."

"It would explain why they broke up."

"Maybe a jealous wife did her in," Quinn mused. "Who would have had access to Molly's friendship bread card?"

"Good question," I said. "I know Opal got a loaf, and Molly said she gave out ten loaves, but I need to get a list."

"Does Rooster know about all this?"

"Most of it, anyway," I told her. "But he didn't want to hear anything from me. He pretty much ran me out of the station," I said as I opened the fridge and located the bacon. I set up the griddle and cut the package open. "Did Krystal ever mention her sister?"

"Not that I can remember," Quinn told me, sliding a batch of cut potato off her cutting board and into a bowl. "Like I said, she didn't talk much about family."

"Brandi left her car in front of the cafe," I said.

"Her *car?*" Quinn set down her knife. "Are you telling me she drove here?"

"Parked the car half on the sidewalk. Just like Nettie Kocurek used to do—only Brandi drives a Kia, not a Cadillac."

"It's a miracle she didn't kill herself—or someone else—on the way here," Quinn said, picking up her knife and neatly halving another potato. "Still . . . I feel terrible for her. She thinks she's coming into town to share in her sister's good fortune, and instead she finds out she's dead."

"I get the feeling it wasn't a super close relationship," I said as I laid the bacon onto the griddle. "Brandi seemed to love Krystal, but I got the impression they hadn't talked in a long time."

"All Krystal talked about was her wonderful, nameless boyfriend."

"But she never said anything about them breaking up?" I asked as I laid the last piece of bacon on the pan.

"No," she said. "Then again, maybe it's recent; she'd been off work the two days before the house fire. She might have stayed home because she was in a funk about it."

"Or because she was poisoned," I pointed out. "You don't usually get out much when you're dead."

"True," she said. "I keep thinking about Buster and his treasure hunting. Do you think maybe he and Krystal found some buried money, then Brandi stole it and killed her sister?"

"Why would she come in and tell us about it, then?"

"Because she's drunk?" Quinn suggested. "But honestly. You'd think if there were any treasure in Buttercup, somebody would have found it by now."

"And if they had, why would they still be digging behind my house?"

"Maybe it wasn't Buster who was digging," Quinn mused. "It could be someone who heard Buster had found those two coins, and was looking for more. Still . . . I can't believe anyone found anything in Buttercup."

"You never know," I said. "They're still finding Roman antiquities in fields in England."

"Yeah, well, there aren't a lot of amphorae turning up in Texas." She bit her lip and grabbed a bunch of the green onions I'd brought her yesterday and rinsed them under the sink.

I checked the bacon; it was turning golden brown on the bottom. "None of it makes sense. I just wish we could talk to her ex-boyfriend."

"You think he knows she's gone?"

"If he did her in, I'm sure he does. Plus, if he lives anywhere nearby, he probably knew fifteen minutes after I did. Did she ever say if he lived in the area?"

"I got that impression, but I don't really know," Quinn said as she began dicing the onions.

Krystal sure hadn't said much, I reflected as the bacon sizzled. Her life was pretty much a mystery.

"How's the puppy doing, by the way?" Quinn asked.

"I haven't had a chance to check. She was okay two nights ago."

Quinn scraped the diced onions into the bowl with the potatoes. "How did it go when you talked to Tobias?"

"It was a bit tense," I said, adjusting the heat on the griddle as the bacon continued to sizzle. "He told me there was nothing going on with Mindy, at least."

"No? Why's she here, then?"

"The official story is that she's looking for property, but Tobias implied there's something more."

"Sounds fishy to me," she said.

"Thanks for the support."

"I'm sorry," she said. "I wasn't thinking . . ."

All my worries about Tobias came flooding back. I sighed. "At least the puppy seems to be stable."

"That's something, I suppose," she said. "What are you going to do if she pulls through?"

"We'll have to find a home for her," I said.

Quinn was quiet for a moment. "Can I meet her?" she asked.

I looked at my friend. "You're thinking about getting a dog?" I asked.

"I don't sleep well at night," she confessed. "Even though I know Jed is behind bars, I still have a hard time relaxing." She opened the fridge and reached for a stick of butter. "I keep thinking about how Chuck warned us when Jed showed up at the farm."

How could I forget? I also remembered how Jed had kicked Chuck into a wall and attacked Quinn.

"Knowing Chuck is there does help me sleep more soundly," I told her. It had been eerily quiet the first few nights at the farm; it had been easier to drift off with my little apricot-colored protector at the end of the bed. "I think it's a good idea."

As she plopped the butter into the pot to melt, Quinn said, "I don't really have a yard with a fence."

"I didn't in Houston, either," I told her. When I'd worked for the *Chronicle* as a reporter, I'd lived in a small condo. I'd taken Chuck for walks by the bayous every night, and that had suited him just fine. "You can take her for walks around the square, or visit Chuck at the farm and let them romp together."

"I've never had a dog," she said.

"Well, then, I think it's about time you got one. Let's finish up this soup and go visit the one Peter saved. Okay?"

"But I've got all the bread to bake, and the market opens at six . . ."

"The stall's already set up, and I can help you carry the breads and cakes out. You can take an hour off. Come on . . . what happened to the slow pace of small-town life? This isn't Houston—or New York!"

She poked at the butter with a wooden spoon and grinned. "We'll finish this up and go visit the puppy."

"And then I think we should check out Krystal's house—or what's left of it."

She looked at me and nodded grimly.

Chapter 13

Tobias's young assistant, Jon, greeted us at the front door of the Buttercup Veterinary Hospital when we stopped by a half hour later on the way to Krystal's house.

"Is Dr. Brandt here?" I asked, feeling butterflies in my stomach.

"He's out on a call at the Chovaneks'," he said. "But the puppy just woke up."

"Can we go see her?"

"Sure!" We followed Jon to the back of the hospital. The little black puppy's nose was pressed to the front of the crate, and she was whining.

"She's adorable!" Quinn said, squatting down and touching her fingers to the front of the crate. The puppy's pink tongue popped through a hole in the crate, licking her fingertips.

"I think she's going to be okay," Jon said. "She's still a bit wheezy, but she's doing much better."

"Can I take her out of the crate?" Quinn asked.

"Of course," Jon said. Quinn sat down and unlatched the front of the crate. As soon as the door swung open, the little puppy bounded out, then nestled into Quinn's lap. "She's so sweet!" my friend said, caressing her silky ears.

"She's got a great temperament," Jon told her, smiling. He'd recently moved from Houston, and Tobias had told me he was really happy with Jon's work. "And she seems to really like you!"

"You think?"

"I do," he said. "By the way, I'm sorry about that young woman who worked at the cafe."

"Thanks," I said. "I just wish we could figure out what happened to her."

"Well, I've got to go give some immunizations, but you're welcome to stay as long as you want."

Quinn didn't even hear him; she was too busy baby talking to the little black puppy, who had turned over to present her pink belly to my friend.

It was love at first sight, I thought, grinning.

"She looks like a black Lab, don't you think?" Quinn asked.

As I was about to answer, the bell above the front door jingled, and I heard a woman's voice ask, "When's Tobias going to be back?"

The hair on the back of my neck bristled. Quinn looked up at me.

"I'll be right back," I told her, and walked to the front of the hospital.

It was Mindy, wearing a pencil skirt and a silk blouse that showed off her fit figure. Jon's eyes widened, and he looked back and forth from the blonde to me.

"You must be Mindy," I said, extending a hand.

"How did you know?" she said, shaking my hand.

"I'm . . . friends with Tobias."

"Nice to meet you," she said coolly.

"I hear you're looking for property."

"Looking for a weekend place," she said. "I was thinking of staying for Christmas . . . just for old time's sake," she said. "I forgot how cute the town is." She smiled, making fetching little crinkles at the corners of her eyes. "And it's been fun catching up with Toby."

I smiled, but I don't think my eyes crinkled. "So," I said, trying to sound friendly, "it must be nice to have parted on such good terms."

"Good terms? Of course we did! We didn't split because we didn't love each other . . . it wasn't an acrimonious divorce. We just wanted different lifestyles." She turned slightly pink. "Why am I telling you all this, anyway? I haven't even asked your name."

"Lucy," I said. "Lucy Resnick."

"Good to meet you," she said, and I got the impression she'd never heard the name before. Which meant she either had a terrible memory for names, or Tobias—Toby—hadn't mentioned me.

"Likewise," I told her, trying to sound like I meant it.

"Well," she said, turning to Jon. "Tell him I

swung by, and that I've got some work to do, but that I'm still up for dinner tonight."

"I'll let him know," the assistant said, looking uncomfortable.

She turned to me. "Nice to meet you, Nancy."

"Lucy," I corrected her.

"Lucy. Right . . . sorry. Anyway, I'm off. See you later!" she said, and pushed through the door, her heels clicking on the tile floor.

"Has she been here a lot?" I asked the assistant.

"A bit," he confessed.

"I see," I said. "Thanks." I drifted back to where Quinn and the puppy were drooling all over each other, feeling slightly sick to my stomach.

"Do you think I'd be crazy to adopt her?" Quinn asked when we left the hospital thirty minutes later. The festive lights strung up around Buttercup didn't seem quite so festive anymore; the afternoon had turned gray, and my mood matched it.

"I think you'd be crazy not to," I said. The puppy had whined when Quinn closed her back in her crate, and her cries had followed us to the front door. "I love having Chuck for companionship—and I think you'll sleep better knowing someone else is keeping watch."

We were quiet as we crossed the railroad tracks. I was trying to be upbeat, but it wasn't working.

"How are you doing with the Mindy thing?" my friend asked.

"What do you mean?"

"You know just what I mean. I didn't want to bring it up at the hospital in case Jon was listening."

"They're having dinner tonight, apparently. And she didn't recognize my name," I said. "Called me Nancy, actually."

"Tobias didn't tell her about you?"

"If he did, she forgot." I shrugged. "We never really made anything official, anyway, so I shouldn't be complaining."

"I'm sure everything between you will be fine."

"I haven't seen much of him lately, frankly."

"It's the holidays," Quinn reminded me. "Everyone's busy. Plus, he's covering two clinics right now."

"You're right," I said, and looked out the window at the overcast sky, trying to put Tobias out of my mind. Brittany was out there somewhere . . . I wished I had some idea where. "Do you think Brittany will come back now that her mother's been arrested?" I asked.

"I hope so," my friend said grimly.

So did I, I thought, saying a brief prayer for Brittany's safety—and Molly's.

It was a short drive to Krystal's house. The fields were green; cold as it was, I knew the bluebonnets that would bloom in the spring had already sprouted, even though we were in what passed for the depths of winter in central Texas. A lazy spiral of smoke swirled up from the chimney of an old farmhouse, and as we passed Peter Swenson's Green Haven, I spotted a few goats nosing the hand-hewn gate.

"How are the new goats, by the way?" Quinn asked as we passed Peter's place.

"They haven't escaped yet," I said.

"Milking going okay?"

"It's not milking time yet," I said. "It won't be until they have their kids."

"Well, get the hang of that chèvre when it is," she said. "I've got some new recipes I want to try."

"Can't Peter supply you?"

"He's got too many customers in Austin already clamoring for his goat cheese," she said. "I snag a few tubs of it here and there, but you'll be much more dependable."

I smiled. The truth was, Quinn could probably get anything she wanted out of Peter; she was just trying to support my nascent farm. We'd known each other less than a year, but Quinn was the best friend I could ever have asked for.

I turned at Skalicky Road; it was only another quarter mile to Krystal's property. The blackened remains of her little house were a blot on the verdant landscape. I pulled my truck in at the end of the driveway; the gate was locked, but we hopped over it easily. There was no sign indicating that it was a crime scene, and Rooster had clearly already been through the place, so I decided not to worry about trespassing.

The pasture around us was pockmarked. "I see what you mean about the holes in the ground," Quinn said as she surveyed the place.

"Maybe Krystal *did* dig up some gold," I said.

"Her sister sure seems to think so," Quinn said as we walked up the driveway. Although pieces of the house's walls were still standing, the windows were burned out, and smoke damage streaked the remaining siding. The door still gaped open from where Peter had kicked it in. We stood looking at what was left of Krystal's little home in silence for a moment. "If Krystal did find something," Quinn said finally, "what do you think she did with it?"

"If it was in the house, it should still be here— if it was gold, anyway. Paper might have burned. That is, unless someone stole what she found."

"Listen to us," Quinn said. "People have been searching for hidden treasure for more than a hundred years, and I've never heard of a single person finding any, but we're talking as if she really found something."

"Well," I said softly, surveying the ruined house, "with the exception of a possible love triangle, it's the only reason I can come up with that someone might want to kill her. What's that on the front porch?" I asked, pointing to something red and green.

"A bouquet of carnations," Quinn said as we walked up to the house. "It looks like a tribute."

"From her ex-boyfriend? Or Dougie Metzger?"

"Or the murderer?" Quinn suggested.

"Could be the same person." I shivered. "Maybe we can ask around at the Word of the Lord Church," I suggested. "Hopefully someone will know something about her mystery boyfriend. Plus, I want to ask one of those church ladies a few questions."

"About what?"

"One of them—Wanda—was about to say something at the Blue Onion, but Brandi barged in just before she could finish."

"About Krystal?"

I nodded. "There may be more to Krystal than we realized," I said, walking up to the empty frame where the front door had been. "Somebody wanted her dead, after all."

I stopped at the top step. The inside smelled like campfire and burned plastic. "Not much here," I said, peering at the interior. "Still, I should probably check it out."

"I'm afraid you might fall through the floor if you go in," Quinn said. "If there was anything valuable, I'm sure Rooster's already found it."

"It doesn't hurt to look," I said. "Just haul me out if I get stuck. Or call Peter to come help."

"Are you sure, Lucy?" Quinn asked as I stepped inside.

"I'll only be a moment," I told her.

Although the back half of the house—the bedroom area, I guessed—had burned clear to the ground, the front was largely intact. A cold wind blew through the doorway, ruffling the damp, charred papers scattered across the floor. An electric bill, a few circulars, and an old copy of the *Buttercup Zephyr*.

"Find anything?" Quinn asked from the door.

"Not yet," I said. "But I don't see any sign of investigation, either." The living room— what was left of it—was sparsely furnished. A blackened overstuffed couch sat next to a shattered glass coffee table, and the remains of an orange rug lay melted on the floor.

In the kitchen, the top cabinets had burned, but the counters, while a bit scorched, were largely intact. Miraculously, an undamaged mail sorter sat a few feet away from a plastic lump I was guessing used to be a phone. Not a cell phone—a landline phone.

I took a step toward the sorter, wondering if there might be some clue to the identity of Krystal's boyfriend. "You okay?" Quinn asked.

"I'm fine," I said, and took another step. No sooner had the words left my mouth than my foot plunged through the floor in a burst of splintered wood.

I said a few colorful words and pulled my foot out as Quinn fussed from the door. "I knew this was a bad idea," she said as I inspected my leg. I had a few deep scratches on the back of my calf, and my ankle was twisted, but nothing was broken.

"It'll be fine," I said, giving the hole a wide berth and limping toward the mail sorter. The floor held the rest of the way, thankfully, and I was able to look through the wad of damp papers that had been jammed into the plastic bin.

Magazines, bills—she was a bit behind on the electric bill, it appeared—but nothing from a boyfriend. There was a big manila envelope, though, addressed to someone named James Smythe on Skalicky Road. Krystal's mystery boyfriend? I wondered, lifting the flap on the envelope and teasing out the damp papers inside. Stuck together was a stack of certificates of authenticity for gold dollars minted in 1862, all signed by a numismatist—which I presumed meant some kind of coin expert—named Kenneth Graham. The envelope was postmarked in Houston.

"Looks like Krystal may have found something after all," I called to Quinn.

"What did you find?"

"Certificates of authenticity for Civil War-era coins," I said. I tucked all of the certificates except for one back into the envelope and slid it back into the mail sorter.

"Huh. So maybe she did find treasure," Quinn said.

I was about to make my way back to the front door when a crumpled ball of damp paper on the counter in front of the mail sorter caught my eye.

The ink had run on most of the page, but a few words were visible: "Wages of sin," "out of wedlock," and "Your mother would be ashamed of you" were quite legible.

"Quinn," I called, scanning the blurred page. "I think someone from that church sent Krystal a nasty letter."

"Can I see it?" she asked.

"Here it is," I said, avoiding the hole in the floor as I tiptoed back to the front door and handed it to her.

She paled as she looked at it. "I got one of these, too," she said as she turned the page over.

"What?"

"A nasty anonymous letter," she told me.

"Why didn't you tell me?"

"It was embarrassing," she said, her face flushing. "The handwriting's the same, though."

"Did you keep it?"

"No," she said. "But I remember what it said. All kinds of terrible things about Peter and me, and how we were . . . well, living in sin. Which is ridiculous; we've barely started seeing each other. But it felt very invasive." She shivered.

"Do you think it's possible that whoever wrote this might have killed Krystal?"

"I sure hope not," Quinn said. "I don't want to be on the list of next victims."

I looked down at the damp letter. "I should probably put this back."

"Probably," she said.

"I'm going to take a picture, though."

"This place creeps me out," Quinn said as I snapped a shot of the letter.

"Me too." I tiptoed back through the house and returned the letter to the counter in front of the mail sorter, then did one more brief scan of the interior, looking for anything I might have missed. There was no sign of a dog bowl or leash, I noticed—although it was possible it had burned in the fire. A few minutes later, I followed Quinn down the front steps.

Together, we walked around to the back of the house, peering at the holes in the ground, which had been dug in regular increments along a series of lines. A wooden shed stood a short ways away from the house.

"Maybe she hid something in there," I suggested.

"Maybe," Quinn said, sounding doubtful. We walked over to the shed together; the door was ajar. "I wouldn't get your hopes up. Somehow I think she'd put a lock on it if there were anything of value inside."

I pulled the shed door open and peered inside. There was a tangle of old farm equipment: rusted machinery, faded garden hoses, and empty bags of fertilizer were heaped in a pile in the middle of the bowed floor. Leaning up against the plywood wall by the door was a shovel, its blade coated in fresh-looking dirt.

"No treasure, but I'm guessing this was what she was digging with."

"If she was the one digging," Quinn said. "It could have been Buster."

"Good point." I still needed to talk to him and warn him off my land, I thought to myself. I wanted to ask him about the certificates I'd found in Krystal's house, too.

We closed the shed door and surveyed the property again. "Not much here, is there?"

"Mary Jane told me the remains of an old homestead are back behind the house somewhere. I'm curious to see them. You think we can find them?" I asked, squinting toward the back of the property.

"There's a path here," Quinn said, pointing to a depression in the grass. "Let's go find out."

Together, we followed the groove in the winter-bleached grass into the woods. We'd gone about fifty yards when we reached a clearing next to Dewberry Creek. A pile of weathered, broken wood that must once have been a barn was at the far end of the clearing; closer to us was a square of foundation stones. I recognized clumps of iris plants under a gnarled oak tree that must have been young when the house was built. I thought of the hands that must have planted them . . . how long ago? A hundred years? Longer?

"It's a little spooky back here." Quinn hugged herself as I examined irises' gray-green leaves; I might check with Mary Jane and see if it was okay to transplant a few to Dewberry Farm. "And somebody's been digging," Quinn added as she walked around the foundation.

"Could be the same person who whacked me over the head," I told her, looking at the holes in the ground. "But why dig at my place if he'd already found gold here?"

"Maybe he thinks there's more," she said, poking at one of the piles with her foot. "Most of the holes seem to be around this tree," she said, touching the rough bark of an ancient oak on the other side of the foundation.

"What's that?" I asked, pointing to a strange marking on the bark.

"Some kind of symbol," she said. "It looks like an arrow."

I walked over and traced the carving on the gnarled bark; whoever had made the mark had made it a long time ago. "I wonder if whoever is digging thought that was a marker of sorts?"

"Maybe there is something to that old treasure legend," Quinn mused.

"One symbol and a bunch of holes doesn't mean it's true," I reminded her. "But it's definitely worth investigating." Together, we walked around the old foundation, but the holes just looked like . . . holes.

Quinn took another look around and sighed. "It's depressing, actually. Let's get out of here."

Chapter 14

"Where are your parents?" Quinn asked as we sat down to tea in my kitchen a little while later. After our trip to Krystal's, she'd decided to come back to the farm with me to warm up and visit the goats.

"I guess they're out taking another trip down memory lane," I said. "Since I'm never here these days, it's probably a good idea."

"Are you glad they're in town?"

"I am," I said. "It'll be good to have them here for Christmas. It's a little tense with my mom, though; she never wanted me to buy the place, and hasn't let go of that."

"Don't listen to her. I'm glad you're here."

"Thanks," I said, smiling at her and reaching for one of the gingersnap cookies I'd laid out on a plate.

We were quiet for a moment, listening to the wind as it swirled around the house. Chuck was stretched out on the rug in front of the wood stove. I took another sip of my tea, thankful for the cozy farmhouse, but still disturbed by the burned-out house we'd visited that afternoon. "I wish we could figure out who Krystal was seeing."

"I know," Quinn said, reaching for a cookie. "Whoever wrote that nasty letter might know."

I snagged another cookie. The gingersnaps were my grandmother's recipe; they were sweet and spicy, perfect for a cold gray afternoon. Sitting in the familiar, warm kitchen where I'd spent so many childhood mornings, I could almost sense my grandmother's benevolent presence.

"I wish we could find out who gave her that necklace," Quinn said. "It looked expensive. I got the impression she wouldn't have been able to afford it on her own."

"The tag on it said it was five hundred dollars," I said. "It wasn't cheap." I took another bite of cookie and thought back to Krystal's body. "She wasn't wearing it when I found her," I said.

Quinn paused with a cookie halfway to her mouth. "Really? She wore it all the time. Couldn't keep her fingers off of it."

I shook my head. "She didn't have a necklace on. I'm sure of it. Then again, maybe she'd taken it off to take a shower or something."

"Or maybe whoever killed her—or burned the house down—stole it," Quinn suggested. "But why leave a defenseless dog? This whole thing is weird." She finished her cookie and took a sip of tea. "Speaking of weird, I had a random thought," Quinn said. "What if Krystal wrote the poison-pen letters, and someone killed her because of them?"

"You mean she wrote, but didn't send, the one I found?" I asked, pulling up the picture I'd taken of the crumpled page.

"I can't read the salutation," Quinn said, looking at my phone. "Can you?"

I peered at the screen. Quinn was right; it was a blur. "Do you have anything with Krystal's handwriting on it?" I asked.

"She filled out an application, but I probably threw it out. I'll check, but we might have to go back and look through the house again to see if we can find anything with her writing on it," she said, and shivered. "I feel like whoever wrote the one I got was jealous of Peter, somehow. But Krystal had a boyfriend, so why would she be jealous of me?"

"Teena Marburger has a crush on Peter," I pointed out. Teena, the local teenager with a psychic streak, had been enamored of the young farmer since he came to Buttercup, and had not been happy when he started seeing Quinn.

"I doubt Teena would write poison-pen letters," Quinn said. "Besides, if she's jealous about Peter, why send a letter to Krystal? I'm the one dating Peter." She sighed. "I just wish I could figure out why someone would want to kill her; she was such a nice young woman."

"What do you know about the Word of the Lord Church?"

"I've met the pastor—Vince Matheson. Good-looking guy, very charismatic. I think half his membership consists of love-starved pensioners."

"I met a few of them at the Blue Onion," I told her. "Wanda Karp and Ethel."

"Ethel?" she asked. "She just moved to town a few years ago. Her last name means 'happy' in German, but it doesn't seem to be working for her."

"She and Wanda seemed pretty close," I said. "I saw Ben O'Neill looking at properties with Faith Zapalac, too. I wonder what he's up to?"

"Our mayoral wannabe and our local real estate shyster," Quinn groaned. "Just what Buttercup doesn't need. Did you talk with them at all?"

"I didn't get a chance," I said.

"He's been a big supporter of the church. If he made a big donation, that would explain how Matheson built that new building so fast," Quinn said, finishing off her tea.

"Why would he donate to the church?"

"To get the church's support," she said. "He's going after Mayor Niederberger's seat, after all."

"I think we should pay the church a visit," I said. "Maybe we'll run into someone who can tell us about Brittany, too."

"I can't today . . . I've got to go to the market."

"How about tomorrow?"

"Two o'clock? You're on."

I'd visit Krystal's Uncle Buster by myself, I decided—but didn't tell Quinn.

She ate the last of the crumbs as Chuck watched, salivating. "Sorry, buddy," she said, then turned to me. "You think he'll like Pip?"

"Pip?" I grinned. "You've already named her?"

She gave me a sheepish smile. "I want to, but it worries me that I don't have all the room you do," she said, glancing out the window at the long rows of my garden.

"She could always come and romp here," I suggested. "Or at Peter's," I added. "How's that going, anyway?"

She flushed a little bit, and her smile told me everything I needed to know. "He's amazing," she said. "I can't believe I ever wasted my time with Jed. Peter's kind, he cooks, he's handsome . . ." She bit her lip. "Of course, Edna down at the Red and White was teasing me about robbing the cradle the other day."

"He's only, what . . . five years younger than you?"

"Seven," she corrected me, blushing a little bit deeper.

"So what?" I asked.

"It's just . . . I don't know," she said, shrugging.

"Silly is what it is. To worry about it, I mean."

Before Quinn could answer, the phone rang. It was Tobias.

"Hey," I said, feeling a thrill at the sound of his

voice, then a rush of insecurity. "We stopped by the hospital," I told him. "I was sorry we missed you."

"I hear Quinn is thinking of adopting the puppy," he said.

"We were just talking about that," I said. "She's going to name her Pip."

"Great name," he said.

"I think so, too," I said, then took a deep breath. "I met Mindy while we were there," I said, glancing at Quinn, whose eyes had gotten wide.

There was a long silence. "Mindy?"

Before he could say more, Quinn sucked in her breath. "Lucy!" She was standing at the window.

"Hang on," I told Tobias, and turned to Quinn. "What?"

"The goats are halfway done with your broccoli patch."

It took twenty minutes and half a loaf of vánočka to round up the goats. I was thinking of Tobias and our unfinished conversation the entire time.

"How did they get out?" Quinn asked as I finally closed the gate behind Hot Lips, who was smacking her lips and looking at me with a hopeful expression.

"I don't know," I said, scanning the perimeter of the fence. Everything looked intact to me. "Thank goodness you saw them when you did," I said.

"Maybe the broccoli will grow back," Quinn said, although she didn't sound convinced.

"At least they didn't get to the lettuce," I said. "Good thing I put the row cover on it."

"I guess that's positive thinking," Quinn said, walking the fence line with me. "Ah," she said, reaching down and touching a loose wire. "Here it is."

"How did that happen?"

"Looks like someone managed to detach it from the fence post," she said, glancing over at the goats, who were nosing their food trough.

"Probably Hot Lips," I said.

"Let's get this fixed. Got a staple gun?"

As she stood guard, I hustled back to the barn and grabbed the staple gun. Quinn pounded a half-dozen staples in, just to be sure, and together we checked the rest of the fencing while Blossom looked on with interest. She seemed a bit disappointed to have missed out on the fun.

"Peter warned me," I said, surveying the repaired fence, then wincing as I took in the damaged broccoli patch. "I just hope I haven't bitten off more than I can chew."

"Are you going to call Tobias?" she asked as we walked back to the house together.

"Do you think I should?"

"It's better to talk about it than let it fester," she said.

"You're probably right," I said. I pulled off

my boots and set them by the back door, then went inside and picked up the phone, dialing the familiar number and trying to keep my heart from racing.

Jon answered the phone. "Buttercup Veterinary Hospital, can I help you?"

"Is Dr. Brandt in?"

"He's with a patient," he said. "Can I take a message?"

"No," I said. "I'll try back later."

"Why didn't you leave a message?" Quinn asked as I hung up the phone.

"I don't know," I said. "I just . . ." I took a deep breath. "It's because I know they're having dinner together."

"I get it," she said, walking over and giving me a squeeze. "I'm sure it will work out, Lucy."

I hoped she was right.

Quinn had just left when the phone rang again. I hurried to pick it up, hoping it was Tobias, but it was Fannie Pfeffer of Fannie's Antiques.

"What's up?" I asked as I looked out the window. Two cardinals were at the feeder, and a cool breeze was making the row cover ripple like water.

"I heard you're looking into Krystal Jenkins's death," she said.

"I am," I said. "I know Molly Kramer didn't do it."

"Me too," she said. "I'm glad someone's looking into it. Pardon my saying it, but Rooster Kocurek couldn't find his derriere with both hands."

"I couldn't agree more," I said.

"Anyway," she said, "Remember how I told you Buster Jenkins called about some coins?"

"I do."

"Well, I'm calling because he showed up with two Confederate-era gold coins today, and I thought you should know."

"Where did he get them?" I asked, gripping the phone.

"He says he dug them up behind his house," she said. "As if I didn't know he's been sniffing around on every property lining Dewberry Creek for years."

"I think he was on my land the other night," I said.

"Maybe that's where he found the coins he brought in," she suggested.

"Maybe; this was the first I've seen of anyone digging back there, although I haven't been down to the creek in a week or two," I said. "But someone's been digging on Krystal Jenkins's property."

"I heard someone had been messing around over there," she said. "That's why I called you."

"Thanks," I said. "He only had two? What kind were they?"

"Two coins from 1862," she said. "If they're real, they should be worth a few thousand each. He told me there's more where they came from. I offered to have an appraiser friend of mine in Houston to take a look at them, but Buster didn't leave them with me."

"There were a few certificates of authenticity at Krystal's house," I said. "Signed by someone named Kenneth Graham. They were addressed to a man named James Smythe, I think. I keep meaning to Google them."

"Never heard of either name," she said. "Maybe he got them appraised somewhere else."

"It's weird that they were sent to Krystal's address, but with a different name." I made a note to myself to ask Mary Jane about it. Maybe he was a former tenant?

"Anyway, I don't know if it means anything, but I just thought I'd let you know."

"Thanks," I said. "You might want to tell Rooster, too."

"I will, even though I might as well spit in the wind," she said. "Any word on Brittany Kramer?"

"Nothing yet," I said, feeling my stomach twist.

"I'm keeping them both in my prayers."

"Me too," I said. "Let me know if Buster comes in again, will you?"

"Of course," she said. "Merry Christmas!"

"To you, too," I replied, then hung up and

grabbed my computer. I searched for Kenneth Graham first; although there were plenty of entries, none were in Texas and none were linked to gold coins. I came up equally blank on James Smythe.

Curiouser and curiouser, I thought, glancing at the clock on the wall. Mom and Dad were out and about for the afternoon, but Dad said he'd grill steaks for dinner at seven; when I found out about Molly, I'd texted them to let them know I was going to be out of pocket. It was still only midafternoon. I still had plenty of time to visit Buster—and maybe swing by the filling station and see if Dougie was working.

It took about fifteen minutes to get to Buster's place, which was well on the outskirts of town, and as I passed the painted 1800s farmhouses and fallow golden pastures, I found myself trying to come up with a game plan that wouldn't end with me peppered by Civil War–era bullets.

Although Buster's trailer was hidden from view behind a bunch of scrubby cedars, it wasn't too hard to figure out which property was his. The battered mailbox seemed to rise up out of a pile of tractor parts and what may or may not have been the remains of a spring mattress. A few yards away, a small oak tree was growing up through the rusted-out remains of an old combine, and a chained, padlocked gate blocked the end of the drive.

The only thing that looked like it dated from later than 1955 was the Confederate flag, which hung limp and bright from a peeling flagpole attached to the gate. The hair stood up on the back of my neck as I pulled over on the shoulder and grabbed the package of fudge I'd taken out of the freezer.

I crossed the road and was about to figure out how to get past the gate when my phone rang. I glanced down at the display; it was Quinn.

"Brandi was just in, complaining about Ethel trying to reform her," Quinn groaned. "What are you doing?"

"Taking some fudge to Buster," I said. I'd made a few batches the week before; I figured it might sweeten him up.

"Are you out of your mind, Lucy? What if he has a gun?"

"I know he has a gun," I told her. "He has lots of them, in fact. But I've got to ask him questions if I'm going to find a way to get Molly out of jail."

"You couldn't wait for me?"

"I'm only going to talk to him. I'll be fine," I said with a breezy confidence I didn't feel. In truth, I had decided it was best to go alone. I knew Quinn was still traumatized by what had happened with Jed, and I didn't want to subject her to anything that would bring back bad memories. "I'll call you when I'm leaving, okay?"

"What exactly are you planning on asking him? Questions like, 'Did you kill your niece?' "

"I'm still working that out," I confessed.

She sighed. "I don't like this. Are you sure you won't wait until tomorrow?"

"I'm already here. I'll call you when I'm done," I said.

"If you don't, I'm coming out after you," she said. "Be careful."

"It's a deal," I said. I hung up a moment later, thankful to have a friend who cared, and confronted the gate. A barbed-wire fence extended from both sides, and the shiny padlock was shut, which meant I was going to have to climb over the gate. Thankfully, it wasn't too high.

As I eased a leg over the gate, glad there wasn't a "No Trespassing" sign, I found myself hoping Buster wasn't the kind of person who shot first and asked questions later. The first barrier behind me, I walked up the rutted driveway, which was lined with debris of all varieties. I spotted a rotting box full of yellowed newspapers, a rusted-out wheelbarrow, the remains of an old bicycle, and a pile of trash bags lurking among the undergrowth. The property had the potential to be pretty, but it would need a lot of cleanup; it felt more like the town dump than a home. As I turned around a bend, the odor of stale beer wafted to me. It smelled like Brandi might not be the only one with an alcohol problem.

I stopped about ten yards from the house. It was a wonder it was standing, since the whole thing kind of sagged to the left. In fact, it appeared to be held up by the piles of debris leaning against it. There were holes dug in a scattershot pattern here, too, I noticed, but none of them were fresh. "Hello!" I called out, just to be sure he heard me coming. There was no response, so I said it again, louder.

This time, there was a loud thump from inside the house. It made me jump.

"I brought fudge!" I announced, feeling adrenaline shoot through my body. Maybe it wouldn't have been such a bad idea to bring Quinn, I thought, pasting a smile on my face and trying to look nonthreatening. A moment later, the rust-stained door banged open, and I found myself facing the barrel of a musket.

"What are you doing here?"

Chapter 15

I swallowed hard. "I just brought you some fudge," I repeated. Buster scowled at me, but lowered the gun a fraction of an inch. He wore dirty jeans and a stained red sweatshirt with bleach spots.

"Didn't you see the 'No Trespassing' sign?"

"No," I said. "There wasn't one."

He eyed the fudge in my hand. "Why'd you bring that?"

"I thought it would be a nice thing to do," I said. "It's Christmas, after all, and I know you just lost your niece."

He grunted.

"I hear Brandi and Krystal used to live with you. Were you and Krystal close?" I asked.

"No," he said shortly.

"I understand you spent some time together recently," I said, "and I was wondering if I could ask you a few questions."

"About what?" he asked, narrowing his eyes in his sallow, leathery face.

"About Krystal, and who might have wanted to hurt her."

"House burned down," he said shortly. "That's what happened."

"Not exactly," I said. "Did you know they arrested Molly Kramer for murder?"

He lowered the gun a little bit more. "I heard something about that. Poisoned bread or something." He looked at the container in my hand. "Did you put something in the fudge, too?"

"Why would I want to do that?" I asked. "I've barely met you."

"Never can tell," he said. He gestured with the gun toward a small rusting table a few feet from the door. "You can put it there," he said.

"Gosh," I said, feeling irritable despite the musket being leveled at me. I didn't follow his instructions; I wasn't fond of being ordered around. "How about thank you?"

He looked a little embarrassed suddenly, and the gun dropped. "I'm sorry, ma'am. You're right. I should say thank you."

"You're welcome," I said, and walked over to set the fudge on the table he had indicated. The metal table had once been painted turquoise; now, it was rusted orange. "I'm sorry about your niece."

He shrugged. "Happens," he said.

"I was hoping you might be able to tell me who her boyfriend was," I said. "I'd like to get in touch with him, too. Do you know anything about him?"

The gun rose a bit again. "I don't know nothin' about no boyfriend," he said. "And why do you care?"

Because they arrested one of my best friends, I thought. "Just wondering," I said, letting my eyes rove over the cluttered front of his trailer. "I hear you know a lot about the history of this town," I said, changing the subject.

"I know a thing or two," he said, the muzzle of the musket dropping another few inches.

"I understand you know a lot about the Confederacy."

"You're right about that," he said. "I've been researchin' it for years."

"No one ever found the buried treasure?"

His mouth snapped shut. "I don't know nothin' about that," he said.

"Fannie said you brought a few coins in the other day," I said. "You must know something about it."

"Found it on my land."

"Are you sure?" I asked. "Someone was digging on my land the other day. Gave me this," I said, pulling my hair aside to show him the goose egg.

He shrugged and looked away.

"Krystal apparently called Brandi, and said she'd come across a windfall. Were you planning on sharing the proceeds of your gold with your niece?"

"Like I said, I only found a little bit, and that was on my land. If you're looking for a big spender, maybe you should ask Ben O'Neill," he said.

Ben O'Neill? That was interesting. What could the hobby rancher turned would-be mayor have to do with a windfall?

"What do you mean?" I asked.

"He's got lots of funds. Maybe he gave some of them to Krystal."

"Why would he do that?"

He shrugged again. It seemed to be his stock response to questions.

"Are you saying he was Krystal's boyfriend?"

"I ain't sayin' nothin'," he said. His hand twitched on the musket, and I felt my stomach twist.

"Krystal had a few certificates of authenticity for Civil War coins," I said.

He blinked rapidly, but said nothing.

"They were sent to someone named James Smythe," I went on. "Did she ever mention finding any coins to you?"

"I wasn't into Krystal's business. I hardly saw her."

"Your truck was there a few times," I said.

"She's kin," he said. "I was checking up on her."

Somehow I doubted he visited her out of family duty. "You know, Brandi's in town," I said.

This news didn't seem to impress him. "Haven't seen her. She hasn't been by," he said.

Looking around, I could see why.

"We weren't close," he said shortly.

I sucked in my breath and decided to be brave. "I'm going to ask you again. Were you out digging behind my house the other day?"

His eyes hardened, and his shoulders tensed; I guessed the answer was yes.

"If so," I added, "don't do it again. I have the right to protect my property, and I'll do whatever I need to." Strong words from a woman whose only weapon was a hoe, but I wanted him to know I meant business.

"I think it's time you headed on out of here," he said.

I took the hint and started backing up. "If you happen to remember anything about those certificates," I told him, "you know where to find me. I plan to do a little more digging myself." I turned around and walked down the dirt road, feeling his eyes burning into my back. There seemed to be no love lost between Buster and the rest of his family. Maybe he had killed Krystal after all.

"You are an idiot, Lucy Resnick."

"Thanks," I told Quinn on the phone as I pulled

away from Buster's house. She'd called just as I got back into the truck.

"So, was your visit worthwhile?"

"He claims not to know anything about the certificates we found at Krystal's, but when I asked him about the windfall Krystal called Brandi about, he said that I should ask Ben O'Neill."

"Do you think O'Neill might have been her mystery boyfriend?" Molly asked.

"He didn't elaborate, but I wondered that, too."

"If she wasn't wearing that sapphire necklace when you found her, maybe she sold it."

"If it was the one I saw in La Grange, it was worth only five hundred dollars, remember?" I said.

"Not exactly a fortune. Maybe he gave her a breakup gift, and that was what she meant."

"Do people do that?"

"They do if they want people to be quiet," she suggested.

"Perhaps I should have a chat with him," I said. "Oh—and I think Buster's the one who was digging behind my house," I said, reaching up to touch my temple. It still hurt, but it was healing. "When I mentioned it, he clammed up."

"Jerk," she said.

"I told him he'd better not do it again, or I'd take any necessary measures to protect my property. I kind of insinuated I had a gun."

191

"You don't, do you?"

"Not yet," I said. "The way things are going lately, though, I might reconsider."

"It won't protect you from poison," Quinn pointed out.

"Thanks for the encouraging words. Any word on Brittany, by the way?"

"Alfie says they still haven't heard anything. I wish there were something we could do to help." She pursed her lips. "I think I'm going to ask around down at the high school."

"Good plan," I said. "And I need to find out who Molly gave friendship bread to. I know Opal and Dougie had a loaf, so at least we have one suspect."

"Dougie? I guess it's something," Quinn told me. "I told Tori to keep an ear out at the Blue Onion and see if she hears anything about Krystal or Brittany. Mindy was in this afternoon, by the way."

"Oh, yeah?"

"She and Faith were chatting over chicken salad. And when they were done, Faith and Ben O'Neill had a hush-hush meeting in the corner."

"That's the second one I've known of between those two. What do you think they're meeting about?"

"It looked like they were going through property listings. I don't trust either of them."

"Do you think it has something to do with O'Neill's bid for mayor?"

"I wouldn't be surprised," she said. "Oh—Faith did mention that there was a squatter out on the Simpsons' ranch."

"Not a surprise," I said. "The Simpsons have had that place empty and up for sale for months. Do they have any idea who it is?"

"Nobody was there when they got there; they must have moved on. There were frozen pizza boxes and empty beer cans all over the place."

"No whiskey?" I asked. "I guess that rules Brandi out. Have you seen Brandi, by the way?"

"She was only in for a few minutes with Ethel, who was buying bread; she didn't look very happy, but I didn't get a chance to talk to her. I thought I'd swing by Ethel's this evening, assuming Brandi hasn't moved out by then," she said. "See what else I can find out."

"Let me know how it goes," I said. I hung up a moment later and pulled into the filling station on the square with a loud thunk. Usually I did the self-service, but this time I pulled into the full-service pump. Dougie Metzger, tall and gangly with a mix of wrinkles and acne, loped up to my truck a moment later.

"Better get that noise checked out," he said as I cut the engine.

"I will," I said. "Any thoughts on what it might be?"

"Sounds like it might be a broken axle."

"Is that bad?"

"It's not good, that's for sure."

"You're Dougie, right?" I asked.

"Yes, ma'am."

"I hear you were friends with Krystal Jenkins."

His spotted face flushed red. "What about it?" His tone was gruff.

"I'm so sorry about what happened to her," I said. "It must have been really hard."

"Regular, or premium?" he asked, ignoring my comment.

"Regular, please," I said. I waited until the pump was running and he was reaching for the windshield wiper. "I hate to bother you, but do you know if she was seeing someone?"

His back stiffened. "Why do you want to know?"

"Because I need to find out more about her," I said. And my friend is in jail and I want to get her out, I added silently.

"She was," he bit out, not turning to look at me.

"Do you know who?"

"I never saw him, and I don't know his name."

"Married?"

"Look. Why are you asking me all these questions? I wanted to date her. She turned me down. I don't know who she was seeing." He turned to look at me, and there were tears in his eyes. "I loved her. She didn't love me."

"I'm so sorry," I said. "I know how hard that is. I hate to ask, but . . . did you ever leave anything at her house?"

"That'll be eighteen fifty-three," he said, ignoring my question, but turning beet red. Which I took as a "yes."

I fished a twenty out of my purse, along with one of the cards I gave out at the market. "Thank you," I said, handing them to him. "If you ever want to talk, or you think of anything, please get in touch with me." He took them both and started to fumble in his pocket for change. "Keep it," I told him.

He looked up at me. "I left carnations after she died. And other things, before."

"Thanks for telling me," I said. "And you don't know anything at all about who she was seeing? Even a guess?"

"I think it was someone from that church of hers," he said. "Drove a white truck. That's all I know."

"Thank you," I said, trying to think of who drove a white truck.

"So someone . . . killed her?"

"That's what the police are saying. Poison."

"I could have given her a good life." He swiped at his eyes.

"I know," I told him. "I'm so sorry."

He crumpled the card in his hand.

"Hold on to that," I said. "Let me know if you think of anything else that might help."

He nodded and turned away as I revved up the truck and clunked out of the parking lot, my heart hurting for Krystal—and for Dougie.

But I didn't rule him out as a suspect.

The farmhouse was redolent of grilled onions and steak when I got back to the house; my dad was making dinner.

"I'm sorry you had such a rough day," my dad said as he transferred onions to a plate. Chuck was drooling on the floor at his feet.

I sank into a kitchen chair. "Thanks; it really was rough. I can't believe Molly's in jail for murdering Krystal Jenkins."

"Do you think she did it?"

"Absolutely not," I said. "The problem is, how do I get her off? I've got a couple leads, but no solid motive."

"Good thing you've got those investigative reporting skills," he told me. "From what your mother's told me, the police force in Buttercup has never quite been Texas's finest."

"That's an understatement," I said. I decided not to tell him that I had been a suspect a few short months ago. "I'm probably going to be busy trying to figure out what happened over the next few days . . . I'm so sorry. Between everything going on and the Christmas Market, I may not be around much."

"No worries," he said as he washed his hands at the sink. "I'll make your mom take me for another tour of the area, so she can tell me stories."

"She really isn't happy with my buying the farm, is she?"

"She isn't," he admitted, slipping Chuck a piece of steak. It disappeared in a flash. "She was looking at the want ads in the DC papers the other day."

"Looking for a new job?"

"For you, of course," he said. "But I can tell you're happier here than you ever were working for a paper—even though I know things are tight. Although you might want to get your truck looked at. It sounds awful."

"I know," I said, "but I don't want to spend the money right now. I'm hoping the finances will get better as I get more established. Where's Mom, by the way?"

"Kibitzing with the goats," he said. "For a woman so averse to farm life, she sure does seem to enjoy being here. I liberated a bit of your lettuce, by the way . . . I hope you don't mind."

"Of course not," I said.

"Glass of wine?" he asked, nodding toward a bottle of red on the counter.

"Absolutely," I said, thankful for my dad's presence—and hoping the alcohol would dull my mother's barbs.

I poured myself a glass and took a big swig. So far, Christmas in Buttercup was anything but what I'd envisioned.

Chapter 16

I finished my chores early the next morning and headed to the Blue Onion. After Quinn gave a few directions to Tori and Olivia, who were covering the cafe for the day, we piled into her car to head to Word of the Lord Church; we'd decided she should drive, since there was less likelihood of her undercarriage falling out. "You really need to get that fixed," she told me.

"I'm afraid to find out how much it'll cost. Did you see Brandi last night?" I asked, changing the subject.

"I did," she said. "She and Ethel Froehlich are not exactly a fit."

"No?"

"Ethel's a teetotaler, and Brandi . . . well, she was named well."

"Did you find out anything helpful?"

"She was still really upset about Krystal," she said. "She told me a little about their childhood. Apparently their mother lived in Buttercup and got pregnant in high school. She left town before anyone found out about it and had the girls somewhere else. Their father—Matt Jenkins— died in an accident when they were fourteen;

that's when they moved back to live with Buster."

"Poor things," I said. "No wonder Brandi's got issues. And I'll bet Krystal was thrilled to have a boyfriend who loved her. If it weren't for the fire—and the friendship bread—I'd wonder if the pain of the breakup didn't cause her to . . . well . . ."

"Take her own life? I had the same thought," Quinn said. "It's tragic in any case. Oh—before I forget, there was one thing Brandi told me that was interesting."

"Really?"

"Krystal mentioned their uncle when they talked. She was feeling some pressure from him to do something she didn't want to do."

"Did she say if it had anything to do with the windfall?" I asked, wondering if the "pressure" had something to do with the certificates of authenticity sent to Krystal's address.

"I'm not sure, but I also ran into Monica Espinoza, down at the bank. She told me Krystal deposited a big cashier's check two days before she died."

"Did she say where she got it?"

Quinn shook her head. "No, but it sounds like she wasn't lying about a windfall."

"That rules out Buster's Confederate gold, then. He just brought the gold coins to Fannie to be appraised—if he hasn't sold them yet, the money must have come from elsewhere."

"Maybe he found a second hoard?" Quinn suggested.

"If so, what did he do with the first one?"

"I wish I knew," Quinn said. "I stopped by the high school and asked a few of Brittany's teachers if she'd said anything about where she was going, but no one knew anything about it. They're going to ask the students for me, though. Oh—and John Chovanek stopped by." John was a local rancher; his daughter went to school with Brittany. "He thinks he saw Bryce Matheson pulling out of the grocery store in La Grange. He told Rooster, but he wanted to pass it on to you and me, too."

"No sign of Brittany?"

"No," she said. "He tried to catch up with Bryce, but got caught at a red light."

I felt a chill. Why was he alone? "Do you think she's okay?"

"I don't know," she said honestly. "I'm hoping we find her soon."

"Maybe we'll get a lead this morning," I said as we turned onto State Highway 71 and headed to Krystal's church. We rode the rest of the way in silence, both fretting over our friend . . . and Krystal's unsolved murder.

I'd never been to the Word of the Lord Church before. It looked like an airplane hangar, but with less charm. The only two things distinguishing the corrugated-metal building as a church were an enormous red cross that had been screwed to the front of the building and a bait-shop-style sign near the highway proclaiming "Jesus Loves You: Faith Healings Every Sunday!" The metal building was located just off 71, and a car backfired as Quinn and I walked from the broad swath of parking lot to the double front door of the church. It was a far cry from the quaint wooden Brethren Church down the road from Dewberry Farm.

"I'm surprised they don't have drive-through communion," Quinn said as I grabbed the door handle.

"Maybe that's phase two of the building program," I told her as we walked into the narthex. "Thanks for coming with me, by the way."

"So, what's our reason for being here, again?" Quinn asked. "Other than sheer curiosity, that is."

"I don't think we need a pretext," I said. "Brittany's missing and Molly was arrested. We just want to see if anyone can help us figure out what happened."

"Got it," she said.

The narthex smelled like burned coffee and new construction, which could not have been further from the cozy scent of wax and furniture polish I associated with the Brethren Church. I peeked into the worship space; the warehouse-like room had metal chairs in a rough semicircle, stadium-like, on a concrete floor. An enormous white screen was in the front of the room, where I was accustomed to seeing a cross, and in front of the low-slung altar was what looked like a small above-ground pool. "I hear they do full-body baptisms," Quinn said.

"No snake pit, though."

"I've heard rumors," Quinn said. She looked up at the ceiling. "Lots of stage lights. It looks like an auditorium."

"That's because of the television show," said a voice behind us.

I turned to see one of the two women from the Blue Onion. She had a helmet of highlighted hair, a blue shirtwaist dress, about three pounds of foundation on her face, and a stack of papers in her hands. It was Wanda Karp.

"When is that starting, anyway?"

"The New Tomorrow network starts broadcasting this Sunday . . . it's so exciting! Pastor Matheson will be spreading the Word of the Lord all across the world!" Her eyes shone through the thick mascara; I got the impression she had a bit of a crush on the good pastor. "Of course, they'll have to do some sound remediation. With that concrete floor, it's a bit echo-y."

Quinn and I exchanged glances. "I'd love

to hear more about his ministry," I said. For some reason, I felt uncomfortable leading with questions about Krystal and Brittany.

"So would I, actually!" came a bright voice from behind us.

I turned to see Mindy Flynn. "Oh," I said. "I had no idea you were here."

"I'm shopping churches," she said brightly, "since I'll be here on weekends. Mind if I join you?"

The secretary's "Of course" seemed a bit feeble.

"I'm sorry, what's your name again?" Mindy asked her.

"Wanda Karp," she said. "If you'll come to the office, I'll get you some literature."

We followed her through the narthex to a long hallway. Her office was the second on the right, a closet-like space with a small window that overlooked the parking lot. "Let me give you some brochures," she said, putting down her papers and gathering up a handful of shiny flyers. "Shoot. I'm missing the one on faith healing. I'll be right back," she said, and bustled out of the room.

"I still can't believe they're running a TV show out of Buttercup," Quinn said.

"I know," I said, my eyes roving around the room. There was something that looked like a stack of checks on the middle of her blotter. I leaned over to look at the one on top; it was a social security check made out to one of the older residents of Buttercup.

"What do you know about the church?" Mindy asked me. "I've heard the pastor is very charismatic."

"He is," I said. "Unfortunately, so is his son; he just ran off with my friend's seventeen-year-old daughter."

Mindy's eyes widened. "Really? What's her name?"

"Brittany Kramer," I told her. For some reason, I didn't feel like telling her that Molly had been arrested.

"When did this happen?"

"Just this week," I told her.

She sucked in her breath, but she looked more excited than sad. "That's terrible," she breathed.

"I know. We went to see the good pastor, but he didn't seem at all concerned."

"Really," Mindy said. Something about her tone of voice reminded me of when I was an investigative reporter.

"You're in entertainment law, I hear."

Mindy's smile got tight. "Only in Houston," she said. "I'm off duty here."

"Any luck finding a house?" I asked.

"Still looking," she said. "Hard to find ten acres with a nice house on it."

"I'm sure Faith will find something for you,"

I told her. "But I'd double-check the contract before I signed it." Faith, I had learned from experience, was not the most trustworthy real estate agent. To say the least.

"I'm sure. If you'll excuse me," she said, "I'm going to find the ladies' room."

"We'll let Wanda know," I said. When she left, I looked at Quinn. "She seems awfully interested in the pastor, doesn't she?"

"He's a good-looking man," she said. "At least that would mean she wasn't after Tobias."

"I guess that's looking on the bright side," I said.

She pointed out the top check. "Did you see that? That's Ursula Mueller's social security check."

"I know. But she has almost no income," I said. "How can she afford that?"

"There are a couple of others, too," Quinn said, glancing over her shoulder and then quickly leafing through the stack. "Huh. All widows."

"Preaching is more profitable than I thought," I said.

"Holy cow!"

"What?"

She showed me a check from Ben O'Neill for twenty-five thousand dollars.

"That'll cover a few mortgage payments," I said.

"No kidding. That's an awful lot to tithe."

"Maybe that's why Pastor Matheson is such a big supporter of O'Neill's campaign."

We heard Wanda's footsteps coming back toward the room, and Quinn quickly straightened the stack of checks out. When the secretary returned, we were both sitting with our hands in our laps. "Where'd the other lady go?" Wanda asked.

"Call of nature," I said. "I'm sure she'll be back in a moment."

"Well, here you go," she said. "I'm glad to hear you're interested in our ministry."

"Krystal Jenkins always said great things about Pastor Matheson," Quinn said lightly.

The smile froze. "Krystal?" she asked.

"Yes," Quinn said. "She was an employee of mine, until . . ."

"Oh, yes. The tragedy," Wanda said. "I heard she was poisoned by a local woman."

"That's one theory," I said.

"That's what the police are saying," she said, the sugar gone from her voice.

"Do you know who she was friendly with?" Quinn asked. "Apparently she was dating someone, but we can't figure out who it was. We were hoping someone here might be able to help us."

Wanda's face seemed to close up. "I'm afraid I can't help you," she said. "We don't talk about parishioners. Now, if you don't have any more questions . . ."

"Actually, I do," I said. "Do you know Brittany Kramer well?"

"She is very active in the program," she said. "A new parishioner."

"I understand she was dating the pastor's son," I said.

"She's a lucky girl," Wanda said. "He's handsome, like his father. Yes, I see them together on Sunday mornings."

"Did either of them say anything about going somewhere?"

"Going somewhere?" She looked confused. "Like on a mission trip? No, I'm afraid not."

"Apparently she and the pastor's son ran off together the other night. Nobody knows where they are."

She blinked at me and pursed her lips. "I hadn't heard that. I'm sure it's just a nasty rumor."

"No," I said. "It's not. I saw the note myself."

"I'm sure it's just a misunderstanding." She began shuffling papers. Our interview, it seemed, was over.

"Are there ever snake-handling Sundays?" Quinn asked. I turned to blink at her.

Wanda was blinking at her, too. "Snake handling? Goodness gracious. Of course not."

"It might make good TV," Quinn said. I stepped on her toe, and she yelped.

"We have faith healings, but no snakes," Wanda informed her.

"Thanks," I said. "We'll think about it."

The phone rang, and she picked up. "Word of the Lord Church, can I help you?" A moment later, she smiled. "Yes, Mr. O'Neill. Of course. If you'll drop them off, we can have the campaign buttons in the narthex for Sunday services. I know you wanted to talk to him about"—her eyes darted to us—"that other matter," she said. "I'll have him call you when he gets back." She hung up a moment later.

Mindy appeared at the door. "Everything okay?" she asked.

"Fine," Wanda practically barked.

"Sounds like the church is a big supporter of Ben O'Neill," she commented.

"Mr. O'Neill is a God-fearing man," she said shortly, handing Mindy a stack of brochures. I noticed a red flush rising from her tight collar. "Now, if you'll excuse me, I have a lot of work to do." She stood up, dismissing us. "Maybe we'll see you some Sunday," she said with a weak smile that I wouldn't call welcoming.

"Before you go, I heard that one of your parishioners recently died in unfortunate circumstances," Mindy said, echoing what Quinn and I had said.

"Yes," she said, looking wary. "I heard her house caught fire. Tragic."

"Have the police been by to talk to you?" she asked.

Before she could answer, Pastor Matheson walked in. He looked a bit pale, and his chiseled jaw was clenched. When he spotted us, there was a brief flash of emotion before he arranged his features into a charismatic smile.

"Ladies! Are you interested in the church?" he asked.

"Why, yes," Mindy said, practically fluttering her eyelashes. "I was hoping to run into you!"

"Well then, it's my lucky day!" he said, brightening; once he saw Mindy, I got the impression that he'd forgotten about the rest of us. I glanced at the secretary, whose mouth was a disapproving moue; it hadn't escaped her notice, either. Jealous? I wondered.

"We're starting live broadcasting this coming weekend," he said. "If you come and sit in the front row, your beautiful smile might make national TV!"

"Maybe you can talk another time," Wanda interjected. "We have a meeting now."

He looked startled. "Meeting? But—"

"It's about the programming for this Sunday. Don't you remember?" Her voice was strained.

"Of course," he said. "Sorry we couldn't talk more . . . what's your name again?"

"Mindy," she said. "Mindy Flynn."

"Mindy," he repeated. "Lovely name. If you'll leave me a card . . ."

"Shoot. I don't have them with me. Why don't I write down my number?"

"That will work," he said as she scrawled a number on a scrap of paper. He smiled when she handed it to him. "Hope to see you Sunday!" he said, glancing over his shoulder as Wanda ushered him into the adjoining office like a shepherd herding a wayward sheep.

The three of us walked into the hallway, which was festooned with invitations to hand our troubles over to Jesus and our paychecks over to the Word of the Lord Church. Mindy hurried past us. "Good to see you," she said. "It's probably best he had a meeting; I've got another appointment with the real estate agent. Wish me luck!"

"Of course," I said.

"She didn't say what kind of luck," Quinn pointed out as Mindy hurried out of the building.

"What did you think of all that?" I asked Quinn.

"Pastor Matheson's a whiz at fundraising, I'll give him that. And he certainly has an eye for the ladies."

"You're right; he sure seems to know how to get big donations," I said. "Is that in return for campaign support? It seems like an awful lot of money for a small-town election."

"I wouldn't be surprised," Quinn said as we walked down the hall. We'd almost reached the end when something caught my eye.

"Look at this," I said, pointing to a Bible verse printed on a piece of construction paper.

"Charming," Quinn said, scanning the verse.

"I don't mean the verse, silly. I mean the handwriting."

She stared at it, looking puzzled.

"Look familiar?"

Her eyes widened as she realized what I was saying. "It's just like the handwriting in the letter I got."

"And the one Krystal got, too," I said. "Think Wanda knows who wrote out the verse? Think she'd tell us if she did?" I pulled up the picture of the letter at Krystal's on my phone, and compared the two. The handwriting on the wall was less jagged, and had been written with less pressure, but was markedly similar. "See the hook on the 't'?" I asked.

"And that weird 'g,'" Quinn pointed out.

I unclipped the page from the wall. "Shall we ask? I'll bet her meeting's over now that we're gone," I said, grinning.

We walked back to the secretary's office together. She was talking on the phone; I put a hand up to stop Quinn, and we paused outside the door to listen.

"Yes," she said. "You can have the microphone at the next rally, and Pastor Matheson told me he'll find a way to work you into the sermon." She paused for a moment. "Hold on and I'll put you through." We waited a moment, then walked back into the office. Wanda's lips thinned when she saw us.

"Short meeting," Quinn remarked.

Wanda just pursed her lips tighter.

"This may seem like an odd question," I said, holding up the piece of paper, "but do you know who wrote this?"

"Why?" she asked.

"It's such unusual handwriting," I said. "I'm interested in handwriting analysis."

She squinted at it. "It must have been done by one of the Sunday school teachers," she said.

"How many of those are there?"

"Twenty," she said.

"And no idea who wrote this?"

"No," she said shortly.

"Do you have a list of teachers?"

"Like I said, we don't talk about parishioners. Now, if you'll excuse me, I'm very busy." Her friendly demeanor had been replaced by iciness bordering on rudeness. She didn't like questions, that was for sure. Was the church this secretive about everything?

"Thanks," I said, taking the page with me as we walked out into the hallway. Maybe someone else at the church would recognize it—maybe this Sunday.

"Well, that was a dead end," I said when we were out of earshot of the office.

"Not completely," Quinn said. "We know the poison-pen writer is a Sunday school teacher."

"And we also know Mindy's up to something," I reflected.

"You think?"

"She looked like an investigator on a trail," I said. Which at least gave her a reason other than Tobias for being in Buttercup. I was glad to get at least a bit of confirmation for what Tobias had suggested to me. "I'm wondering who hired her—and why?"

Chapter 17

Opal Gruber looked unusually rattled when we walked into the little house that operated as the sheriff's office.

"How's Molly doing?" I asked.

"Poor thing hasn't slept a wink," she said. "And I'm still trying to figure out where Brittany went."

"I heard someone saw Bryce in La Grange," I said.

"I heard that, too, but I'm coming up blank," Opal said, adjusting her cat-eye glasses. "And I still think Sheriff Kocurek's got the wrong woman. Like I said, Molly brought me a loaf of bread just last week, and we ate the whole thing. Don't see anything wrong with me, do you?"

"So Dougie shared it with you?" I asked.

"He did."

"Did you make any more with the starter?"

She squinted at me. "Why?"

"I was just curious what it tasted like is all. I've heard it's delicious."

"It is. Anyway, I can't seem to convince the sheriff to look any further than Molly," Opal said, her round face looking grim. "He said the instructions that came with the loaf were from her."

"Molly copied the instructions onto card stock," I said. "Anyone could have used the starter and baked a new loaf to give to Krystal. I was hoping to get a list of people she gave it to."

"Well, I didn't do it," Opal said, "so you can count me out."

"Of course not," I said, not mentioning my suspicions about her cousin, Dougie.

"Sheriff Kocurek thinks Molly's gone round the bend, but I don't buy it," Opal said. "She was upset about her daughter gallivanting around with that Matheson boy, and she blamed Krystal for introducing them."

"I've heard that, but I still can't believe he's taking that seriously," Quinn said.

"I know. You'd think she'd poison the boyfriend instead, wouldn't you?"

As Opal finished talking, Rooster strode into the room, his thumbs in his belt, his prodigious paunch spilling out over the silver buckle. He squinted at us as if we were two flies who had showed up on his barbecue sandwich. "What do you gals want?"

"We're here to see Molly," I said. "And find out if you've made any progress on finding Brittany."

He shrugged. "Nothing yet."

"Do you really believe Molly poisoned Krystal?" Quinn blurted.

"What are you, the FBI?" he asked. "Little lady, if I were you, I'd get back to your kitchen and mind your own business."

I resisted the urge to take the letter opener off of Opal's desk and plunge it into Rooster; instead, I smiled and said, "I'm curious. What was Molly's motive?"

Rooster reached for a handful of M&M'S from the bowl on Opal's desk and dismissed the question. "That's police information."

"A woman's life is at stake," I said. "I think it's a reasonable question. Did you talk to Buster Jenkins about the coins he found?" I asked.

His infuriatingly blasé look was temporarily replaced by a flash of mild confusion. "What coins?"

"He brought them into Fannie at Fannie's Antiques. And Monica Espinoza said Krystal deposited a big cashier's check a few days before she died; you might want to talk to the folks at the Buttercup Bank."

"How do you know that?"

"Word travels in a small town," I said vaguely. "There was a nasty letter in her house, too," I told him. "I have a picture of it on my phone. Whoever wrote it is a Sunday school teacher at Word of the Lord Church; the writing matches up. Quinn got one from the same writer—anonymously—also."

"How do you know Krystal Jenkins got a letter?"

"I found it when I was trying to find information on the puppy we found in her house. There were some certificates of authenticity for some Civil War–era coins, too. Someone's been digging out back of my house and hit me over the head with a shovel the other day; it could be related."

"You went into Krystal's house?" he asked, ignoring what I'd said about the certificates—and my head.

"We were just trying to figure out who the puppy belonged to," I lied.

"Well, if you were snooping around pretending to be an investigator, you shouldn't have wasted your time. I already found the killer," he said. "Now, if you little ladies will excuse me," he said in a very nasty tone, "I have real work to do."

"You're not even going to check out the cashier's check—or the gold coins?"

"You can leave the info with Opal, if you want," he threw over his padded polyester shoulder as he tossed another handful of M&M'S into his mouth and sauntered past us to the door.

"Hmm," Opal said as the door swung shut behind him. "That didn't go very well."

"Not surprising, really," I sighed. "He's not going to check anything out, is he?"

Opal pursed her lips. "I hate to say it, but I doubt it. I'll keep pestering him, though . . . I promise."

"Thanks," I said. "Can we see her?"

She glanced toward the door Rooster had just walked through.

"Officially Rooster told me no, but what he doesn't know won't hurt him."

She opened a desk drawer and pulled out a key, then led us to the back of the station. "She's in here," she said, unlocking a door at the end of the hall.

The cell was a small white room with a high, barred window. Molly sat on the narrow bed in the corner, looking like she hadn't slept in days.

She rose as soon as she saw us. "Did you find her?"

"Not yet. Oh, Molly." I sat down next to her and hugged her solid shoulders. "I wish I could do more to help."

"You could find Brittany, for starters," she said with a forlorn look.

"I'm working on that," I said.

"I just want my baby back," Molly said, her eyes filling with tears. I'd never seen my perky, can-do friend look like this before; it made my heart twist.

"Molly," I said, taking her gently by the shoulders. "We'll find her. But we also need to find out who killed Krystal so you can get out of here."

She sniffed, and Quinn fished in her purse for a tissue and handed it to her. Molly wiped her eyes and blew her nose, then apologized. "It's just . . . I can't believe all this has happened."

"I know," I said, squeezing her shoulder gently. "We're going to do everything we can to solve this, but we're going to need your help. Okay?"

She nodded.

"Now," I said. "Do remember who you gave bread to?"

"Why?"

"Because whoever gave that poisoned bread to Krystal had access to your recipe card."

Her face lightened a fraction. "Oh," she said. "Why didn't I think of that?"

"You've had a bit on your mind, my friend," I said.

"The list is on the computer," Molly said, "but I remember."

I turned to Quinn. "Do you have a pen in that bag?"

"And paper," she said, producing an empty envelope.

"Okay," Molly said. "Let's see. Myrtle down at the library. Edna Orzak. One of Ethan's teachers—Deb Gehring—Quinn, Tobias, Father

Mikeska, Mayor Niederberger, Opal Gruber, Peter Swenson, and the Mathesons, of course."

"The Mathesons?" I asked.

"It's the season of Christian giving," she said. "I was trying to be civil. Open lines of communication."

"A card would have been easier," I pointed out. "And it's hard to poison someone with a card."

She gave me a look.

"You didn't give one to Krystal?"

"No. I didn't know her that well, to be honest. She only came over to the house once."

"When was that?" I asked.

"She came for Thanksgiving dinner, actually. Buster wasn't exactly rolling out the red carpet for her, so I told Brittany to invite her to join us."

"No turkey with Uncle Buster?"

"I get the impression he's not much of a cook," Molly said. From what I'd seen of his place, I was guessing she was right. Which didn't bode well for my suspect list. Although maybe he made an exception for poisoned friendship bread.

"She did say she'd seen him recently, though. I got the impression it didn't go well."

"What do you mean?"

"He was trying to talk her into something, I think. Brittany would know more." Her face crumpled, and I gave her a squeeze.

"We'll find her," I said, thinking that was the

second time I'd heard about Buster trying to convince Krystal to do something.

"I know Krystal was twenty-five, but I always thought of her as younger—more like Brittany's age. Naive, somehow. I guess that's why she was taken in by the whole church thing."

"She's not the only one. A lot of women—of all ages—seem to be drawn to Pastor Matheson," Quinn said.

"And a lot of people seem to be donating a lot of money, too," I said. "Unless he's got a trust fund, that is. That wasn't a cheap house."

"You're right about that," Molly said.

"Quinn and I were at the church office, and the donations are rolling in. O'Neill gave a ton of money, and a lot of the older women are signing over their social security checks."

"O'Neill gave twenty-five thousand dollars," Quinn said.

"Which sounds suspicious to me," I said, thinking of what Buster had said about Ben O'Neill. He seemed to be throwing around an awful lot of money. But why?

"I still can't believe someone put poison in my friendship bread," Molly said, and I put my thoughts about O'Neill aside. "I keep going through that list in my head . . . I can't think of anyone who would want to kill Krystal. I liked all those people—except the Mathesons—and I can't think why they'd want to poison anyone."

"Just a thought," I said, "but what about the Mathesons? Is it possible Krystal was seeing the pastor?"

"If his wife found out about it—or he was worried about the scandal—that would explain why he called it off," Quinn suggested.

"But why kill her?" Molly asked.

"Maybe she threatened to talk about it," I said. "That would kill the TV contract—and maybe his position as pastor."

"Not to mention his marriage," Quinn added. "Although having met the woman, that might be considered a plus."

"Besides," I said to Molly, "there's no love lost between you and the Mathesons. Why not frame you?"

"That's terrible," Molly said, "but it makes sense."

"So who do you think is most likely? The pastor, or his wife?" Quinn said.

Molly's brow furrowed. "It could be either one. I didn't leave it at their house; I dropped the bread and the starter off at the church," she said. "The secretary put it on the pastor's desk."

"If he brought it home, either one of them could have used the starter to bake the poisoned loaf," Quinn said.

"Except I'm not sure the pastor knows how to operate an oven," I pointed out.

"Or a coffeemaker," Molly said. "Assuming

it was the Mathesons, I'd put my money on Phoebe." She looked more hopeful than I'd seen her.

"The thing is, how do we prove it?" Quinn asked.

"She must have bought the datura—Jimson-weed seeds—somewhere," I said.

"Maybe check down at the Red and White," Molly suggested. "They have all kinds of seeds."

"What does datura look like, anyway?" Quinn asked.

"I've seen the plants; they're called Angel's Trumpet or Jimsonweed. They've got beautiful trumpet-like flowers; they do pretty well around here," I said. "The whole plant is poisonous. I'm guessing whoever made the bread may have substituted the seeds for poppy seeds."

"I just wish we had a starting point for finding Brittany," Molly said.

"We're still working on that," I told her. "But John Chovanek thought he saw Bryce in La Grange, so they may be close by."

She sagged back down. "All I want is for her to come home," she said in a low, defeated voice.

"We'll find her," Quinn said.

"Any word on when you'll get out of here?" I asked.

"There's a bail hearing today," Molly said. "Alfie's ready to cash out our retirement; I told him not to, but he's insisting."

"He loves you," I said. "You'll get the bail money back; it's better for you to be home."

"I'm so worried about Brittany," she said.

"I know. And we're worried about you, too," I said.

"Remind Alfie to make sure Ethan's getting his homework in, okay? And give the kids a big hug for me."

"Of course," I said. "Can we get you anything?"

"A file?" she said wryly, glancing up at the barred window.

"We'll get you out of here," Quinn said. "No files needed."

"I hope you're right," she said. "And I hope Brittany comes home soon."

So did I, I thought, trying to stay optimistic.

Chapter 18

The thumping from the undercarriage of the truck was beginning to sound like a high school drummer having a temper tantrum by the time I made it back to the farm. I rolled up to the driveway just as the mail carrier, Alma Holz, was pausing at my mailbox. She waved to me; I slowed down to greet her. I liked Alma; she was just a few years older than me, and despite the rather punishing temperatures she endured, she always had a smile on her broad, tanned face. She lived with her father, Gus, whose passion was the birdhouses he made and sold outside the post office. I'd bought one for the back fence; I was hoping a bluebird would take up residence this coming spring.

"What's up with your truck?" she asked.

"I'm afraid to ask," I said. "It sounds too expensive."

"I'd get it checked out before you get stranded," she warned. "I heard about Molly Kramer, by the way," she added, grimacing. "Bad news."

"I know," I said.

"Unfortunately, I've got more bad news," she said, handing me a stack of mail.

"Bills?" I said.

"Always," she said. "But it looks like you got one of those poison-pen letters."

My stomach sank as I looked down at the handwritten letter on top of the stack of seed catalogs and bills. "How did you know that's what it is?"

"I've delivered about ten of them," she said.

"Any idea where they're coming from?"

She shook her head. "They all get sent from the box at the main post office," she said. "I haven't gotten one yet, but we'll see. Whoever it is seems to be targeting every woman in town."

"Only women?" I asked.

"So far," Alma said. "I only found out what they were when Quinn mentioned it to me."

I looked down at the letter as if it were a dead mouse. "Wonder what's in it?" I asked, feeling a bit of foreboding.

"Nothing good, that's for sure," she said, and glanced at her watch. "I've got to push on, but I hope your day improves."

"Thanks," I told her, and turned into the driveway before ripping open the letter.

It was every bit as nasty as Alma had suggested.

To the new harlot in town . . .
    You are living in sin . . . and living a
lie. Your "boyfriend" is just using you . . .

227

he is still in love with his wife. You aren't welcome in this town. Take your immoral big-city ways and go back to Houston where you belong. He's been sleeping with his ex-wife on the side, anyway. You are a scourge on Buttercup.

I put the letter down; the anger and hatred bled through not just in the words, but in the slashing letters and heavy pen strokes. No wonder Quinn had been so upset. As I shoved the letter back in the envelope, I got a whiff of lavender . . . I might have been imagining things, but it comforted me all the same.

I jammed the letter into the glove compartment—I didn't want it in the house—and carried the rest of the mail inside to where my mother was busy putting up dishes. She wore jeans and a gorgeous red wool sweater with a snowflake pattern. Christmas carols played on the radio I kept on the shelf above the microwave, and Chuck came over and wagged; I noticed when I reached down to pet him that he smelled suspiciously like bacon.

"Hey, Mom," I said. "You look festive; I love the sweater."

She smiled. "Thanks. I didn't know if I'd get to wear it, but it's pretty chilly this year."

"Where's Dad?"

"Out checking your fence," she said, then

gave me a compassionate smile. "He told me it's been pretty awful for you . . . I'm so sorry about everything that's going on with your friend."

"It hasn't been the best," I agreed. I decided not to mention the letter I'd just gotten.

She poured herself a mug of coffee and offered me one; I took her up on it. We adjourned to the kitchen table; I put Molly's list of bread recipients on the table and wrapped my hands around my mug to warm them. The heat was another thing that was going out in the truck. "How's your head?" she asked.

"Better," I said. "No headaches, no focus issues, no more absentminded than normal, which isn't saying much, but it probably means I don't have a concussion."

"That's good, at least."

"I guess."

Again, I got that whiff of lavender. My mother seemed to smell it, too; she sat up a little bit straighter and looked around. "Did you smell lavender?" she asked.

I nodded. "Happens sometimes," I told her. As I spoke, there was a sudden breeze, and the list I'd put on the table wafted to the floor.

"You should get that door weatherized," my mother said as I bent to pick up the paper. Was Grandma Vogel sending me a message? I shivered.

"It's almost like Grandma's here sometimes," I said as I looked at the paper in my hand.

"It'd be nice to think so, wouldn't it?" my mother said dismissively. She never was one for superstition. "By the way, you got a call from Margaret Marburger. Unfortunate name, isn't it?"

"Hard to forget," I said.

"Anyway, she called to invite us to a cookie exchange," she said.

"Us?"

"Yes," she said. "I'm in the mood to make Grandma Vogel's *Lebkuchen*, but I don't have the recipe."

"That's one of my favorites, too! I was planning to make some this week, actually," I said, opening the pie safe and retrieving my grandmother's cookbook from the bottom shelf.

"I haven't seen that in years," my mother said in a soft voice. "Where did you get that?"

"It was here when I got here," I said. "Sometimes it just shows up on the kitchen table."

"Weird," she said, flipping through it. "Ah. Here it is. Do we have everything?"

"I think so." I'd picked up the ingredients last time I was in Austin; the recipe was one of my favorites. "I was going to make some fudge balls, too. Give me a few minutes, and I'll join you." I wanted to look through Molly's list of friendship bread recipients again before I did anything else. I loved my mother, but my friend was in trouble.

As my mother began assembling ingredients for the Lebkuchen, I reviewed the list of names, wondering if the murderer's name was on the list.

Other than Dougie, and possibly the Mathesons, there were no other obvious suspects. Had Buster somehow gotten his hands on some friendship bread? Buttercup was a friendly town; it was always possible that someone had been feeling charitable and passed it on.

I set the list down on the table and walked over to join my mother, my thoughts still on Krystal's murder—and Brittany's disappearance.

"Why don't you heat the honey and molasses, and I'll get going on the lemons?" I asked my mother, who had assembled all of the ingredients on the tile counter. I felt guilty for taking time away from helping Molly, but I couldn't think of anything else to do. Besides, how often was my mother in town?

"It's going to smell great in here," she said. "You know, from a practical standpoint, I still wish you were in Houston, but I have to admit I'm enjoying being here. Farm life is not my cup of tea, but I have fond memories of this kitchen."

"I was always jealous of the way you grew up, to be honest," I said. "Not that we didn't have good times in Houston, but it always seemed magical out here."

"That's because you weren't mucking out the chicken coop on Saturdays and getting up at the crack of dawn to milk cows and weed the garden," my mother said with a grin. "I spent half my childhood knee deep in animal manure. I didn't want you to have the same experience."

"The funny thing is, that's what I crave," I said as I reached for the lemon zester.

"Animal manure?"

I laughed. "You know what I mean. But you're worried I'm going to end up a bag lady, aren't you?" I asked. My tone was light, but the truth was, the thought had occurred to me more than once. In fact, if I had to replace the truck, I wasn't sure how I was going to manage.

"I do worry about your financial security," she admitted. "And if you're thinking of getting married . . . well, the pickings can be slim in a small town."

"I'm seeing someone, actually."

"I heard. The vet, right?"

"How did you know?"

"It's Buttercup, Buttercup," she teased. "I also hear his ex-wife is in town, looking for property."

"Yes," I said, feeling deflated. "And to be honest, Tobias and I haven't seen much of each other lately. It *is* the holidays, and he's covering a second vet practice . . ."

"Why don't you invite him over to dinner?"

"You don't think it would be too much pressure—the meeting-the-parents thing?"

"We'll stay out of your hair," she said. "You can always suggest the two of you have dinner at Rosita's. The tamales are to die for, and they're only around through Christmas."

"That's a great idea," I said. I put down the bowl and reached for the phone. "I'm going to call now."

"Good for you," she said as I picked up the phone and dialed the vet hospital.

Tobias's assistant, Jon, answered the phone.

"Hi, Jon," I said, feeling butterflies in my stomach. "It's Lucy. Is Dr. Brandt around?"

"He's in surgery right now. Can I take a message?"

"Could you tell him I called?" I asked.

"Actually, he just finished," he said. "Hold on a moment." Without waiting for me to respond, he put me on hold, and I stood in my kitchen listening to the tinny sound of "Jingle Bell Rock."

It seemed like forever before there was a click, followed by Tobias's deep voice. "This is Dr. Brandt."

"Tobias? It's Lucy."

"Hey, Lucy," he said, sounding tired. "Calling about the puppy?"

"How is she?" I asked.

"She's doing great," he said. "Full of beans. If Quinn adopts her, she's going to have her hands full."

"I'm glad to hear it; I'll let her know," I said. "Actually, though, I was calling to see if you wanted to join me for dinner at Rosita's tonight."

"That sounds great. It's been busy, but it looks like I'm free. Will six work?"

"Works for me," I said. I'd ask Quinn to cover for me at the Christmas Market.

"Unless an emergency comes up, let's plan on it. Normally I'd pick a lady up, but is it okay if we meet there? My last appointment is on that side of town."

"Works for me," I said.

"I'll see you at six, then." There were voices in the background. "See you soon!"

My mother nodded approvingly. "Now that that's taken care of, let's get these cookies in the oven and start on the fudge balls."

"Aye, aye," I said, reaching for the nearest pan and trying to banish the butterflies from my stomach. I thought I'd feel better after setting up a date with Tobias, but it seemed to be just the opposite.

It was a surprisingly conflict-free few hours in the kitchen with my mother—the brown sugar pecan fudge balls were another childhood favorite of mine—but guilt nagged at me. My friend was missing a daughter and on the hook for murder, and I wasn't doing anything about it. I had called Alfie to see if he needed help with the kids, but he hadn't picked up the phone. Quinn hadn't answered, either, and as I stared at the list of names Molly had given me, I felt despair creeping in. Everything seemed like a dead end.

Buster hadn't been particularly helpful, and as far as I knew, he had no way of getting his hands on Molly's friendship bread starter. I suspected the pastor, but all I knew for sure about Krystal's ex was that he was probably married. Buster had implied that O'Neill might be the source of Krystal's funds, but the only information I had on her supposed windfall was that she put a cashier's check in the bank not long before she died. I knew the poison-pen letter writer was a Sunday school teacher at the Word of the Lord Church, but I couldn't see how that was linked to Krystal's death—or Brittany's disappearance. I kept thinking about Ben O'Neill. Was it possible that he was the mystery boyfriend—and paid Krystal off to keep her quiet after he broke up with her? O'Neill wasn't on Molly's friendship bread list, but it was the only thing I could think to follow up on.

"What's on your mind?" my mother asked as she finished rinsing the last bowl. My dad had come in from fixing the fence and was in the shower, and Chuck was sleeping on the rug in front of the wood stove.

"My friend Molly," I said. "I only have a few potential leads, and they're flimsy at best; I feel like I'm not helping at all."

"Then all you can do is follow the leads," she said. "It may come to nothing, but you might turn up something good. You never know!"

Chapter 19

I took some time getting ready that evening; I didn't want to look like I'd tried too hard, but I didn't want to seem unkempt, either. Apparently what I picked out—a tapered button-down blouse with a gold necklace, jeans, and cowgirl boots—wasn't quite what my mother had in mind.

"Don't you have a dress?" she asked.

"It's cold," I said, shrugging on a jacket. "Besides, Tobias is used to seeing me like this."

"Think about Mindy," she reminded me. "I'll bet she's loaded with dresses."

"Thanks for the pep talk, Mom," I said. I resisted the urge to go and change—I'd be late—and pulled my jacket tight as I headed out to the truck, praying it wouldn't fall apart on the way to the restaurant.

Fortunately the truck and I made it to Rosita's, even if we were a few minutes late. But when I pulled into the parking lot, there was no sign of Tobias's truck. Had he forgotten? I wondered as I parked near the front entrance. Despite the appealing scent of cooking fajitas wafting from the restaurant, my appetite had vanished.

"Table for one?" Tammy, the curvy young

server, asked as I pushed through the door into the restaurant, which was filled with the scent of tortilla chips and sizzling meat. I recognized the server as a friend of Brittany's.

"Two, actually," I said.

"Ooh. Got a date?"

"Yes, actually," I said, flushing. She grabbed two laminated menus, and as she led me to a booth next to a window, I asked if she'd heard anything about Brittany.

"Not since she ran off with that boy from the big new church," she said.

"Her family's worried sick."

Tammy seated me, then lingered, still holding the menus. "I also heard Mrs. Kramer went to jail for killing that waitress who worked for Quinn. Why do you think she did it?"

My stomach churned. "Molly Kramer hasn't done anything to anyone," I said. "But she's worried sick about Brittany. Has anyone at school heard from her?"

"Not that I know of," she said. "It's scary, really. You don't think Mrs. Kramer did in her daughter, do you?"

"Of course not!" I said, shocked. "Are people suggesting that?"

She shrugged, which meant the answer was yes.

"Is there any gossip about where they might have gone?"

"Not really," she said. Just then, a server put a

basket of chips and a bowl of salsa on the table, and she put her hostess smile back on. "Can I get you something to drink?"

"A margarita," I said. With everything that had been going on—not to mention my impending date with Tobias, who was late and still hadn't called—I needed one.

Maybe more than one.

"I'll be right back," she said, and trotted back to the kitchen, leaving me alone with my thoughts and the basket of chips.

Despite my fluttery stomach, I'd managed to make my way through half a margarita and two baskets of chips before I saw Tobias pulling into the parking lot. I glanced up at the clock by the door; he was twenty minutes late.

"I'm so sorry," he said as he hurried to the table. "It was a more complicated case than I expected." He gave me a peck on the cheek and slid into the seat across from me. He wore blue jeans and a button-down shirt with a worn leather jacket, and looked good enough to eat, but I still felt wary. I took another sip of my margarita. "How's the investigation going?" he asked.

"Not too well, unfortunately," I said, I reaching for a chip. "How are things with you?" I asked, still feeling hurt that he was late and resisting the urge to grill him about Mindy. "You've been slammed lately, haven't you?"

"It has been crazy," he agreed, giving me a tired smile that made me want to wrap my arms around him and kiss him. "I'm sorry I've been so hard to pin down the last week or two. I've missed you. Are you doing okay?"

"I've missed you, too," I told him. "I guess I'm okay."

"Any word on Brittany?"

I was about to answer when Tammy arrived at the table. She gave Tobias a big smile. "Can I get you something to drink, Dr. Brandt? A strawberry margarita like you had the other night?"

"Actually, I think I want a Shiner," he said.

"Got it," she said, and sashayed away.

I looked up at Tobias. "The other night?" I asked, unable to resist.

"Mindy and I had dinner," he said. "She wanted to talk over some properties she was looking at."

"Oh," I said, looking down at my drink.

"Lucy," he said, reaching for my hand. I looked up into his blue eyes, feeling uncomfortable, and wishing he looked a little less handsome. "There's a reason she's my ex. Things between us are over; they have been for years."

"Are you sure? Even though she's buying a place in Buttercup?"

"Positive," he said, giving my hand a squeeze.

"Where's she staying, anyway?" I asked, feeling a little bit better. "The hotel on the square?"

He gave me a rueful smile. "My guest bedroom, actually. The hotel was booked up."

Something inside me curdled. "Ah," I said, looking down at my margarita. Why hadn't he told me this before? What else was he keeping from me?

"I know I should have told you earlier, Lucy, but really, there's nothing more to it than friendship."

"Right," I said, forcing a smile as I poked at my drink with a straw and stared unseeing at the menu. "So, are you going to get the tamales?"

"Of course," he said. "But I don't really care about tamales right now." He reached out and lifted my chin. "Lucy. Please believe me; there's nothing between Mindy and me. I swear it."

I took a deep breath. "Okay," I told him, but I still didn't feel any better.

"Have you two decided?" Tammy said, appearing at the table with a pad in her hand.

"I think we're going for the tamales," Tobias said, looking at me.

"Two orders?"

"Yes, please," I said. As she sauntered away, I turned back to Tobias. "I'll call Fannie tomorrow," I said. "See if Buster's come by again."

"Let me know what she says. How's Chuck, by the way? Getting along with your parents?"

"Yes, but my dad keeps slipping him bacon."

"Bad habits run in the family," he replied, grinning. For a moment, I almost forgot Mindy. Almost.

"How's his weight?" Tobias asked. Chuck had been on diet food for more than six months now, but he still retained his roundish profile.

"The Light 'n' Lean doesn't seem to be working out too well."

Tobias fixed me with a hard look. "Are you sure you're not giving him too many treats?"

"He doesn't like carrots," I said. "Or vegetables in general."

"But still fond of cheese, I'll bet."

"I don't give him much!" I protested.

"You have to be strong, Lucy," he said with a grin. "More exercise, then." He reached out for my hand. His touch felt electric, and for a moment, I forgot all about Krystal and his ex-wife and the Christmas Market. I leaned forward over the table. Our lips were just about to touch when my cell phone rang.

"Hold that thought," I said, and grabbed my phone.

"Lucy, is that you? It's Quinn!" I could hear the sound of Christmas music in the background.

"What's going on?" I asked.

"I think Hot Lips just stole a packet of burnt almonds out of Bessie Mae's hand and climbed a tree."

Chapter 20

"But . . . I just checked on them two hours ago," I said.

"Two hours is a long time," she said. "And apparently they cover a lot of ground fast; they made it to the Christmas Market. Gidget's heading for the roasted corn stand now."

"I'll be right down," I said.

"What's wrong?" Tobias asked as I hung up.

"Hot Lips just stole a bag of almonds from Bessie Mae," I said.

"Are you sure it was Hot Lips?"

"I think I need to go find out," I said. "Should we cancel the tamale order?"

"We'll just come back and get them to go," Tobias said, sliding out from the seat across from me. "Come on; let's go round up some goats."

Thank goodness Tobias was with me tonight, I thought . . . if only for a little while.

By the time we got there, the Christmas Market had turned into chaos. Peter had rounded up Gidget and lassoed her with a hand-knitted scarf, which he was now trying to keep her from eating.

Hot Lips, however, was still halfway up one of the oak trees, and was alternately bleating and mouthing the Christmas lights; apparently she'd dropped the bag of burnt almonds somewhere along the way. Peter was crouched down, calling to her and trying to get her attention with an ear of roasted corn from the Kosmetskys' stall, but she seemed too intrigued by the Christmas lights to respond.

"We'd better unplug those lights," Tobias said.

"You're right," I said, hurrying over to yank the cord as Tobias helped Peter replace the scarf with a rope collar. Mayor Niederberger was at the base of the tree, looking up at Hot Lips, who was precariously balanced on a long knotted branch about halfway up. "Sorry about this, Mayor Niederberger," I said. "We're still having trouble with the new fence, apparently."

"Oh, it's no problem," she said. "If anything, we could use a little excitement to get people's attention on something other than that." She tipped her head toward the protest contingent, which was chanting something about Jesus and candy canes. I recognized Ethel Froehlich, who was looking very downtrodden, and her pal, Wanda Karp, but neither the Mathesons nor the O'Neills were in attendance.

"Maybe we should try luring her with some of Quinn's vánočka," I said. "It's how we got her into the enclosure the other day."

"Do all of your animals have a thing for baked goods?" Tobias's eyes twinkled.

"I don't give Chuck vánočka."

"But I'll bet he steals it when he can." Tobias grinned, then waved to Quinn, who was watching the action from her stand. "Quinn, can I have some vánočka?"

"Sure," she said, cutting a slice from the sample loaf. "Is this enough?"

"Why don't you give me two, just in case," he said, and she sliced off another chunk and handed both to him.

"Need something to tie her with?" Tobias asked Peter.

"That would be helpful," he said.

"Here you go," Tobias said, handing him the bread and some more rope. "Maybe if we can get everybody to back off a bit, she'll stop freaking out and come down."

"She's crafty," Peter warned. "She'll make a break for it if you let her."

"I'll help corral her if she does," Tobias assured him. He turned to the crowd that had gathered. "Would y'all step back a bit? Give her some space?"

As everyone backed away, Peter crooned to Hot Lips, lifting the bread up so she could smell it. "Can I help?" I murmured to Tobias, who was standing a few feet from the base of the tree, his eyes on Hot Lips.

"If she runs, see if you can help me box her in," he said quietly as the goat took a tentative step toward her former keeper.

"That's it," Peter said in a soothing voice. "Come this way."

She tried to lift her hoof, but it was caught in the Christmas lights. She reared up, almost losing her balance, and backed up a few more feet.

"It's okay, girl," Peter said, proffering the bread again. She tossed her head a few times, but then took another step forward.

"See? Here is proof that Satan is in league with this commercial 'Christmas Market,'" someone bellowed. Hot Lips backed up, agitated, as I looked over to see Wanda Karp, thin lips pressed together. "If baby Jesus had been the parade marshal, none of this would have happened."

"What?" the mayor asked in her soft drawl. "I don't know about you, Wanda, but I'm getting a real kick out of watching two grown men trying to coax a goat out of a tree. In fact, I could go for another Glühwein. Bubba," she said, addressing the proprietor of the mulled wine booth, "do you mind getting me a cup?"

Bubba beamed at her. "Coming right up, Mayor."

Wanda drew herself up and attempted to look down her nose at the mayor, which was a challenge, since Mayor Niederberger was at least six inches taller. "You're in league with Satan, then?"

"I am a card-carrying member of the Brethren Church," Mayor Niederberger said, steel in her voice. "The whole point of this market is not just to celebrate Christmas, but to make it possible for a member of our community to continue to live in the house she's been in her whole life." She looked down at Wanda, who had tilted her head back and was still trying to look morally superior. "If helping out a disabled woman means being in league with Satan, then I guess I'm guilty as charged."

The entire square burst into applause, and Wanda turned stiffly and marched back to the picket line, looking like someone had rammed a broom up the back of her brown dress.

"Well done, Mayor Niederberger," I said.

"I don't much hold with the old ways," she said as Bubba handed her a cup of mulled wine, "but there are moments when I wish tarring and feathering were still legal."

I glanced up at Hot Lips, who, thanks to Wanda, had climbed farther up the tree, and then at the cluster of sign-carrying people over on the corner of the square. "Not quite sure how they were planning on getting baby Jesus here for the parade, but I guess they have First Amendment rights."

"I know. And so does Buster Jenkins, who

247

keeps flying that Confederate flag and blabbing on about Civil War conspiracies." She sighed. "I just have to tell myself it adds to the local color."

"You know Buster?"

"We've had a few run-ins over the years," she said. "He behaves . . . most of the time. Still, I wouldn't be sorry to see him move out of town. Shame about his niece, though."

Peter cooed at Hot Lips, but she wasn't interested in moving.

The mayor sighed. "Christmas is coming, and we've got picketers at the Christmas Market, a homicide, a goat stuck up in a tree, and a good woman arrested for poisoned friendship bread. What in heaven's name is Buttercup coming to?"

"You don't believe Molly did it?"

"Molly might be feisty, but she's not a murderer," she said.

"Is there anything you can do to persuade Rooster to consider other options?"

"I'm afraid he's as stubborn as an ass. I told him that only a fool would include a personalized card with a poisoned loaf of bread, but that man doesn't have the sense God gave a goose." In a low voice, she leaned over and added, "The only thing I can think to do is for someone else to figure out who did it." The mayor shook her head and took a long sip of wine.

"I've been wondering about Ben O'Neill," I said. "I've seen him with Faith Zapalac a few times. Why do you think he's so keen on being mayor?"

"He's got plans for Buttercup," she said. "I have a feeling he's got some money-making scheme up his sleeve. There's been talk about rerouting 71 through Buttercup for years . . . that would ruin the town, but up the property values."

"That would be terrible for Buttercup!" I said.

"I know, but I don't think he's too concerned with quality of life."

"That would explain why he's buying up property. Why don't you put that on your campaign material?" I asked.

She shrugged. "I don't have any proof; it's just a gut feeling." She looked over at Rooster and sighed. "But I've got other things I'm worried about, like Molly. To be honest, I was kind of hoping you might do some of that magic you did when ol' Nettie got herself skewered."

"Quinn and I are looking into it," I confessed. "I was wondering: You've known Buster for a long time. Do you think he might be capable of poisoning his niece?"

"Poisoning a loaf of home-baked bread?" the mayor asked. "I would have figured him more for a six-shooter, but I guess anything's possible." She put a finger on her nose. "You know what? He did have a loaf."

"What do you mean? He wasn't on the list."

"Father Mikeska's cutting out sugar, so he's been giving all the home-baked goodies he's gotten to the less fortunate. I remember him saying he gave his loaf of bread and starter to Buster after church the other day. Although I doubt he'd have the wherewithal to follow the recipe."

"You never know," I said, thinking of the certificates I'd found at Krystal's house. I was beginning to think Buster was capable of a lot more than people gave him credit for. "Thanks for letting me know about that. I hope you'll tell Rooster about it, too."

"I think I'll do that as soon as we're done watching the show," she said, nodding toward the goats. "I hate to think of Molly rotting away in jail." She finished her mulled wine and crumpled the cup, and we both watched Hot Lips as she inched down the tree toward Peter. The entire town stood silent, mesmerized, as she put one hoof, then a second, down onto the ground, reaching her nose out toward the bread. She tore off a chunk and was starting to chew it when Tobias slid the noosed rope around her neck and grinned at me.

The town square burst into applause for the second time that evening.

It was late by the time Tobias and I drove back up the drive to Dewberry Farm, two frustrated goats bleating from the truck bed. It wasn't the most romantic ride I'd ever experienced.

Despite the excitement of the goat rescue, my thoughts were still with Molly. "Turns out Buster got Father Mikeska's friendship bread," I told him as we got out of the truck and headed over to the goat enclosure. "And Opal shared hers with her cousin, Dougie Metzger."

"Well, at least that's something," Tobias said. "Not that Rooster's going to bother looking into it."

"True," I conceded as we searched the fence perimeter. The wire was intact, but the gate was unlatched.

"I'm sure I latched it—and I can't imagine my mother didn't. How did this happen?" I asked.

"Either someone didn't close it, or your goats figured it out."

"Figured it out?"

"You might want to get a more complicated latch," he said. "Maybe a sliding bolt."

"I'll add it to the list. That's twice now you've helped me rescue my livestock," I said once we'd gotten the goats back into their home under Blossom's wistful gaze, securing the gate with an extra length of wire. It had been at least a month since she'd gotten out. I hoped she didn't pick up any tips from Hot Lips and Gidget.

As I finished securing the fence behind me, my eyes drifted down to the creek.

His gaze followed mine. "Any more digging?"

"I don't know," I said. "I haven't looked."

"It's dark, or I'd say let's go have a look now." He turned to me, then encircled me with his arms, pulling me close to his muscular chest. The rest of the world seemed to melt away as he reached down and tipped my chin up, then kissed me.

I have no idea how long we stood there, but a tug on my jacket caught my attention. Hot Lips had nosed through the fence and was trying to eat my sleeve.

Tobias released me and took a step back. "I guess we should get back and get our tamales," he said.

"I suppose," I said. "I'd almost rather stay here."

"Me too," he said, and there was a huskiness in his voice that made me shiver.

He leaned down and gave me one last lingering kiss, and we turned back toward the truck, hand in hand.

At least something was finally going right, I thought, trying to push down the thought of Mindy that kept trying to bubble to the surface.

Chapter 21

After chores and a quick breakfast with my parents the next morning, I climbed into my truck and headed to the O'Neills' house to ask some questions. They lived in a sprawling, Frank Lloyd Wright–inspired house with expansive views of the countryside. It was located up a long, winding drive; the O'Neills lived on a huge piece of property—and an expensive one, according to Quinn. I hadn't called ahead, but I'd learned since moving to Buttercup that most people didn't bother. The truck made a series of jarring clunks as I pulled in next to the O'Neills' sparkling white Ford F-250, and as I turned the engine off, I prayed it would start again when I wanted to leave. Dougie had mentioned Krystal's beau having a white truck. Could it be Ben O'Neill?

The front porch was wreathed in garlands, and a gorgeous balsam wreath adorned the stained-glass front door. I might not agree with the O'Neills' politics, but they had good taste in architecture, I thought as I admired the limestone porch and the large bungalow-style windows that lined the front of the house.

I knocked on the front door, a small tin of Lebkuchen in my hand, and hoped someone would answer.

I was in luck.

A puzzled-looking Hope O'Neill opened the front door, a wine glass filled with what looked like orange juice in her left hand. "Can I help you?" she asked.

"I just wanted to drop off some Christmas cookies and see if you had a minute to visit," I said, smiling.

"Oh," she said. "For a moment I thought you were a salesperson."

I decided not to be offended. "We're both still adjusting from Houston, aren't we?" I said lightly.

"Yes, I'm sorry. Please come in . . . and remind me of your name again?"

"Lucy. Lucy Resnick," I said.

"Oh, yes. You bought your grandmother's farm, didn't you?"

"I did," I said, following her into the house. It was as beautiful inside as outside, with wide-planked, honey-colored wood floors and cherry built-in shelves. A huge Christmas tree stood next to the tile fireplace, sparkling with white lights, and the air smelled like cinnamon and oranges—and liquor.

"Can I get you a drink?" she asked, raising her glass and walking into the kitchen. "I'm

254

on my second mimosa. Would you like one?"

"Actually, if you have any tea, that would be lovely," I said.

"I'll put a kettle on," she said, and gestured toward a chair as she put a copper kettle on the stove.

"Thanks for the cookies," Hope said as she fished in a canister for a tea bag. "The kids should be home in a day or two. They'll disappear quickly."

"How old are they?" I asked.

"They're both nineteen, and at college," she said. "They should be finishing up finals now, and they'll be home with their laundry soon."

"Do they like being in Buttercup?"

"They miss their Houston friends," she said. "I kind of do, too, to be honest. When you're not from around here, it's hard to break in."

"I hear you're pretty active at Word of the Lord Church," I said.

"We are," she said. "But to be honest, that's more Ben than me. I'm not much of a Bible-thumper."

"He's a big donor, too, I understand."

Her smooth forehead creased. "What? I mean, we give a little bit, but nothing huge. After all, we've got two kids in college."

Interesting. "How did you two meet?" I asked.

"Oh, we were set up by a friend in Houston,"

she said. "We've been married what . . . twenty years now?"

"That's a long time," I said.

"It is. I'm a lucky woman."

"First marriage for both of you?"

"For me, anyway. We actually met while he was still married to his first wife. Of course, we didn't start seeing each other until he divorced . . ."

"Of course not," I said, although I wasn't convinced.

"And of course," she continued with a grim smile, "I told him if I ever found him cheating, I'd kill him before I divorced him."

My eyebrows rose. "Well, at least he knows where he stands," I said.

"Oh, he'd never cheat on me. I'm the best thing that ever happened to him." She slugged down the rest of her mimosa.

"Are you and Phoebe Matheson close?"

"Heck no," she said. "All she talks about is her husband, and how everyone in the congregation is after him. I swear, it's gotten worse lately, too. She's like Velcro." She added another slug of champagne to her glass. "I can see why, though. He's good looking, and half the women at that church are swooning over him."

"Do you think he's a faithful man?"

She grinned at me. "To the church? Absolutely. To Phoebe? I couldn't say, but that woman would drive me insane."

"Was he sweet on anyone in particular?"

"Oh, he laid it on thick all around. Got all the widows in town paying his mortgage for him. He's a smooth operator, that one."

"Your husband seems to be looking at buying more land."

"Oh, he and Faith have their heads together all the time. He's full of big plans—he just has to win the mayoral race."

"What plans?" I asked.

She was about to say something else when the door opened.

"Hope, honey?" It was Ben O'Neill.

"Oh, hi, sweetheart. I was just telling her about Pastor Matheson's harem—and your plans for our little town."

O'Neill's face went dark. "Looks like happy hour started a little early." He turned to me. "I'm sorry, Ms. . . ."

"Resnick," I supplied.

"Ms. Resnick. It looks like my wife isn't feeling too well."

"I'm just fine, Ben. You just don't like my talking to people is all."

"Perhaps another time?" he asked, ignoring her and looking at me.

"Sure," I said.

"Come on over anytime," Hope called to me as her husband ushered me to the door. "It was nice talking to you!"

He walked me out and lingered on the front porch. "I don't know what she told you, but when she's like this . . ." He shook his head. "She's liable to say anything."

"I understand," I said. "So . . . I understand you're a big donor to Pastor Matheson's church?"

"Who told you that?" he barked.

"Oh, a little bird," I said.

"I think it's time you left," he said, the pretense of friendliness gone.

"Merry Christmas," I told him, and headed down the steps to the truck, glancing back over my shoulder. What had Hope O'Neill been about to tell me about her husband's plans? I wondered. As I opened the door to my own truck, I heard the sounds of raised voices from inside the house. I wasn't sure what kind of marriage the O'Neills had, but I got the feeling it wasn't very happy.

The truck's thumping took on a new, ominous rhythm as I pulled out of the O'Neills' driveway. As I drove toward town, the sound got louder, and the car started to drag to one side. I was still a half mile from town, surrounded by bleached pastures, when I hit a pothole. There was a very loud thump, followed by the sound of the engine revving up and metal scraping against pavement.

I said a few choice words as I steered toward the shoulder. When the car rolled to a stop, I killed the engine, then got out and peered under the truck. To my dismay, a large piece of the undercarriage seemed to have fallen off the bottom of the truck and was now wedged into the gravel shoulder. I stood up and scanned the area; the closest house was about a quarter mile away. I started walking, telling myself I could use the exercise and trying not to think about how expensive it was going to be to fix whatever had happened to my truck. Or whether it was fixable.

I reached for my phone, planning to call my parents, but it had died somewhere between the O'Neills' house and here.

The wind picked up as I got closer to the house, a low-slung brick ranch set about one hundred yards off the road. A giant cross adorned the front yard, along with a fading plastic manger scene surrounded by a few scraggly bushes.

I walked up the concrete front walk to the door, pulling my coat close against myself as a gust of wind hit me. The inside door was ajar, and the wind rattled the glass storm door. I knocked, then sucked in my breath.

A crumpled form lay on the linoleum floor of the front hall, a hand curled like a claw.

I reached for the handle of the door and yanked it open—thank God it was unlocked—and rushed to the prone figure. It was Ethel Froehlich, Wanda's friend from the Blue Onion. She wore a brown velour bathrobe that zipped up to her neck. Now, it was bunched up around her knees. Her pale legs were askew on the tan rug, riddled with dark veins.

I knelt to check for a pulse.

Nothing.

I dropped her arm—still warm—and ran to the kitchen, where I grabbed the phone and dialed 911. As I reeled off the details to the dispatcher, I surveyed the room. Two teacups were in the dish drainer; on the table was a plate with a few cookies and some crumbs. Who had Ethel been entertaining? I wondered as I told the dispatcher what I'd found and she promised to send an ambulance. I had just hung up when there was a knock on the front door.

That was fast, I thought.

I hurried to the front door to find the mail carrier, Alma Holz, holding a package. I should have known it wouldn't be Buttercup's finest.

"Lucy. What are you doing here?" she asked, looking puzzled as I opened the storm door.

"My car broke down. I was walking to borrow a phone, and when I got here . . ." I pointed to the prone form behind me in the hallway.

"Oh, no. Is she okay?"

I shook my head. "I called 9-1-1; an ambulance should be here soon. Or at least in the next hour or two," I amended, remembering that I wasn't in Houston anymore.

Alma looked at the package in her hand, and

then at me. "I was just going to drop this off, but I hate to leave you here alone . . ."

"I'd love the company, to be honest." It was creepy being alone with a dead person—particularly one you suspected might not have died of natural causes. I wondered what had happened to her. Heart attack? Stroke? Or something else?

As we stood on the front porch, the wind kicked up; I hadn't put a jacket on, and the chilly air cut right through my cotton shirt.

"Let's get out of the cold," she said.

"Are you sure?"

"The door's already open. As long as we don't touch anything, I'm sure we'll be fine."

As I followed her into the mothball-scented front hall, a cold breeze followed us. "When will they be here?" Alma asked.

"They're sending someone from La Grange," I said. "It'll be a few minutes."

"What should I do with this, do you think?" Alma held up the Harry & David box.

"Put it on the hall table, I guess," I said, pointing to the chunky oak table just inside the door. We both gasped at the same time. A letter addressed to Brandi Jenkins lay propped up against a porcelain angel. I recognized the jagged script immediately.

And so did Alma. "So that's who's been sending them," she said.

I looked back down at the prim-looking woman on the rug. "I never would have guessed."

"Me neither," the mail carrier said.

My eyes were drawn to a writing desk tucked into the corner of the living room, which opened up off the front hall. "Think that's where she composed them?"

"I'm guessing so. Looks like she was working on one when she died," Alma said. She was right; there was a half-full page on the desktop. I walked over and looked at it.

"This one's to Hope O'Neill," I said. It suggested, as usual, that her husband had not been particularly faithful, and chided her for not being a good wife. It seemed to be a common theme for Ethel. Her last name might mean "happy" in German, but she seemed to be anything but.

"Spreading the Christmas cheer, wasn't she? Look," Alma said, pointing to a half-crumpled sheet addressed to Phoebe Matheson in a trash can next to the desk. "I just delivered one to her last week."

"The pastor's wife, too?" I glanced down at the page. Several words had been crossed out; the letter looked like a draft. I skimmed the text; evidently Ethel felt that Phoebe had been an inadequate wife, and that because of her, the good pastor was being tempted into sin. I wondered if she was referring to Krystal.

"Because when a husband strays, of course it's

his wife's fault, right?" Alma said sarcastically.

"That's what she seemed to think," I said, looking at the letter. "It doesn't go into specifics, though."

"At least not in the draft," she said. "What a piece of work. Sending nasty letters anonymously isn't exactly the most Christian thing to do. And wasn't she picketing the Christmas Market just the other day because it was immoral?"

I glanced back at the prone figure in the front hall. "Think she died of natural causes?"

Alma's eyes widened. "Do you think someone killed her?"

"Someone killed Krystal," I said. "It might be a heart attack . . . or it might be because she knew something she shouldn't have. Or maybe one of her letters hit a little too close to home."

"What do you mean?"

"Maybe someone found out who was writing them and killed her because she knew something she shouldn't have," I suggested, thinking of the two cups in the kitchen. Someone had been here—and Ethel hadn't put away the cups or picked up the cookie plate. Had she fallen sick while her guest was still in the house? That would explain why the plate was out when everything else in the house was neatly tidied away. "I wonder if she was poisoned?"

"Poisoned?"

"That's how Krystal was killed," I said.

"I heard it was Molly Kramer's friendship bread."

"It was somebody's friendship bread," I said, "but I doubt it was Molly's. Did Molly get any letters?"

"No," Alma told me, "but her daughter did."

My heart sank. I looked over at Ethel. I was fairly sure what had killed her wasn't natural causes—and it wasn't Molly, either.

I looked down at the desk again. There was another piece of paper, one that had been covered in strange doodles. The numbers "1-2" appeared again and again, along with the initials "BK" inside a heart. Was she in love with a man with the initials "BK"? If so, who?

I turned to Alma. "Know anyone with these initials?"

She reflected for a moment. "Not offhand, but I'll think about it," she said. "What do you think the numbers mean?"

"I don't know, but she seemed pretty obsessed with them." I looked back at Ethel; she was full of secrets, it seemed. "Will you come with me?" I asked Alma. "I want to look at the kitchen again."

"Is that okay? I mean, if what you're saying is correct, this may be a crime scene."

"We won't touch anything," I said. "I just want to look."

With Alma trailing behind me, I walked through

the living room into the dining room, which was furnished with dark oak antique furniture, and into the small, brightly lit kitchen.

There was no friendship bread in evidence, thankfully—or much of anything else outside of the plate of cookies on the table. Four ceramic canisters were lined up neatly against the back of the green Formica backsplash, and a dish drainer sat next to the sink. With the exception of the plate on the table, the kitchen was spotless. "She was a good housekeeper, I'll give her that," Alma said.

"Brandi Jenkins was staying here," I said. "Do you think . . . ?"

"Think she killed Ethel? I mean, staying with her would probably be a nightmare, but other than that, what's her motive?" Alma asked.

Maybe Ethel found out Brandi had killed Krystal, so Brandi poisoned her to keep her quiet, I thought. But how had Brandi gotten hold of Molly's recipe card? I didn't say what I was thinking.

"Ethel got the cups, but she forgot the cookies—and this," I said, grabbing a napkin and using it to pick up a flowered ceramic teapot on the counter (I didn't want to leave fingerprints). Still using the napkin, I opened the top and looked inside. "This doesn't look like black tea to me," I said, pointing to the murky dregs of whatever was in the teapot.

"Probably herbal tea," she said.

I bent down to sniff it; it had a minty, almost medicinal smell. "I hope they analyze it," I said.

"You think it's poisoned?"

"I have no clue, but it wouldn't be a bad idea to find out," I said just as an ambulance pulled up outside.

Chapter 22

"I hope that's not a new perfume you're wearing," Quinn said, wrinkling her nose as I walked into the Blue Onion.

"No. My new scent is a perk of using Fred Sanger's loaner," I said. Alma had given me a ride to town in the mail truck, and I'd arranged with Fred to tow my truck. He'd taken pity on me and loaned me an old Ford pickup that smelled like gasoline and cigars. Which meant that I now smelled like gasoline and cigars.

"I found another body," I said.

Her hand leaped to her throat. "Oh, no," she breathed. "Who?"

"Ethel Froehlich."

She listened wide eyed as I recounted what Alma and I had found. "So Ethel was the poison-pen letter writer!" Quinn exclaimed. "How did she know all that stuff?"

"Nosy, I guess. Maybe too nosy."

"You think someone killed her?"

"If she found out something someone wanted under wraps, I can see a good motive. I hope Rooster looks into it; there were a lot of drafts at the house."

"Does he even know about the letters?"

"I mentioned them to him, but I doubt he paid any attention to me." I hung up my jacket and reached for an apron. "What can I help you with?"

"Just keep me company," Quinn said as she heaved dough onto a floured board. "You think the murderer struck again?"

"I think there's a good chance of it."

"You said she had company before she died. Any sign of who it might have been?"

"Nope."

"Brandi, maybe?" Quinn asked. "Although I heard she moved out. Is Rooster checking it out?"

"One of his deputies showed up. He asked if we'd touched anything and told me he was viewing it as a crime scene for now."

"I hope they don't find any friendship bread."

"I didn't see any, but I thought the same thing. There were a few drafts of letters on her desk, including one to the good pastor's wife."

"Really? Did it accuse her of sleeping with half the church's congregation?"

"Actually, it accused her of being such a bad wife that her husband was tempted to sleep with half the congregation."

"Nice. But no specifics?"

"No names mentioned . . . I was hoping it would call out Krystal."

"You really think the pastor and Krystal were together?"

"I don't have any proof, but I have a hunch. Who else but a pastor would get his girlfriend a sapphire cross?"

"True," she admitted.

"Speaking of poison-pen letters, I got one yesterday, too. Telling me that I was a harlot."

"Ouch. Don't tell Rooster that, or he'll think you're the one that killed her."

"At least it would get Molly off the hook."

"Your letter sounds like what I got, by the way," she said. "I don't understand, though; Ethel barely knew either of us. Why would she send us nasty letters?"

"It's a mystery," I said. "I asked Alma who else she remembered delivering letters to. I figured it wouldn't be a bad idea to have a list."

"Did Molly get one?"

"No," I said, "but Brittany did."

"I never thought I'd say this, but thank goodness Molly's in jail."

"I'm pretty sure Alfie bailed her out," I said. "Besides, even if she was in jail, you don't have to be there to poison someone."

Quinn grimaced. "That's not a happy thought."

"I know," I said glumly. "But still, why would Molly kill Ethel? Her daughter's missing . . . why would she care about what someone she barely knew wrote?"

"Maybe she thought the letter set Brittany off?" Quinn suggested.

"We're talking as if she actually did it," I said, "when what we need to be doing is figuring out who did."

"Are you sure it wasn't just a heart attack?"

"Maybe," I said, "but she was pretty young for that. Oh—and I found something strange."

"What?"

"A piece of paper with the numbers '1-2' on it, and the initials 'BK' inside a heart, over and over again.

"Someone she had a crush on?"

"That's what I'm thinking," I said. "I just don't know who."

"I'll think about it," she said. "It's not Buster . . . his last name is Jenkins. Besides, I can't imagine falling in love with Buster."

"No accounting for taste," I said.

"Well, yours is excellent. I know it's not at the top of your list right now, but are things any better with Tobias?"

I nodded. "We had dinner last night, and it went well. Except for the goats."

"We'll be talking about that for years," Quinn said, grinning. "Speaking of Tobias, he called. He thinks the puppy is ready to go home."

"Are you taking her?"

"I am," she said, smiling at me. "She's my Christmas present to myself."

"I think it's a terrific idea," I told her.

"How's the visit with your parents going, by the way?"

"Not too bad, but maybe that's because I've hardly been home. It's nice to have help with the chores, even if it does come with a healthy dose of advice from my mother. And my dad grilled steaks for dinner the other night; I think they feel sorry for me." I sighed. "I just wish we could figure all of this out before Christmas."

Quinn grimaced, a dab of flour on her nose.

"You know, maybe Krystal told Ethel something she shouldn't have," I mused.

"I can't imagine anyone telling Ethel anything."

I shrugged. "Krystal didn't have a proper mother. Maybe Ethel kind of filled in for that."

"Sad," Quinn said. "What are you up to, by the way?"

"We've got a cookie exchange this afternoon."

"The one at the Marburgers'? I wanted to go, but I've got too much to do before the market. Maybe you can ask Teena if she knows anything."

"I still haven't figured out that flower comment she made," I said. "Maybe she was talking about the datura in the poisoned bread? But that isn't right; she said to look *under* the flowers."

"Maybe she'll have more info today."

"Even if she does, I doubt it will hold up in

court," I said. Evidence provided by psychics generally didn't.

"She might at least be able to point you in the right direction," Quinn suggested.

"It's worth a shot. I'll take what I can get."

"What time's the exchange?"

"Three," I said.

"I'd take your mom's rental car," she said, wrinkling her nose again. "Unless you like gasoline-flavored cookies."

My mother and I pulled up at the cookie exchange at three that afternoon. The Marburgers' house was an old Victorian a block from the square, with gingerbread trim on the porch and a shingled roof that looked like it was made of slate. I could hear a happy bustle of voices inside as we rang the doorbell, and a moment later, Margaret opened the door.

"Lucy!" she said, smiling at me. "And Linda. It's been a long time, hasn't it? I'm so glad you could come!"

"Thanks for including me," my mother said.

"Of course!" she said. Despite the traditional house, Margaret's personal style was very modern; she wore her graying blonde hair cut short and a chunky modern necklace around her slender neck. She and my mother didn't look too dissimilar, actually—only my mother preferred pearls. "I'm glad you could make it," Margaret said with a smile. "I'm so sorry about Molly and Brittany. Any word?"

"Not yet," I said.

"And I heard you found Ethel Froehlich today," she said, her hand going to her necklace. "So tragic. Any idea what happened?"

"Nothing yet," I said. "Is Teena around?"

"Teena?" She looked confused for a moment. "Oh. You're thinking she might be able to help. She'll be home in a few minutes, I think."

"She's got an amazing talent."

Margaret shivered. "I know, and I wish she didn't. It's unreliable, but I guess it's worth a shot. Y'all come on in," she said, inviting us into the fragrant house. "Everyone's in the kitchen." The sound of "Jingle Bells" mingled with chattering voices floated in the air, and a huge tree decorated with handmade ornaments stood in the bay window of the living room.

"Thank you," I said, and we followed her through the house to the small, bright kitchen. The white counters were covered with colorful platters of cookies, and a throng of women in Christmas sweaters were gathered, coffee mugs and plates of cookies in hand. The voices dwindled away as I walked in, and everyone looked at me with wide eyes.

"Lucy!" Edna Orzak hurried over to me, breaking the silence. "I heard about Ethel. What happened?"

"I'm not sure," I said, "but hopefully the sheriff will investigate."

"I'll bet it was that woman, Molly, again. If it was poison, she didn't need to be there," Wanda Karp piped up. I resisted the urge to strangle her; we'd had enough deaths in Buttercup already.

"Good to see you again," I lied. "I didn't know you knew Margaret."

"We're in a knitting group together," Margaret supplied. "Wanda brought the gluten-free almond crescents." I glanced over at the platter she pointed at; the almond crescents looked more like concrete chunks than cookies, and I made a mental note to avoid them. From the large pile on the platter, it looked like I wasn't the only one who felt that way.

"You were friends with Ethel, weren't you?" I asked Wanda.

"Yes," she said, her face drooping. "I still can't believe she died. Do you think it was more of Molly's poisoned bread?" My stomach twisted.

"What did she put in the bread?" Edna asked.

"Jimsonweed seeds, from what I hear," Wanda said. "I've been trying to remember who had some growing in their yard last year."

"I guess we should steer clear of poppy seed cookies," Ursula Mueller joked, but there was a brief, uncomfortable silence as we all looked at the home-baked goods. Molly might not

274

have poisoned Krystal—and possibly Ethel—but someone had.

"You don't think Molly did it?" Wanda said, looking at me. "She wasn't very happy with her daughter hanging out with that girl. Maybe Brittany disappeared so she wouldn't have to testify against her mother."

"There's something funny about that church," Edna Orzak said. "Two parishioner deaths in a week now. I can't believe they're filming a television show there."

Wanda's mouth puckered, but she didn't say anything.

"Maybe, maybe not," Betty Zapp chimed in. "I think there's some kind of investigation going on."

"Investigation?" Wanda asked. "What kind?"

"My daughter works for the network in Dallas. She told me the company got burned a few shows ago, and now they're being super careful," Betty said.

"What do you mean, burned?" I asked.

"Big scandal with the priest—apparently he had a second wife up in Arkansas. The show went under after only about four episodes; the network pulled it. So now they're being extra careful."

"They're investigating Pastor Matheson?" I asked, thinking of the family's low-key response to their missing child . . . and Mindy's interest in Word of the Lord Church.

Was she the investigator? "Do you think the network knows the pastor's son has run off with Brittany?"

Betty nodded. "All of Buttercup knows. It's not exactly a state secret."

"True," I said, feeling a twist in my stomach at the thought of Brittany. Where was she? Was she safe?

"Pastor Matheson is beyond reproach," announced Wanda, who was clutching a gingerbread cookie and looking as if we'd just told her the church would be replacing the communion wine with vodka shots. "You seem to have something against Pastor Matheson," she said, looking at me.

She wasn't wrong. Not only did the good pastor seem totally unconcerned about the disappearance of his son with my friend's daughter, but from what I could see, he was using his charisma to get pensioners to sign over their checks and fund his lifestyle. But I decided not to share that. "I don't really know him," I said. "I'm mainly worried about my friend's daughter—and my friend."

Wanda's nostrils flared. "The girl who tempted his son?"

"We all know how young love is," Margaret said, stepping between Wanda and me.

"Speaking of love," Wanda added in a tone of voice that could have burned holes in her almond

276

crescents, "I hear your boyfriend's ex-wife is looking for a place in town."

What did this woman have against me? The rest of the women had quieted down again and were watching us intently. I didn't know what to say. I turned to Margaret. "When does the cookie exchange start?"

"We're just waiting for Faith," Margaret said. "She should be here any minute."

"We'll ask her about the house hunt, then," Wanda said with a malevolent look. "I hear Mindy's been spending a lot of time with Dr. Brandt lately."

"Wanda," Margaret said sharply. "Let's remember the reason for the season."

Wanda pursed her lips tightly, but she kept them shut. I reached for two coffee mugs, wishing there was something a little stronger available. Thankfully, the conversation had started again, although I could feel a few curious glances darted in my direction.

"What did you bring, by the way?" Edna asked.

"My mother's Lebkuchen," my mother said, taking the wrap off the tray. "And Lucy made some pecan brown sugar fudge balls."

"Ooh," Ursula said. "Lebkuchen with the icing? My mother used to make that; I haven't had it in years!"

"Why don't we head into the dining room?"

Margaret suggested, herding Wanda and the other ladies away from me.

A moment later, Teena burst into the kitchen, cheeks pink from the chill outside. Thankfully, my mother and I were the only two still there. "Oh. Hi, Ms. Resnick—and Ms. Resnick," she added, looking at my mother.

I smiled at her. "Hi, Teena."

Her mother came back in. "Teena!" She gave her a proud smile and said, "How did your chemistry final go?"

She groaned and reached for a cookie. "Don't ask. But the worst is over; all I've got left is English and PE."

"I'm sure it went better than you think," her mother said.

"Let's hope so." She took a bite of cookie and turned to me. "You're here about Brittany, aren't you?"

"Well, officially I'm here for the cookie exchange, but . . ." I nodded. "Yes."

"I can't believe she missed finals," Teena told me. "It's not like her at all."

"I know. We're all worried about her."

"Ms. Resnick was wondering if you had any inkling of where she might be," Margaret said.

Teena pursed her lips. "Actually, every time I think of her I get an image of a fireplace."

"A fireplace?"

She nodded. "I don't know what it means,

either. I don't get the feeling she's in danger, though. I get a sense of . . . confusion."

"Not in danger is good. But you have no feeling for where she might be?"

"She's not far, but she feels very far away," she said, and pursed her lips. "I wish I could be more helpful. That's the frustrating thing; I have no control over what I see or don't see. My great-grandmother had the sight, too."

"Anything about Krystal? Or Ethel?"

Teena was silent for a moment; I got the impression she was far away, somehow. "There's love," she said, her eyes looking blank. "Secret love. Hidden for a long time. It was going to come out . . . that's why they both died." Her brow furrowed. "But there are two loves, not one."

"Can you be more specific?"

"One feels passionate, tortured. The other . . . protective. Like an umbrella. I see lots of hearts."

Hearts. I thought of the paper on Ethel's desk. "Do the initials 'BK' mean anything to you?"

She was quiet for a moment, her eyes still staring into the middle distance. "Nothing, I'm afraid," she said. "Just a feeling of love and loss."

I stifled a sigh. "Thanks, Teena. If anything comes to you, will you let me know?"

"Of course," she said, and turned to leave the kitchen. "I hope you find Brittany soon." She cocked her head as if listening. "And don't forget the flowers."

"Flowers? What does that mean?" Was Teena talking about the Jimsonweed seed?

"Whatever it is, it's under them," she told me. "I think it's your grandma who keeps bringing it up."

I glanced at my mother, whose hand was at her throat. "My mother?" she said in a soft voice. "Can you talk to her?"

"I can try," she said.

"Tell her I love her," my mother said, her eyes looking misty. "And that her granddaughter's doing a great job with the farm."

My own eyes stung a bit as Teena smiled and said, "I'll do my best to pass it on."

I squeezed my mother's hand, but then Ursula called from behind me, "Do you have the recipe for these fudge balls? They're amazing!"

We turned to face the throng. "I'll get you a copy," I said, still thinking of Brittany—and of my mother's kind words.

I had no idea what to make of the flowers my grandmother seemed so insistent on telling me about, though—or the bit about two loves. Not for the first time, I wished the spirit world, or whatever it was that gave Teena her inside info, could be a bit more specific.

Chapter 23

Despite the smell of mulled wine and the crisp, fresh air, the Christmas Market felt much less festive that night when I swung by to drop off another batch of mistletoe. I'd called Molly before; she was finally home with the kids. "Alfie had to empty our retirement fund to pay bail," she said.

"We'll get everything figured out," I said.

"How?" she asked, sounding miserable.

"I used to be a reporter, remember?" I reminded her. "We'll figure it out. Hey . . . did Brittany tell you she'd gotten a poison-pen letter?" I asked, thinking of the handwriting I'd seen at the church.

"What? No," she said. "Why?"

"There have been a lot of them going around," I said. "And the writer just turned up dead—I found her in her house today."

"What? Who? We've been so caught up in the bail thing that I haven't talked to anyone today."

"It was Ethel Froehlich," I said.

"Poor thing," she breathed. "I met her a few times, but I didn't really know her. I'm so sorry to hear it."

"Me too. I'm hoping she died of natural causes, but . . ." I shivered, thinking of her claw-like hand. "She was pretty prolific. Krystal got one, Quinn got one, Brittany got one, and so did I."

"How do you know she sent them?" she asked. I told her about the handwriting we'd seen on the wall—and what I'd found at her house that afternoon.

"Very Christian of her," Molly said tartly. "Of course, that doesn't mean I wanted her to die."

"I know," I reminded her, hoping Rooster wouldn't accuse her of murdering Ethel Froehlich, too. "Anyway, Quinn and I are planning to visit the church again and see what we can find out."

"Do you think someone there might know where Brittany went?"

"I'm hoping," I said. "I did talk to Teena, though. She said something about a fireplace—and that Brittany's not far away. That she's safe, but confused."

"Not far? She didn't have any more information than that?"

"I'm afraid not," I told her. "She said she'd tell me if anything else came through."

"I hate this," she said. "Brittany's gone, and I don't know where to find her, the police believe I killed that poor girl . . ." She let out a small sob. "Last week, I was worried about getting Christmas cards out on time, and now . . ."

"I know," I said. "We'll get Brittany back, Molly. And we'll find out who did this."

"I'm beginning to think we're going to need a Christmas miracle," she said.

Now, as I arranged more mistletoe along the front of the stand, I realized I was afraid she was right.

My parents were doing the rounds of the stalls, my mother catching up with old schoolmates and doing a little bit of Christmas shopping. Over the past few days, she'd given me her expert advice on field rotation, fence building, and the condition of the farmhouse—which I knew could use a paint job—and to be honest, I was glad to have a break.

Unfortunately my mind kept turning back to Brittany—and Molly.

The picketers were still in force at the far end of the Christmas Market, and my eyes drifted to them. I felt a pang not seeing Brittany and her boyfriend among them. Where could they be? And why was the pastor so determined to keep their disappearance quiet? Either he knew where they were and was trying to convince them to come back quietly, or he was too worried about the impact on his church—and his upcoming TV program. Would the network think twice about inking the deal if they knew the pastor's son had run off with an underage parishioner? And was Mindy in town to investigate Pastor Matheson—

or was she really looking for property, possibly with an eye to rekindling things with Tobias?

I scanned the small group again. Wanda stood on one side of the pastor, looking even more self-righteous than usual, with his wife on the other. In the front were a few young people I didn't recognize and two families that must have been from La Grange.

Quinn and I had just sold another two Christmas cakes when Fannie walked up to the stall, looking remarkably merry. "Hi, Fannie," I said. "Any word on the coins?"

"Buster came and met with the appraiser and brought one of the coins with him," she told me. She was a thin, energetic woman with bright brown eyes and close-cropped hair. Her antique store drew tourists from Houston to Austin, and she was a pro at discovering valuable finds at estate sales. "If he has as many coins as he says he does, it's looking like Buster's got a fortune on his hands."

"And he's claiming he found them on his property?"

"He said he was using a metal detector on his twenty acres, and it went absolutely haywire. He dug, and turned up a jug full of Confederate coins. I think it's worth thousands. Maybe tens of thousands."

"That will help with Christmas shopping," I said.

"It does look like it's going to be a great Christmas . . . despite all the tragedies," she said, her face falling a bit. Then her eyes lit on the pile of vánočka bread, and she looked at Quinn. "Ooh, speaking of Christmas, can I have a loaf of that bread?"

"Of course," Quinn said, handing it over to her. She paid, and as she drifted away, Quinn said, "I don't think he found those coins on his property."

"And I don't know why he's still looking if he's already found a jackpot."

"Maybe it is someone else."

"I don't think so," I said.

"If it weren't for the fact that he didn't have access to Molly's friendship bread starter, I'd put my money on Buster."

"He did, though," I said. "Father Mikeska's cutting out sugar; he gave his loaf and starter to Buster."

"Really?" Quinn said. "So he's in the running after all."

"He and Dougie Metzger. And the Mathesons."

"You think?"

"I'm not ruling it out," I said. "I really think the pastor was Krystal's mystery boyfriend, though, which puts the Mathesons at the top of the list."

Before Quinn could respond, Brandi stumbled up to the stall, smelling strongly of liquor. She reached for the table and knocked two loaves of bread onto the ground.

"Why don't you come sit down?" I offered as Quinn scurried to pick up the fallen bread. I guided her into the stall and settled her onto the folding chair Quinn kept behind the counter. She wore a tank top and capri pants, and the skin of her arms was icy cold and covered with goose bumps. "Can we get you a drink of water?" I asked.

"Any of that mulled wine around?" she slurred.

"No," I said, glancing at Quinn. "But I'll go get you a hot chocolate. You must be freezing. I've got a blanket in the truck," I said. "I'll be right back."

I hurried to get the wool blanket, then bought a small hot chocolate from Bubba. I draped the wool blanket over Brandi's skinny shoulders and handed her the foam cup, hoping she didn't spill it on herself.

"Is there anything in this?" she asked, looking up at me with bleary eyes.

"Marshmallows," I said.

"Can I have some of that hot wine?" she asked.

"Hot chocolate's all I've got," I said as she slurped some of it down.

"It's good," she said. "Krystal always liked marshmallows."

"Did she?" I asked as Quinn turned to help a customer. "Were you two close as kids?"

"Yeah," she said, chewing up a marshmallow. "Had to be. Mother was gone, and Dad was always working, and then he died. Krystal always tried to take care of me. Even now," she said, tears welling up in her eyes. "Things were finally going to be good for us, and then she died. Just before our birthday, too."

"I'm so sorry," I said. "When is it?"

"The day after New Year's," she said.

"That's got to be so hard," I said.

"It's not awesome," she agreed, taking another sip of hot chocolate. As she lifted the cup, some of it sloshed over the side, splattering the blanket.

"You stayed with Ethel for a bit, didn't you?" I asked.

"Yeah, but I moved out; it was terrible. No liquor, and nothing but oatmeal and meatloaf. I'm sorry she died, though." She took another swig of hot chocolate, giving herself a foamy mustache. "I think she kind of took Krystal under her wing."

"That was awfully nice of her," I said. "Did she know your sister well?"

"She was sad that she died," she said. "Kept asking me about her. And asking about me, too. Nosy." Brandi drained the rest of the hot chocolate. "Sure I can't get some of that wine?"

I ignored the question. "Have you talked to your uncle about a memorial service?" I asked.

"I tried," she said. "But he wants nothin' to do with me," she said.

"Was he always that way?" I asked.

She shrugged. "After my dad died, we spent a few years at his house, and it was just awful," she said. "It's why Krystal and I moved to Houston."

"What happened to your parents?" I asked.

"My mom took off right after we were born, and my dad died in an accident when we were teenagers."

"I'm so sorry," I said. "Sounds like you had a really hard childhood."

"Probably why I started drinking. I know I shouldn't—Krystal always wanted me to stop—but once you're hooked . . ." She shrugged. "I was hoping rehab might help me get straight."

"Maybe you'll find a way," I said gently.

"Not now I won't," she said, her eyes welling with tears. She swiped at them and took another drink of hot chocolate.

Chapter 24

I had just finished milking Blossom and feeding the goats the next morning when the phone rang. I put down the pail and hurried to answer, hoping it wouldn't wake my parents.

It was Opal. "What's going on?" I asked. "Did you find Brittany?"

"No, but I got the report on what killed Ethel," she said.

"It wasn't natural causes?" I asked.

"Oleander," Opal told me.

"Oleander?" The long-leafed flowering bush grew all over the place; it could have come from anywhere. Including the Kramers'.

"It was in the tea," she said in a low voice.

"Molly's got an oleander bush in her yard," I said, feeling my heart sink. "Is Rooster trying to pin this on her, too?"

"Knowing him, he will," she said.

"You know Ethel was the poison-pen letter writer, don't you?"

"Yes," she said. "And I got a look at some of the drafts. She seemed to think everyone was having an affair. The mayor, the pastor out at that church . . ."

"I didn't know about the mayor, but I saw the one where she accused Phoebe Matheson of not paying her husband enough attention. Also, Father Mikeska gave Buster a loaf of friendship bread—and the starter, probably." I thought about the coin appraisal certificates I'd found in Krystal's house. Although Fannie had told me the coins Buster had brought in were the real deal, it didn't explain the strange certificates. Was Buster into some kind of counterfeiting business—maybe something that Krystal knew about? If so, it's possible that Buster decided to shut her down. Did he know anything about plants? I wondered.

"And I'm still trying to track down that cashier's check," Opal said. "But don't say anything to Rooster. If anything comes of it, I'm going to have to make him think this was all his idea."

"So . . . datura and oleander. Whoever did this knows plant poisons pretty well."

"Maybe a botanist?"

"Know any of those in Buttercup?"

"No," she said, crestfallen. "A lot of gardeners, though."

"That doesn't narrow it down much. I have the list of people Molly gave friendship bread to, though," I said.

"Read it to me," she said. "I know just about everybody in town."

I spooled through the rest of the names, but she came up blank. "I don't know about Mayor Niederberger and Pastor Matheson—why on God's green earth would she give that man a loaf of her bread, anyway?—but the rest of them wouldn't know a petunia if it jumped up and bit them."

"I'm pretty sure the pastor was Krystal's mystery boyfriend."

"I wish we could just ask him, but I doubt he'll fess up."

"Brittany might know," I suggested.

"Problem is, no word on where she is, either."

"Did Rooster file that missing person report?"

"I did," she said. "Sent out the license plate number of the Mathesons' SUV and everything. Not a peep."

"I just feel like everywhere I turn I'm at a dead end," I said. "But Krystal's and Ethel's deaths have to be connected, don't you think? Both poisoned by plants, both attend the same church . . ."

"Can't imagine we've got two poisoners runnin' around Buttercup. Leastwise, I hope not."

"Did Rooster ask the neighbors if they saw any cars at her house?" I asked. "There were two tea cups in the dish drainer; it looked like she had company."

"I know the cups and the teapot are in evidence, but I didn't hear anything about a visitor. I'll hint that he might want to talk to the neighbors. You'd think he'd figure that out himself, but with Rooster, you gotta tell him."

"Thanks," I told her.

"We'll get it figured out, Lucy."

"I hope so. Thanks for calling. Let me know if you hear anything more about that cashier's check—or about Brittany."

"Will do. You keep me posted, too." She paused for a moment. "And good luck with those goats."

"Thanks," I told her. "Obviously I need it."

I'd just hung up the phone when it rang again. I picked it up; it was Fred Sanger's gravelly voice.

"I wish I had better news for you," he said.

"What's the damage?"

"Broken axle," he said. "And you've got a huge oil leak."

I winced. How was I going to afford that? "How long will it take you to fix it?"

"I have to order a few parts, but I can get it done by the end of the week."

"I guess I don't have much choice, then," I said, feeling my stomach churn. Maybe my mother was right and I should have stayed in Houston, I thought as I hung up the phone and reached down to pet Chuck.

My dad walked into the kitchen, yawning. "Who was that?" he asked.

"Fred Sanger down at the repair shop," I said.

"What's the word on the truck?"

"Not good," I said. "It's going to be expensive."

"This hasn't been your best December, has it?"

"No," I said. At least things were going better with Tobias, I thought—even though Mindy's presence was still nagging at me.

I was just finishing up watering the lettuce when a red SUV came rolling up the driveway. I stood up and squinted; I didn't recognize the car. When Mindy stepped out of the driver's side a moment later, looking like a runway model in sleek jeans and a jacket that highlighted her curvy figure, I wished I'd put on something other than holey jeans and flannel.

I turned off the water and walked over to the driveway, where Mindy was waving at me.

"Hi," I said as I approached. "What brings you here?"

"You're good friends with the Kramers, right?" she said.

"Yes."

"I went by their house, but they're not home, so I came here."

"Why?"

"I think I know where their daughter is. Hop in and I'll take you to her."

Mindy's Lexus was a far cry from Fred's loaner. Instead of gasoline and cigars, it smelled like mint gum and perfume. I was almost relieved to see stacks of papers in the back and a bit of dirt on the floor mats; at least she wasn't entirely perfect.

"How did you find them?"

"I've been looking at houses," she said, "and we looked at one this morning that had a squatter in it."

"Was it the Simpsons' place?"

She nodded. "There'd been a recent fire in the fireplace, and there were dirty dishes in the sink. The logs were still warm."

I thought about what Teena had said about a fireplace, and goose bumps rose on my arms. "So someone's been there recently. Why do you think it's Brittany?"

"The boy she was with was driving a Range Rover, right?"

"He was. How do you know that?"

"I make it my business to know a lot of things," she said with a grim smile. "I saw the SUV parked a little bit off the road about a quarter mile away from the place. The house has been vacant for four months and it's out of the way, so I'm sure they thought no one would be by."

My heart leaped. "Oh, I hope you're right," I told her. "Thank you so much for thinking of Brittany."

"Well, I still haven't seen her, but I think the

odds are good that she's there—or at least she was. I just hope we haven't scared her off."

"Even if you have, they must still be close. We can call the police."

She nodded as she turned onto Kometzky Road. "I understand you and Tobias are seeing each other," she told me. "I hope it's not a problem that I'm staying in his guest room." She glanced over at me.

"Of course not," I said, trying to sound casual.

"He's a good man," she said. "He seems to really like you. I hope things work out for the two of you."

I blinked, not knowing what to say. I felt terrible for being so jealous . . . and jumping to conclusions. "Thanks," I croaked finally. "I have to admit I felt a little threatened when I found out you were in town. You're gorgeous, accomplished . . ."

She laughed. "Thanks, but I'm also a pain in the neck to live with. No, Tobias and I had a good run, but we're better not together." She glanced over at me again. "And don't worry . . . I'm not planning on a weekend house in Buttercup."

I'm a little ashamed to admit it, but I was flooded with relief. "No?"

"No," she said. "I'm here on business, actually. It's quiet, though. Can you keep a secret?"

"Of course," I said. "Why?"

"I'm only telling you because I think we have

a common cause. You want to find out who poisoned Krystal Jenkins and Ethel Froehlich, and I want to find out if the murders are linked to Pastor Matheson."

"You're working for the network, aren't you?"

"I'm in entertainment law," she said. "You can connect the dots."

Well, now I knew who was investigating Pastor Matheson. And I had confirmed why Mindy was in town—a reason that, thankfully, didn't have to do with Tobias.

"What do you know about the pastor?" she asked. "You can't say anything, though—I don't want anyone to know what I'm doing."

"Well, I know lots of widows are signing over their social security checks to him," I said. "I also know that would-be Mayor O'Neill gave the church a very big donation recently."

"How big?"

"Twenty-five thousand."

"That seems like an awful lot to give someone to support your political campaign," she said. "Unless you were planning to use the office to make more money, somehow . . ." she mused.

"Like getting Highway 71 diverted to Buttercup and selling off a lot of land?"

"That's a pretty good reason. Could there be another?"

"Good question," I said. "Could it be blackmail?"

"That's definitely a possibility," she said. "I keep looking for reasons someone might want to blackmail the good pastor, too. I get the impression that he's a big hit with the ladies—and that he's pretty fond of them, too."

I remembered how he'd lit up when he met Mindy. "Do you think maybe he took things a bit too far with someone? I don't want to talk out of school, but I'm beginning to suspect he and Krystal Jenkins were together."

"That's what I'm hoping Brittany Kramer will be able to tell us," she said. "We're both trying to figure out what's going on, and I thought we'd do better if we worked together. You used to be an investigative reporter, didn't you?"

"I did."

"I think we might be able to figure this out, then," she said, slowing down as we approached the house. "Look," she said, pointing to a narrow driveway leading into a copse of trees. "It's still parked there."

"And somebody's got a fire going," I said, looking at the smoke spiraling from the chimney.

"Let's go find out who it is, shall we?" she asked, parking at the end of the driveway.

Together we walked up the gravel drive. The curtains were drawn in the windows of the house, a '60s ranch, and as we approached the front door, my nerves started to act up. What if it wasn't Brittany and Bryce?

"Ready?" Mindy asked when we got to the front door.

I nodded, and she knocked.

Nothing.

She knocked again, and I heard the sound of footsteps from inside.

"Brittany?" I called. "Are you in there?"

Still nothing.

"Your mom is worried sick about you," I continued. "She's been arrested for Krystal's murder. I just want to ask you a few things."

Silence. Mindy and I exchanged glances.

"Please," I said. "I need you to help me save your mom."

There were a few more footsteps. We waited. A moment later, we heard the sound of a dead bolt snicking back, and Brittany opened the door.

Chapter 25

"Brittany," I said, feeling a rush of relief.

"Ms. Resnick, I'm so happy to see you. Is my mom okay?" she asked. Her face was wan, and she looked like she'd lost weight.

"She's worried to death about you," I said, and pulled her into a hug. Her thin frame relaxed in my arms.

"Brittany?" She tensed as a male voice called her name.

"I'm here," she said. "It's my mom's friend. Ms. Resnick."

Bryce Matheson walked up behind her, looking rumpled and angry. "You weren't supposed to answer the door!"

"Who's this?" Brittany asked, suddenly noticing Mindy.

"A friend of mine," I said without thinking. "Can we come in? It's chilly out here."

She looked back, uncertain, but then said, "Yes."

Bryce folded his arms over his chest. "Brittany!"

"They already know we're here . . . what harm can it do? Besides, my mom's in trouble."

"But . . ."

"Come in," she said, ignoring Bryce.

"Fine," he said, and stormed away. Brittany rolled her eyes. It looked like a few days in close proximity had swept away some of the magic.

"Thanks," I said, and Mindy and I stepped into the musty-smelling house.

"How's my mom?" Brittany asked as we followed her to the kitchen.

"Rooster thinks she killed Krystal," I said.

"That's ridiculous. My mother would never do something like that."

"I know that and you know that," I told her. "But we need to know more about Krystal so we can find out who really did kill her."

"How did she die? We've been holed up here without TV and phone . . . I have no idea what's going on."

"Poison," I said. "Someone put datura in a loaf of friendship bread and passed it off as your mom's."

"And Rooster believed it? What an idiot."

"Can you help us?" Mindy asked.

Brittany bit her lip. "I don't know what to do," she said. "I promised Krystal I wouldn't say anything, and Bryce . . ." She glanced over her shoulder.

"We're talking about your mom," I reminded her. "If you know something that might help, please tell me."

"Who is this?" she asked, looking at Mindy.

"She used to be married to Dr. Brandt," I said. "You can trust her."

"All right," she said, then leaned forward. "Krystal and the pastor were having an affair."

Mindy smiled like a cat who'd caught a canary, but said nothing.

I wasn't surprised to have my suspicions confirmed. "So Pastor Matheson was the mysterious boyfriend?"

She glanced nervously toward where Bryce had disappeared.

"Does Bryce know?" I asked.

"No," she said. "And I don't want to tell him. But do you think his dad's the one who killed Krystal?"

"I don't know," I said. "Do you know if his wife knew about them?"

"She found out," Brittany said. "That's why he had to break it off with her."

"Ouch," I said. "Just in time for Christmas."

"Krystal was devastated," she said. "Just before Thanksgiving, he told her he wanted to marry her."

"He's the one who bought her the sapphire necklace, then?"

She nodded.

"Did she say anything about a sudden windfall?"

Brittany looked puzzled. "Windfall? No."

"She didn't find buried treasure with her uncle?"

"Not that I know of," she said. "Of course, he was always over there digging around. It's possible he found something, I guess, but I always thought he was half-crazy."

"How did Mrs. Matheson find out?" Mindy asked, bringing us back to the topic of the affair.

"She got a letter that made her suspicious, and then she followed them," Brittany said. "She tracked them to Krystal's house."

"Her name was on the list of people your mom gave friendship bread to," I told her. "Do you think she would be jealous enough to kill Krystal?"

"That's awful," she said. "I don't know. I guess it's possible."

"Is there anyone else in the church who might have had it in for Krystal?"

"Most of the women in the church didn't like her," she said. "Everyone knew Pastor Matheson was sweet on Krystal."

"Did anyone in particular seem to have an issue with it?"

"Ethel and Wanda seemed upset about it. I used to call them his admiration society. I think half the women there had the hots for him, though, to be honest."

"Ethel's dead," I told her.

302

Her hand leaped to her mouth. "No. Poor thing. She was so broken up about Krystal."

"She was poisoned, just like Krystal." I didn't tell her she was the one who had sent Brittany the nasty letter.

Brittany's eyes widened. Just then there was a thump from the back of the house, and I was reminded of Bryce. "How are things going between you and Bryce?"

She grimaced. "Not great, honestly. The problem is, I don't know what to do. It was a stupid thing to do, but now I've missed my finals, and my parents are going to kill me."

"We'll get that worked out," I said. "I think they mainly want to know you're safe. How's Bryce feeling about things?"

She glanced back toward the hallway. She looked very tired and worried. "I think we're both ready to go home. I need to make sure my mom is okay."

"I think she's fine," I said.

"She won't be if she spends the rest of her life in jail," Brittany pointed out.

"Do you want us to talk to Bryce?"

"No," she said decisively. "Let me talk to him."

As Mindy and I waited in the run-down living room, she disappeared down the hallway. There was an urgent-sounding exchange of words, then silence. A few minutes later, Brittany reappeared, trailed by Bryce, who looked like a sullen twelve-year-old. They weren't holding hands anymore, I couldn't help but notice.

"We're ready," she said.

Alfie was beside himself with relief when Mindy and I rolled up the driveway with Brittany in tow a while later. Bryce had taken the Range Rover home. I had some qualms about sending him home to a suspected murderer, but I figured the odds were low that the Mathesons would do in their own child.

As Brittany stepped out of the SUV, Alfie rushed out of the house and pulled his daughter into a hug that lasted longer than any hug I'd ever seen. Then he stepped back and took her by the shoulders, peering into her eyes. "Are you okay? He didn't hurt you, did he?"

"I'm fine," she said.

"And you're not married?"

"No," she said. "We're not married. And nothing happened, don't worry." She gave a little shrug. "It was a dumb idea. Is Mom okay?"

"She's been better," he said, "but she'll be happy as a hog in mud now that you're back." He hugged her again. "Head in and give her a hug."

"She's not in jail?"

"Out on bail," he said with a grimace. As Brittany headed into the house, he turned to us. "Thank you, Lucy . . . and Mindy? Is that right?"

Mindy nodded.

"How on earth did you find her?"

"Mindy realized there was a squatter in one of the properties she and Faith were looking at, and scouted around. She found the Range Rover and figured out whose it was."

"I can't thank you enough, ma'am."

"My pleasure," Mindy said.

"And we found out something that might help Molly. It turns out the good pastor was having an affair with Krystal," I told Alfie. "Brittany told us about it when we found her. Pastor Matheson broke up with Krystal a few days before she died."

His eyebrows rose. "Do you think he killed her?"

"It's possible," I said. "Or more likely his wife did."

"Lucy's right. I get the impression he wouldn't know how to turn on an oven, much less bake something in it," Mindy said. "Since Brittany said the missus found out about her husband and Krystal, it's worth looking into." She paused for a moment. "If she did kill Krystal, though, why burn the place down later?"

"Maybe she wanted to make sure she was dead before destroying any evidence she might have left behind—poison isn't immediate. Or maybe her husband found out about what she'd done and went back to cover her tracks," I suggested. "The necklace was gone, too."

"What's up with the necklace, anyway?"

"Krystal got it from her boyfriend—the pastor. I think whoever burned the house down took it off of her after she died. But it still doesn't explain the dog."

"Molly did give the Mathesons a loaf of bread, so they would have had the card and a batch of starter," Alfie said. "I told Molly she was crazy to bake bread for them. She said she was just being Christian."

"So we have means, motive . . . and opportunity. I wish there were some way to find out if Phoebe Matheson ordered Jimsonweed seeds, though," I said. "Oleander's everywhere, but Jimsonweed is harder to come by."

"The sheriff should be able to look into that, shouldn't he?" Mindy asked.

"You've met Rooster?" I said with a sigh, and looked at her. "Although *you* might be able to charm him into it. And there's always Opal, thank goodness."

"So what do we do first?"

"I'll go check out the Red and White—I've been meaning to, anyway," I said. "It may be a long shot, but maybe Edna remembers someone buying seeds."

"What about Buster?" Alfie said.

"He may be doing illegal things, but I'm not convinced he's the one who did in his niece."

"And who killed that woman who was writing poison-pen letters?" Mindy asked.

"I figure she knew something she shouldn't have," I said. "She wrote a letter to the Mathesons; maybe one of them did her in so she wouldn't tell Mindy what the pastor had been up to. And since both Ethel and Krystal were poisoned, I'm betting the same person killed both of them. I know Ethel was friends with Wanda Karp; maybe she'll know something."

"I was planning to do a bit of digging on the connection between pastor and O'Neill today," Mindy said. "But is there anything I can do to help you out?"

"Yes, actually," I said. "There was a big deposit in Krystal's account recently. Opal was going to try to figure out where it came from."

"I'll see what I can find out," she told me. As we exchanged cell phone numbers and parted ways, I found myself feeling hopeful for the first time in days.

"How are things going out at Dewberry Farm?" Edna Orzak asked as I walked into the Red and White Grocery a half hour later.

"Just added goats to the menagerie," I said.

"I noticed," she said, eyes twinkling. "They're regular party animals, just like your cow. And big fans of Quinn's vánočka, too."

"Oh, that's right," I said, blushing as I remembered their Christmas Market outing. "Hopefully I've got them under control now."

"We'll see about that," she said as I drifted over to the seed rack. "What can I help you with?"

"I was wondering if you remembered anyone buying Angel's Trumpet seeds," I said, inspecting the rack. Sure enough, the slot was empty.

"Are we out?" she asked.

"Looks like it. Do you remember who bought it?"

"I don't think I was here when it sold," she said. "I can ask Milt, though." She gave me a curious look. "Why are you so interested?"

"Angel's Trumpet is also known as datura."

"That's what killed that girl, isn't it?" she asked.

"Exactly. If you can remember who bought it . . ."

Her eyes grew rounder. "You think the murderer bought them here?"

"You plant Angel's Trumpet in the warm season, not the cool season—it wouldn't be the time of year to buy seeds." I looked at the rack again. "But it's the only thing that's sold out."

"When Milt comes to spell me at lunch, I'll ask," she said. "Is that what killed Ethel, too?"

"Apparently not," I said. "Oleander was the culprit in that case."

"Do you think Molly Kramer really did them both in?" Edna asked.

"No," I told her. "I think someone set her up."

"That's mighty un-Christian of them," she said.

"So's murder," I pointed out.

"Of course," she said, with a shiver. "I just got back from a cookie exchange at the Lutheran church, and now I'm nervous about eating any of the cookies. What if we've got a lunatic in town? Like that awful man who filled those Pixy Stix with poison all those years ago? Or that Tylenol killer?"

"I don't think this is random," I told her, thinking of Phoebe and trying to imagine her baking datura seeds into bread for her husband's mistress, "but I guess it can't hurt to be extra careful."

Edna shivered. "And here you moved from the big city to get away from all that. Lots of excitement in town lately," she continued. "What with Buster finding Confederate gold after all these years."

"I'd heard about that," I said. "Did you talk to him?"

"Came in here and bought four cases of Shiner Bock," she told me.

"When was this?" I asked.

"Day after you found his niece. He didn't seem at all upset about what happened to the poor girl." She paused, and her eyes widened. "You know what? I remember who bought those seeds."

"Do you?"

"Yeah. It was one of those women from that new church—I remember because I asked why she wanted so much Angel's Trumpet. She told me it was for the church grounds; they were going for a Christian theme in the landscaping."

"Do you know who it was?"

"That's the thing. I know it was a woman, but she had on sunglasses and a hat, and a big coat. I thought it was kind of funny, like she didn't know if it was gonna rain or shine, so she just got ready for both."

"Anything else?"

"Not super young, but that's all I remember. I didn't know her; she's not a regular. My memory isn't as good as it used to be."

Although I was pretty sure I knew who it was, I still had one more person to talk to, just to confirm my suspicions. "If you think of it, will you let me know?"

"Of course," she said.

Still thinking, I said good-bye to Edna and headed out to the truck.

Chapter 26

When I pulled up outside Wanda Karp's house a few minutes later, I found myself thinking that it looked like something out of a storybook. Roses climbed over a trellis surrounding the front door; in season, I could tell they would be beautiful. Calendula bloomed along the front walk, interspersed with Johnny-jump-ups, and I recognized the gray-green leaves of poppy plants. The gardens were lush despite the winter weather; they looked like they'd been transported from England. There were a few dug-up spots here and there—she must have been working in the garden recently. I wished I had the time to make the front of my house look so beautiful, but between the livestock and the veggies, landscaping would have to wait.

I knocked on the door, hoping I'd find her home. I was in luck; a moment later, the sour-faced church secretary answered. Something about her reminded me of the witch in the gingerbread house in *Hansel and Gretel.*

"Can I help you?" she asked in a tone that sounded like she'd like to "help" me by directing me back to my truck at the end of a pitchfork.

"I was hoping to ask you a few questions about Ethel and the Mathesons," I said. I was hoping she could confirm that Phoebe Matheson had taken the bread and the starter home with her. "And I have to say your garden is just gorgeous. I'm jealous!"

"Thank you," she said, softening a bit.

"Do you have a few minutes to talk? I know you and Ethel were close."

"I have an appointment soon," she said, her eyes shifting to one side, "but I guess I have a minute."

"Thanks," I said. She opened the door enough to let me in, and I followed her through a dim, dusty-smelling front hallway into her Laura Ashley–esque kitchen. She sat down on a ruffled chair and gestured to one across the wooden table. Like the Mathesons' house, one wall was adorned with crosses, but although homey lace curtains framed the windows and flower pots with herbs sat in the kitchen windowsill, there was little in the way of Christmas decor. An antique hutch displaying crystal vases stood at the end of the homey kitchen next to my chair; on the wall beside it was a framed picture of Wanda with the pastor. She had a smile on her face, and it made her look softer, somehow— younger.

"Why are you concerned about the Mathesons?" Wanda asked. She didn't look particularly soft now, I noted, in her buttoned-up blouse, SAS shoes, and dark A-line skirt.

"Well, I was the one who found Ethel dead," I said. "And I know the two of you were close. I wanted to ask you about her relationship with Mrs. Matheson."

"We were close," she admitted, and her mouth turned down. "I was sad to lose her. It must have been her heart . . . I know she was having trouble."

"Actually, it's looking like she was poisoned."

Wanda swallowed hard, and after a tiny delay, her hand flew to her throat. "Poisoned? Who would want to kill poor Ethel? She wouldn't hurt a fly."

"I just found out she was writing poison-pen letters," I said. "I was wondering if that had something to do with her death."

Her lips thinned. "That's a rumor," she said.

"I found drafts of the letters in her house," I said. "I think it's more than a rumor."

She sighed. "If people followed the Lord's commandments, she wouldn't have had to write them."

That was one interpretation. "So you knew she was writing them?" I asked.

"She mentioned it to me," she said. "I told her it was a bad idea; if someone found out who was writing them, she could be endangered." Wanda sighed. "It looks like I was right, as usual."

"Did she ever write one to you?" I asked.

"Of course not!" Wanda said. "I would recognize her handwriting—besides, I knew she was doing it. And this town may be a hotbed of sin, but I assure you, I am not one of those . . . loose women. Plus," she added as she arranged her long skirt, "we were friends."

"There was also a piece of paper with the initials 'BK' inside a heart, and the number '1-2.' Do you know what that's about?"

Her eyes widened a fraction, but she shook her head firmly. "She never said a word about it."

"Sorry," I said, raising my hands. "I'm curious, though . . . how did she find out about all of those secrets?"

"It's a small town," she said. "Everybody knows everything, don't they?" She stood up abruptly. "Can I get you something to drink?"

"Sure," I said. "I thought you were late for an appointment, though . . ."

"I realized it was later today," she said. "I could use a cup of tea, anyway."

"Was Ethel friendly with the pastor's wife?" I asked as Wanda stood up and began bustling with tea things.

She gave me a sharp look. "Why?"

"It looked like she had a visitor before she passed."

"Why do you think it might be Mrs. Matheson?"

"Pastoral duties?"

"I doubt that was it." Wanda's fingers played with a slender chain around her neck; the rest of the necklace was hidden under her blouse. "If she was there, it was probably because she found out about that little hussy her husband was seeing—and figured out Ethel knew about it."

"What hussy? Do you mean Krystal Jenkins?"

"That's the one," she said as she filled the kettle. "It wouldn't surprise me if Phoebe did Krystal in herself. In fact, she probably used that starter Molly Kramer dropped off at the pastor's office to make the bread."

"Did you ever see them together? The pastor and Krystal, I mean?"

"I saw them kissing once, in the bride's room at the church. They didn't know I saw, but I saw how she lured him in. He would never have done such a thing if she hadn't seduced him."

Remembering how he'd lit up at the sight of Mindy, I wasn't sure I agreed with her assessment, but I suspected Wanda couldn't bear to think of her pastor pursuing someone other than herself.

"I know Mrs. Matheson was jealous of that girl." Wanda sniffed. "She did dress rather provocatively. And she practically threw herself at our pastor . . . but he's too much of a man of God to be truly tempted by a slattern like that." The vitriol made me want to scoot my chair back a little bit.

"Word is that he broke things off with her."

"I wouldn't be surprised," she said. "She wasn't quality, and Pastor Matheson is a quality man. Besides, he's a man of the cloth. He must have come to his senses."

Right. More likely he was worried discovery would interfere with his broadcasting contract. "So the pastor's wife knew about them?"

"Of course she did," she said. "She's not blind."

"Did Krystal and Phoebe ever have words about it?"

Wanda's eyes glittered. "I did see them arguing, now that I think about it. Yes. Mrs. Matheson told Krystal if she didn't keep her hands off her husband, she'd make her regret it."

"So she threatened her," I said. "When was this?"

"Oh, a few weeks ago," Wanda said.

"And you didn't tell the sheriff?"

"I guess I didn't think it was important. I figured the sheriff already found the killer. The police know what they're doing, after all. We should leave them to their work," she said in a tone of voice that indicated the subject was closed.

I sat in awkward silence for a moment, then said, "I noticed you were doing some digging in the front yard. Planting something new?"

"That wasn't me," she said. "It was a—" She

stopped herself. "An animal. It seems to have let up, thank the Lord. It got to a whole row of daffodil bulbs."

The kettle whistled, and she poured water into a flowered teapot.

I glanced around; the hutch drawer was slightly ajar, and I spotted something sparkly and pink inside. I looked closer; it was a cell phone. As Wanda busied herself with the tea things, I reached in and grabbed the phone. When I touched the "On" button, a beaming picture of Krystal and Brittany showed up on the screen. A blue-sapphire cross hung from a chain on Krystal's neck. Goose bumps rose on my arms, and I tried to look neutral as I lowered the phone beneath the table. I watched Wanda squeeze half a lemon into two cups before bringing them and the teapot to the table along with a plateful of cookies from a foil packet. I'd been barking up the wrong tree all along.

"Thanks," I said, eyeing the cookies and trying to act as if I hadn't just found a dead woman's cell phone in Wanda's hutch. A moment later, Wanda poured tea into the cups and pushed one over to me.

"I'm not really a big tea drinker."

"You should try it. It's my special blend," she said.

I raised the cup to my lips and pretended to take a sip as Wanda watched me with keen eyes.

"To be honest," I told her as I put the cup down, "I'm here because I was hoping you could tell me what you think of Phoebe Matheson." Maybe if she thought I suspected the Mathesons, I could get out of here in one piece.

"What about her?"

"Do you think she might have been jealous enough of her husband to kill someone?"

Wanda gave me a grim smile. "You think Mrs. Matheson killed Krystal Jenkins? It could be," she said, staring at me in a way that made me want to squirm in my seat. "But it really doesn't matter what we think, does it? The police said it was Molly Kramer," she said. "They found her recipe card, and her poppy seed bread."

"Was it poppy seed bread?" I asked, trying to sound casual. "I never got my loaf."

"The one Molly dropped off at the church office was poppy seed," she said, her fingers playing with the chain around her neck. "I just assumed they all were."

"Is that a new necklace?" I asked.

"Oh, no," she said, dropping her hand. "I've had it for ages."

I couldn't resist. "I'd love to see it."

She hesitated for a moment, then seemed to make a decision. "It belonged to my mother," she said, and withdrew a sapphire cross from the neck of her blouse.

It was a dead ringer for the one in the picture of Krystal.

"Very pretty. So," I said, "who owned that black dog that was digging up your garden, anyway?"

"I think it was just a stray," she said, then clamped her mouth shut. "How did you know it was a black dog?"

"Someone mentioned seeing it," I said. "Glad it's not bothering you anymore." I felt a bit queasy as I looked down at the tea. What had Ethel found out that made her friend kill her? I wasn't about to ask; it was time to get out of here. "At any rate," I said, standing up, "thanks for the tea. I should let you get to your appointment."

"Oh, it can wait," she said, with an edge to her voice I didn't like. "Why don't you finish your tea? I'll get some more cookies." She stood up and walked over to the counter.

"I'm good, actually," I said, heading toward the hallway, Krystal's phone in my back pocket. "Plus, my parents are in town . . . I really should go."

"I don't think so," she said as she lifted the lid of a canister on the counter. Something about her voice gave me chills. "Sit down."

I turned to see her aiming a small gun at me.

"It's loaded," she said. "I keep it in the cookie jar, just in case. And my daddy taught me how to use it. Now. Be a good girl. Sit down and drink your tea."

I sat down slowly, chastising myself for getting it all wrong—and for not telling anyone where I was going. "Why Krystal?" I asked. "She'd already broken up with Pastor Matheson."

"She was planning to tell that Mandy Vargas at the *Zephyr* that Ben O'Neill had an affair in Houston—a one-night stand with one of her friends," she said. "She was probably going to ruin the pastor's career next. Now, drink." She gestured toward the cup.

"Oleander?" I asked.

"I had extra from my visit to Ethel. I can shoot you, but this is easier."

I picked up the cup and pretended to take a sip. She was satisfied—for now.

"How did you find out Krystal was going to spill the beans about O'Neill?"

"I hear lots of things in the church office," she said. "The walls are thin between the pastor's office and mine."

"I guess that would have blown the big donations the O'Neills were making to the church . . . no point in giving money if it's not buying political support. And once she and the pastor broke up, you were afraid she was going to do the same thing to him?"

"Exactly. First she seduced him, and then she was going to ruin his career."

"He gave her that necklace you're wearing," I pointed out. "He must have had some feelings for her."

"She bewitched him."

"Why did they break up?"

"He came to his senses, like I said. Besides, if it came to light, it would interfere with the mission the Lord sent him to do."

"The television show?"

"Yes. She was a wicked woman," Wanda said, her eyes narrowing. "She deserved to die."

"Just like the dog that was digging up your garden?"

"That was just convenient," she said. "Drink more."

I took another fake sip and set the cup down. "You were in love with him, weren't you?" I asked, looking at the picture on the sideboard. "And Ethel figured it out."

"Ethel had secrets of her own," Wanda told me with a twisted smile.

"Like 'BK'?" I asked.

"Her daughters," she said. And it all clicked.

"Brandi and Krystal," I said. "She was their mother. But what was the '1-2' about?"

"Their birthday," she said, and I remembered Brandi telling me Krystal's birthday was the day after New Year's. "Ethel knew the pastor and Krystal were having an affair. She was trying to save her from what happened to her: pregnancy out of wedlock, and the shame of it. That's why she wrote all those letters, too—trying to save people from themselves."

Funny way to do it, I thought. But not something to die for.

"Ethel was always buddying up to Krystal. She even sent her an anonymous cashier's check when she found out she was having money troubles."

That explained the mysterious windfall. "Was she planning on telling her?"

"I think the shame was too much for her, to be honest."

"Why did you kill her? Did she figure out you'd poisoned her daughter?"

"At first she thought it was Phoebe who did her in, just like you. But she saw the friendship bread in my kitchen, and found out the pastor hadn't gotten his. She invited me over to ask me what I knew."

"And you poisoned her."

"I didn't plan to," she said. "But she figured things out . . . she knew about the dog digging in my garden. When she found out there was a dog in the house that burned, she put two and two together. She was going to tell the police."

"But she didn't."

"Fortunately, I brought some oleander with me, just in case. I'd sensed she might be a problem.

I had to stay for hours until she passed, though. Had to keep her from calling anyone."

"Why did you go back to Krystal's to burn the place down?" I asked.

"I dropped off the bread, but I didn't know when she'd eat it. I stole her cell phone when she was at church, and I'd cut the phone line at the house." Another thing Rooster hadn't figured out—or bothered to look at. "It takes a few hours to kick in," she said, "so I had to keep checking back, just to make sure it did its job."

"Thorough," I said.

"Always. Drink," she ordered. As I reached for the cup, I pretended to accidentally knock the handle, tipping the contents out onto the table.

She tightened her lips and raised the gun, training it on my head. "I can see I'm going to have to take a firm hand with you," she said. She refilled my cup from the teapot and handed it back to me.

"Drink it," she said, "or I'll shoot you now."

"That would be hard to explain away."

"I'll figure something out," she said, nodding toward the cup. "You can shoot someone for breaking and entering, you know. I'll say you were trying to steal my spoons."

I didn't have much choice. I drank it, letting as much as I could spill down my face. I put the cup down with about two inches left in the bottom.

"Finish it," she said.

I swallowed more, slopping it around, and put the cup back down again. She peered into it. "That was enough for Ethel, so it should be enough for you."

"What now?" I asked, feeling my heart beat fast. "How long does it take to work, anyway?"

"A few hours," she told me.

"So, we just sit and chat?"

"No." She opened the back door and waved me toward it. "Let's go."

I was wondering if I could get back to the loaner truck before she shot me when I felt the cold gun barrel nudge my back. The answer, evidently, was no.

"Where are we going?" I asked as I stepped out into the cold December afternoon. There were no other houses in sight, unfortunately . . . and a good portion of the fenced yard was ringed with oleander bushes. She hadn't had to go far for materials.

"The shed," she told me, pushing me toward a small gingerbread-decorated structure in the corner of the fenced yard. I walked over slowly, wishing I'd brought my jacket. If the poison didn't get me first, hypothermia might.

She opened the door. It was a gardening shed; the walls were lined with hoes, rakes, and trowels, and a stack of pots sat neatly in the corner. It didn't look like it belonged to a homicidal maniac, but I was learning that appearances could be deceiving.

"So, is murder part of Pastor Matheson's Sunday sermons?" I asked. "It doesn't seem a very Christian practice, to be honest."

"The goal is for his word to reach as many souls as possible," she said.

"Even if you have to extinguish a few?"

"If you've lived a wholesome life, you shouldn't be worried."

"No?"

"You'd be looking forward to heaven," she said. "Although in your case, I can see why you'd be nervous."

"I'm not the one committing triple homicide," I pointed out.

"The Lord will forgive me," she said.

"Well, I won't."

"You won't be around for me to worry about. Stand still," she ordered me. The next thing I knew, there was a sharp crack and the lights went out.

Chapter 27

It was still dark when I opened my eyes. It took me a moment to remember where I was; when I did, panic set in.

I sat up quickly, my head throbbing and nausea roiling my stomach—poison, or concussion?—and realized my hands and feet were bound together with duct tape. There was a strip of light outlining the shed door, but no windows.

At least it was still daylight; I hadn't been out too long. But if I didn't get medical attention soon, I'd be in trouble—if I wasn't already.

I heaved myself to my hands and knees, thankful she hadn't taped my hands behind me, and began inching around the plywood floor of the shed, ignoring my throbbing headache and searching for something to cut the tape from my hands.

My hands landed on a plastic bag—fertilizer or mulch, probably—and I tried to remember where I'd seen the garden tools hanging. To the left of the door, I decided as my stomach churned. Was it the oleander? I wondered, feeling panic rising in me. How long did I have before the damage was irreversible?

I lurched over to the other side of the shed, scraping my palms and knees against the rough wooden floor, then knelt and flailed my bound hands around. I could feel the smooth handles of the longer tools—rakes, hoes, and cultivators—but what I really wanted was garden shears. I felt around for another several minutes, knocking a rake onto my head in the process, before I gave up and started grabbing the long handles, hoping one of the tools was sharp enough to cut through duct tape.

The hoe was dull, and the rake's teeth were about as sharp as marshmallows, but the cultivator had some promise. I positioned my hands over the sharp tines, swallowing back bile, and rubbed the taut tape over a long tine, pushing down hard.

It punctured the tape on the third try, scraping my wrist and leading me to wonder when I'd last had a tetanus shot. Then I reminded myself that since I'd just been given a nice dose of oleander tea and was tied up in a maniac's garden shed, tetanus really wasn't my primary concern at the moment.

It took longer than I expected to weaken the tape enough to pull it off; my stomach felt like it was trying to turn itself inside out, and my head seemed to be on the brink of exploding, but if I stopped, I knew I was dead.

I fumbled until I got the tape off of my ankles, then crawled over to the door.

Locked. Of course.

I threw myself against it a couple of times, just to see what would happen, but only ended up with a bruised shoulder to go with the rest of my ailments. I gave up after a few minutes and paused to think, picking bits of adhesive off of my skin.

I could wait for Wanda to come back and bean her with a hoe, but there was no guarantee that the poison wouldn't kick in first. Ideally, I'd call 911, but my purse—and my phone—were still in Wanda's kitchen.

As I sat back down on the wood floor, I realized something was still in my back pocket. A moment later, I pulled out Krystal's phone.

The battery had been low—5 percent—when I'd opened it in Wanda's house, but maybe there was enough juice to call for help. I gripped it hard and touched the button, hoping the screen would light up, but nothing happened.

It was dead.

I squeezed my eyes shut, ignoring the shivers that had begun to course through my body. The poison was setting in. "Please, God, get me out of here so I can get Molly off the hook and spend Christmas with my parents," I prayed. A moment later, I caught the familiar scent of lavender. The hair stood up on my arms; I knew my grandmother was here.

"What now?" I asked the darkness.

All of a sudden, the phone in my hand vibrated and lit up.

"Thank you," I whispered, and dialed 911 with a shaky hand.

"Emergency services, can I help you?"

A human voice had never sounded so sweet. "Yes," I breathed. I told her my location and what was going on, hoping someone would get here in time to save me.

"How long ago did you ingest the oleander?"

"I don't know," I told her.

"We'll send the police and emergency services right out," she said. "Hang in there."

There was just enough time to say "thank you" before the phone went dead.

I tucked the phone back into my pocket and sagged against the wall of the shed. Help was coming. I just hoped I'd make it to the hospital in time to counteract the poison.

Less than five minutes had passed before I heard the sound of a door slamming shut.

It was too soon for EMS to have arrived. And if Wanda discovered I had pulled off the duct tape, she might go ahead and shoot me to be on the safe side.

As the sound of footsteps approached, I fumbled around the floor for the cultivator. I could hear the sound of a chain rattling against wood before I found it; as quietly as I could, I stood up and crept to the wall beside the door. When it swung open, I pressed myself against the rough wood.

She stood outside the door; I couldn't see her, but I could hear her, and her voice made my skin crawl. "I was right about you. You are trouble," she said as I stood with the cultivator raised over my head. After a long moment, she extended the gun into the space. I didn't wait for the rest of her to follow.

I brought down the cultivator on her hand as hard as I could. She swore—a most un–Christian oath—and the gun went off as it clattered to the floor. I felt a sharp pain in my leg as a bullet bit into it—but before I could do anything else, the door swung shut again, and I heard the click of a padlock.

I fumbled on the floor for the gun, trying to ignore the pain in my leg. A moment later, my hand grazed cold metal. I picked up the gun, wondering what to do with it. I couldn't shoot my way out of here—even if I did hit the lock on the other side of the door, the bullet might ricochet. And now that I was armed, she wasn't coming back anytime soon.

EMS was coming, I told myself. All I had to do was wait. As I leaned against the wall again, I heard shuffling from outside.

"What are you doing?" I asked.

She didn't answer, but a moment later, the sharp smell of gasoline reached me.

Wanda Karp was going to burn me alive, I realized, breaking into a cold sweat.

"Don't do it," I said. "The police are on their way. Please. If you let me go, I'll tell them it was an accident."

She didn't answer, but kept shuffling around. The smell of gasoline was stronger now. "Please," I begged, but it was no use.

There was a scraping sound, then the rushing sound of flames. A moment later, the scent of gasoline was eclipsed by the hot, sooty smell of smoke.

I banged the cultivator against the door as hard as I could, hoping I could knock the door off its hinges, but it held fast. Wanda had lit the far corner of the shed; as I watched, the wall turned orange, silhouetting the shelves leaning against it.

Was there fertilizer in here? I wondered. Was it explosive? I didn't know, but I didn't want to find out. I crouched down in a corner of the shed by the door, trying to avoid smoke inhalation and hoping I'd find a way to get out of here before the ceiling came down on my head. Already flames were licking the top of the shed's back wall.

What should I do? I wondered. I began beating the wall to my left with the cultivator, hoping it would knock it down so I could get out. It would probably bring the flaming ceiling down onto my head, but if I did nothing, the ceiling would come down anyway.

I hit the wall as hard as I could, but nothing happened, and the flames grew closer.

"Help!" I called out as the air around me grew thicker. My lungs burned; I knew how the puppy must have felt, I realized.

All of a sudden, I heard a voice that wasn't Wanda's. "Is anyone in there!"

"It's me!" I called, hope flaring. "Please . . . help me!"

"Lucy?" It was Peter.

"Get me out of here!" I yelled.

A moment later, there were three sharp blows—the ringing sound of metal against metal—and the shed door burst open. I took a step forward and filled my burning lungs with cold winter air as Peter stood in the doorway, the light shimmering like a halo around him. I'd never been so happy to see anyone in my entire life.

"Lucy," he said, only his voice sounded warped and strange. My stomach heaved, and the world seemed to spin around me. I let the cultivator slide from my hands and fell into Peter's arms. "She poisoned me," I gasped. "Oleander."

"When?" he asked, but before I could answer, the world went black for the second time that day.

Chapter 28

"Lucy?"

I swam up from a dream involving Wanda wearing a frothy dress and goat horns, chasing me around Dewberry Farm with a teakettle, and opened my eyes to Tobias.

"Oh, thank God," he breathed.

"Where am I?" I asked, moving my hand to touch him. I was attached to a tube—more than one, in fact. I was trying to remember what had happened, and why I was here. There was tea, and something about a dog . . .

"You're at the hospital," he said. "Peter brought you here himself when he found you in Wanda's shed. She poisoned you, then tried to burn the shed down with you in it."

It all came back to me. Thank God Peter had shown up, I thought. "And Wanda?"

"In custody."

"Rooster knows Wanda killed Krystal and Ethel?"

He nodded. "She was raving about it when he came to pick her up."

I felt tension I didn't know I was carrying seep out of me.

"I'm just glad you're okay," he said. "If you'd had any more of that oleander, or gotten here any later . . ." He shivered.

"She's awake!" my mother sang out from behind him as she and my dad squeezed through the door. "Oh, thank goodness. We were so worried about you!"

"I seem to be doing okay," I said, "except for all these tubes."

"We had to keep you hydrated," Tobias said. "But you should be out of here in time for Christmas."

"I didn't have time to finish making presents— or shop!" I said, struggling to sit up.

"You've had enough on your plate," my mother said.

"How long have I been here?" I asked, suddenly realizing I had no idea how much time I'd spent away from the farm. "Is Chuck all right? Are the goats and chickens okay? And Blossom?"

"You've been out for about twenty-four hours, but don't worry about the farm. Your mother and I have been taking care of everyone," my dad said.

"Oh, thank you," I said, sagging back into the pillows.

"It's kind of fun being on the farm when you're an adult," my mother said. "I can see why you like it out here."

"Really?" I asked.

"Really," she said. "And to see the community rally around you . . ." She turned to point at the shelf, which was covered with vases of flowers and plates of baked goods.

"Wow," I said. "Those are all for me? Everyone is so kind!"

"They all want you well," Tobias said. "And we checked them all for poison, don't worry," he added with a grin. "Mindy says thank you, by the way. She headed back to Houston with enough evidence to make the network have second thoughts."

"No TV show?"

"It's not looking like it. Mindy discovered Pastor Matheson was using much of the church funding to support his personal lifestyle—plus, the network didn't want the scandal of his affair to hit the news."

"I wonder if the church will survive?"

"A few folks are talking about returning to the local churches," Tobias said. "And some of the pensioners are looking to get their donations back."

"I hope there's still money left," I said, looking out the window at the gray sky. "That's a lot of news for one day."

"Oh, there's one more thing—Ben O'Neill has withdrawn from the mayoral race."

"Wonder why?"

"I got the impression there was a whiff of a

scandal with him, too," he said, "but I don't know the details. Mindy knows, I think, but she's not saying."

"Krystal knew O'Neill had had a fling with one of her friends. I think the pastor knew, too . . . that's why O'Neill was donating so much. That, and the political support; I think he was planning to support rerouting Highway 71 to Buttercup."

"Thank goodness he's out of the race then," my mother said.

Tobias turned to me. "Well, at least Buttercup is safe, but I can't get over Wanda. I can see killing her rival if she was in love with the pastor, but why Ethel?"

"Ethel was Krystal's mother."

He blinked. "What?"

"She was trying to do right by her girls. That's why she was so angry with Wanda when she figured out what she'd done—and why Wanda killed her."

"What about Krystal's windfall?"

"Ethel gave it to her, actually. Poor thing; her daughter died without knowing who her mother really was."

"So Krystal didn't find treasure after all. Speaking of treasure," Tobias said, "there's some news on those gold coins Buster brought to Fannie."

"What about them?"

"Well, according to Fannie, one of them was bona fide, but the rest? They're counterfeit."

"No wonder we found some fishy certificates of authenticity at Krystal's house," I said. "I'll bet he was having them sent to Krystal's address so no one would connect them with him. And that's why he was still digging."

"I do wonder what became of the infamous general's treasure, though. You think it was all a story, or do you think it's still out there somewhere?" my mother asked.

"And then there's that doomed man who was in love with a New Orleans girl," I said.

"I remember that, too," my mother said. "He died before he could come get her, right? And had lots of gold from pirating?"

"That's the gist of what Mary Jane told me," I said.

"We'll probably never know," Tobias said.

"Where is Quinn, anyway?" I asked.

Tobias grinned. "Walking Pip, probably."

"Who's Pip?" my mother asked.

"My new dog," Quinn announced as she swept into the room with a tray of maple twists. She smelled like bakery and lemon verbena. "You're up! I'm so glad to see you!"

"I'm glad to see you, too," I said. My head still hurt a bit, but my stomach seemed to be fine; in fact, it started growling as soon as I saw the rolls. "So she's officially yours now?"

"Yes, and I'm so happy she is. She sleeps curled up next to me at night . . . she's such a snuggler."

"That's wonderful!" I told her. At least someone in Wanda's crosshairs had had a happy ending, I thought. "I know how she ended up in the house now, by the way."

"Was she Krystal's pet?"

"Nope. She was a stray who was digging up Wanda's garden. When she went back to burn the evidence, Wanda put her into Krystal's house before she set it on fire."

"That's terrible!"

"I know," I said. "But what do you expect from a woman who thinks it's okay to poison a young woman and frame a mother?"

"Not to mention murder her friend," my mother added. "Or so I've heard. Why did she kill her, after all?"

"Because she was onto her," I said. I relayed what I had told Tobias earlier.

"Ethel knew about everyone else in town, too, from what I hear," Tobias said.

"And sent lovely little missives to them. But in a weird way, she was trying to help. She suffered from having children out of wedlock; I think she was trying to help others avoid the same thing, in a twisted sort of way."

Quinn shivered. "To think Wanda Karp almost killed you, too. How did you get Krystal's phone, anyway? Peter found it on you when he got you out."

"It was in a drawer in Wanda's kitchen," I said. "I have no idea why she left it there, but that's how I knew it was her. I never would have gone over there alone if I'd realized she was the killer. I thought it was Phoebe Matheson." I thought about how the phone had leaped back to life in the shed. "I'm really lucky it worked; I thought it was dead, but it came on just long enough to call 9-1-1."

"Think your grandma was looking after you again?" Quinn asked, and goose bumps rose on my arms.

"I think she may have been," I said, remembering the whiff of lavender in the shed. "Although having Peter around didn't hurt, either. How did he find me, anyway?"

"He was down at the fire station when the 9-1-1 call came in. When he and Walt Koch pulled up at Wanda's house, he saw the smoke."

"And all's well that ends well, or at least as well as it can, considering the circumstances," Tobias said. It hadn't ended well for two of the residents of Buttercup. "You're okay, Molly and Brittany are back with their family, and it's looking like it might even snow for Christmas."

"Snow? You're kidding."

He grinned. "I am, actually. About the last bit, anyway."

"How long until I get out of here?"

"Now that you're on the mend, we'll see," my mother said. "If you take it easy, it'll go faster."

"Got it," I said, fingering the cotton coverlet. "Well, sounds like things in Buttercup are doing well without me."

"For the most part, even though we missed you." Tobias grimaced. "There is a bit of bad news, though—other than what happened to Krystal and Ethel."

"What?"

"The Christmas Market fell five thousand dollars short; there's not enough to refurbish Bessie Mae's house."

"Oh, no. What's she going to do?"

"Mayor Niederberger's still working on it," he said. "I haven't given up hope yet. Something tells me it's going to come together. Teena thinks so, too. She says there's a last piece that hasn't fallen into place."

"Who's Teena?" my dad asked.

"The local psychic," my mother answered. "She's in high school and cute as a button; I met her at the cookie exchange the other day."

And she'd said something about flowers, too, I thought. What could she mean? Had she been talking about Wanda's garden, and the daffodils? Or the poison? I now knew what she meant about "two loves," at least. Poor Krystal. And poor Ethel.

"If I'm not careful, you're going to want to move back to Buttercup," my dad teased my mother.

"Why move back when I can just visit my daughter?" She reached out and squeezed my hand, and I smiled at her, a bit baffled.

"I'll have to get poisoned more often," I joked, although I was still rattled by how close I'd come to sharing Krystal's fate.

"Not on my watch," Tobias said, and my dad looked at him approvingly.

They discharged me from the hospital on December 23, and as my parents bumped up the long driveway to the farmhouse, I squinted at an unfamiliar red truck in the driveway. "Whose truck is that?" I asked.

"Yours," my mother said.

I blinked. "What?"

"Merry Christmas, Lucy," my dad said.

"You got me a new truck?"

"It's got twenty-five thousand miles on it, so it's not brand-new," he said, "but when I talked to the mechanic and he told me the repairs on your truck would cost more than the car . . ."

"You guys are amazing," I said, feeling a swell of gratitude. Tears pricked my eyes. "But I feel terrible. I'm behind on finishing my Christmas presents!"

"Don't worry about it," my mother said. "You

rescued a family and managed to avoid dying of poison or burning alive. From my perspective, I think that's gift enough."

"There's still another day," I said as my mother parked their rental car next to the truck. It was a zippy red, with a big cab and a cover for the truck bed.

"I can't believe you guys did this for me," I said, wiping my eyes as I got out of the rental car and walked over to the freshly washed truck. "It's . . . it's too much!"

"Nonsense. We figured you needed a bit of help getting started," my mother said. "Hop in and see what you think!"

"Are you sure?"

"Positive," my mother beamed, giving me a squeeze.

Even though the truck was used, the inside still had that new-car smell. It wouldn't for long, I knew, particularly with goats, but I'd savor it while it lasted. I ran my hand over the smooth dash and sank back into the seat—no duct-tape-covered rips. "This is amazing," I said, completely blown away by my parents' generosity. "I can't thank you enough."

"Let's go in and get some dinner," my dad suggested. "It's chilly out here, and I've got a batch of Quinn's baked potato soup warming up."

"Are you sure you two have to go home?" I

asked as I followed him into the farmhouse and bent down to pet Chuck, who was leaping as high as his portly body would allow. Which was about two inches.

"We'll be here until after New Year's," my mother said. "To help you get back on your feet." As I stepped inside, I smelled the scent of pine needles. A tree stood in the corner of the living room, right where my grandmother used to put hers.

"It looks just like it did when I was a kid!" I said, admiring the familiar ornaments. There was a felt cardinal on a holly branch, a wooden Christmas tree, a rotund porcelain Santa . . . "Where did you find these? I haven't seen these in years."

"I found the box tucked away in the attic yesterday," my dad said. "While your mom was with you at the hospital, I went out to get a tree and some lights."

"It's beautiful," I said, admiring the twinkling tree.

"Tobias should be here in a few minutes—I hope you don't mind," my dad said.

"Mind? Of course not . . . although I look awful."

"Nonsense," my mother said. "He's a really nice man, by the way. And he seems totally smitten with you."

I felt my face heat up. "You think?"

"She's right," my dad agreed. The phone rang before I could answer him. I grabbed it on the third ring; it was Molly.

"You're home!"

"I'm home—and thanks to my parents, I have a new truck."

"I wish I could buy you a new truck. I can't thank you enough for finding Brittany—and for getting Rooster to drop all the charges against me. But why on earth did you go over there all alone?"

"I didn't know she was the killer until I got there; I thought it was the pastor's wife. After all, you gave friendship bread to her, not to Wanda."

"How did she get it, anyway?"

"Didn't you drop it off at the church office?"

"Of course," she said. "Duh."

"How's Brittany?"

"Just fine. Apparently she and Bryce got into a big fight the first night, and neither of them could figure out how to call it off. They were embarrassed."

"So that's one more worry off the table," I said. "I'm so glad everything's working out—and in time for Christmas, too."

"That's why I was calling, actually. I wanted to invite you and your parents to Christmas dinner. And Tobias, too, if he'll come."

"That would be wonderful," I said.

"I've got to run, but I can't thank you enough."

"Just one thing."

"What?"

"Don't give any more friendship bread out, okay?"

She laughed. "As long as you don't drink any more tea!"

"It's a deal," I said, and we hung up.

The next morning dawned cold and clear. Frost sparkled on the tree outside my window, and the house smelled like bacon and coffee.

I slipped on my bathrobe and slippers and padded downstairs to where my dad was making breakfast. As I entered the kitchen, my mother came in from the back door carrying jars of milk, her cheeks pink.

"Did you just do my morning chores?" I asked.

"Knock 'em out before breakfast is what your grandpa used to say." She grinned. "Milking's done, and I've got more eggs if you need them, Ronald."

"I could use a couple," he said, and turned to me. "Scrambled, or fried?"

"Scrambled, please." I sat down at the table and did a mental survey of my Christmas gift situation. I had a tea cozy for Quinn, an unfinished scarf for my mother . . . and nothing for my dad, Molly, or Tobias.

"I was looking around the place the last few days. What happened to the clump of irises that used to be near the front door?" my mother asked.

"That's what I meant to do!" I said. "There are a whole bunch of irises by the old homestead behind Krystal Jenkins's house. I asked Mary Jane when she stopped by the hospital, and she told me I could go dig some up."

"I'll bet if we get them in now, they'll bloom this spring."

"And I could give a few as gifts," I said. It might not be fancy, but it was in my budget—and if I added some homemade soaps and some jams, it would make a nice basket.

"Are you sure you're feeling up to it?" she asked.

"Let's finish breakfast and head out," I said. "I haven't tried out the new wheels yet anyway. Maybe we can finish our shopping in town."

"The market's over," my mother reminded me.

"I know, but there are always some cute things at Fannie's Antiques," I said.

"Sounds like a plan," my mother said as my dad cracked eggs in the pan.

It was beginning to feel a lot like Christmas, I thought as the scent of cooking eggs filled the warm kitchen.

Despite the festive beginning to the day—and the luxury of driving a new truck—I felt a pang of sadness as my mother and I drove past Krystal's burned-out house.

"Poor thing," I said.

"I'm glad the person who did it got caught," my mother said.

I parked just out of sight of the partially blackened shell, and the two of us got out and walked over to the stone foundation.

"Who's been digging?" my mother asked.

"Probably the same person who was digging down on my land," I said as we returned to the truck and retrieved two shovels from the bed. "Buster Jenkins is my guess."

"Isn't he the one who tried to pass off counterfeit coins the other day?"

"The same one," I said, handing her a shovel. "He was Krystal's uncle," I told her as we approached the clump of gray-green irises by the remains of the foundation. "See that oak over there with the weird symbol in the bark?" I pointed to a tree about ten feet from the house.

"What about it?"

"See the holes all around the bottom? I'm guessing he thought that was a clue. The story is that it was buried by a tree marked by a fleur-de-lis."

"Well, I don't see any markings," my mother said.

"It was a long time ago. Who knows?"

We turned our attention from the oak and looked at the broken stone foundation. "Wow," my mother said. "When was this house built?"

"I have no idea. Late 1800s, maybe? It could be earlier, even; I have no idea."

"These irises must have been here ever since," my mother said. "These plants are probably older than your grandmother would be . . . isn't that weird?"

At the mention of Grandma Vogel, I thought again of the phone—and that whiff of lavender. "I wonder if whoever lived here brought them from wherever they came from?"

"They might be from Germany or Czechoslovakia, I suppose.

"I think we should leave some of them here, don't you?" she asked.

"We should probably divide them, though, so they have a bit more space."

"I think you're right," she said. "I'll go from this end if you'll take that end," she said, positioning herself at the far end of the clump.

Together, we dug, being careful not to cut through the rhizomes—which was challenging, because the plants were very dense—and separated the plants by hand.

"We'll have enough for every house in Buttercup," my mother said as I gently lined up the irises I had dug up and picked up my spade again. "Do you mind if I take some with me?"

"I hope you will," I said. "I wonder what color they'll be?"

"It'll be something to look forward to," my

mother said just as my spade hit something hard. "What's that?"

"A rock, I'm guessing." I knelt down and used a trowel to clear the dirt away. It didn't look like a rock.

"That looks like a jar, Lucy," my mother said as she peered into the hole.

"Maybe someone was making sauerkraut and forgot," I joked as we cleared the dirt away from around it. Together, we levered it out of the hole.

It wasn't sauerkraut.

"Is that what I think it is?" my mother asked as we gaped at the dirty jar. I looked at the irises. "Fleur-de-lis," I realized, was another word for "iris." That's how William had marked the treasure: not with a carving, but with flowers.

"I think we found Buster Jenkins's treasure," I said as the gold coins gleamed dully through dirt-caked, clouded glass.

"These are the real deal!" Fannie said two hours later as my mother, Mary Jane, and I stood at the counter in her store.

"How old are they?" I asked.

"They're not Confederate gold, if that's what you're asking."

"I didn't think so." I turned to Mary Jane. "Remember that story you told me about the man who buried his gold under a tree and marked it with a fleur-de-lis? Buster was looking for a carving, but it turns out the man meant he marked it by planting irises." I thought about it for a moment. "That's what Teena meant when she told me to look under the flowers!"

"Well," Mary Jane said, "maybe this gold didn't launch William and Violette's life together, but I bet we can use it to set a few lives right around here. How much do you think this is worth?" she asked Fannie.

"I'll have to research it, but I'd guess you're looking at a hundred thousand dollars, maybe more."

"A hundred thousand?" I asked, letting out a low whistle. "Really?"

"Well then," said Mary Jane. "That will go a long way toward fixing things."

"What do you mean?" I asked.

She looked at Fannie. "Officially, this belongs to the property owner, right?"

"From what I understand, yes, it does."

"Well then, it's mine to do with as I please, right?"

"That's the general idea."

"I think we should split it three ways," Mary Jane said. "A third to you, Lucy, as a finder's fee. A third to the town—that should take care of Bessie Mae's house, and put a new roof on the town hall besides. I'll take a third and salt it away for my grandkids' college education."

"A third as a finder's fee? That's way too much," I said.

She gave me a look. "I know how hard it is to start a farm from scratch. Take half to pay down your mortgage, and put the rest in a savings account for the lean years."

"I'm still not sure I can accept it," I said. "It's not mine. It belongs to you."

"Your grandmother wanted you to find it," Mary Jane said. "That's why Teena was telling you to look under the flowers. It's what she would have wanted."

"I feel guilty taking it," I said. "Maybe we can use some of it to get Brandi some help," I said, feeling a pang for the young woman who had died at the hands of one of her fellow parishioners. "That's what Krystal would have wanted."

"I think that's a great idea," Mary Jane said, and grinned at me. "I'll pitch in, too. Merry Christmas."

"It certainly is now," my mother said, beaming.

By the time Christmas Eve rolled around, I had something for everyone, and my heart was full as we drove to the Brethren Church for the candlelit service.

The Kramers were just walking in as we arrived; Molly broke away from her family and ran over to me, her heels clopping on the pavement. "You are the best friend ever," she said. "I hope you and your parents are still planning to come to Christmas dinner with us. Tobias said yes, too."

"We'd love to," I said. "I'll bring a pie. How's Brittany?"

"Her teachers are letting her make up everything over the break. I think she's back on track."

"Thank goodness," I said. "I'm so glad."

"Tobias is waiting for you," she said. "He saved a pew on the right side."

"Terrific," I said, smiling.

"I heard Mindy's gone back to Houston. And that Pastor Matheson's empire came crashing down."

"I just hope the pensioners get their money back," I said.

"Speaking of money, it looks like Krystal still had that cashier's check in her account. She had a handwritten will, too: once her bills are paid off, everything else goes to put her sister into rehab. Brandi's staying with us now; she seems to be doing better now that she can talk to Brittany about her sister." She pointed to where Brandi and Brittany were heading into the church together.

"Really?"

"It's like Krystal knew she was in danger, somehow," Molly said, shivering.

"Sad," I said, thinking of the young woman whose life was cut short so early. I hoped my grandmother—wherever she was—would take care of her like Krystal had tried to take care of her sister. "But at least maybe her sister will have a chance."

"Let's hope so," she said, grabbing my arm and turning to my parents. "I'm so glad your daughter is in Buttercup."

"Me too," my mother said as we stepped through the door of the church together into a room filled with greenery, candles—and Tobias's welcoming smile from a pew on the right.

It was going to be a merry Christmas after all.

Grandma Vogel's Lebkuchen Bars

Dough:
1/2 cup roasted hazelnuts
1/2 cup almond meal
2 3/4 cups sifted all-purpose flour
2 tablespoons unsweetened cocoa
1 1/2 teaspoons baking powder
1/2 teaspoon baking soda
2 teaspoons cinnamon
1 teaspoon ginger
1/2 teaspoon nutmeg
1/2 teaspoon cloves
1/2 teaspoon allspice
1/4 teaspoon cardamom
1/2 teaspoon salt
1/2 cup tightly packed chopped candied orange
    rind
1/4 cup tightly packed chopped crystallized ginger
4 tablespoons unsalted butter
3/4 cup dark brown sugar
1 cup honey
2 large eggs
1 tablespoon pure vanilla extract

Glaze:
3 cups confectioners' sugar
1 tablespoon kirsch, rum, or vanilla extract
3 – 4 tablespoons warm water

Combine hazelnuts, almond meal, flour, cocoa, baking powder, baking soda, cinnamon, powdered ginger, nutmeg, cloves, allspice, cardamom, and salt in a medium-sized bowl. Put the candied orange rind and crystallized ginger into a food processor along with 1 cup of the dry ingredient mixture and pulse until very finely chopped. Add the remaining dry ingredients and pulse to combine.

In a large bowl, cream butter with brown sugar at medium speed, then add honey and beat until smooth. Beat in eggs and vanilla to combine, then add dry ingredients by the heaping spoonful and beat at a very low speed until combined (a paddle attachment on a standing mixer is ideal for this). Scrape sides and bottom of bowl and beat again until evenly combined.

Line a half-sheet pan (13" x 8") with parchment paper, extending paper a few inches over the short sides. Lightly spray the unlined sides of the pan with nonstick cooking spray. Spread the dough into a thin, even layer and bake in the center of the oven about 25 minutes, until surface is dimpled and a toothpick inserted into the center comes out clean. The cake should be springy but firm. Cool on a rack.

While the cake is cooling, whisk confectioners' sugar with kirsch, vanilla extract, or rum, and add enough water to make a thin but spreadable glaze. Spread glaze on just-warm cake and let cool completely. When cool, slide the cake (with parchment) from the pan onto a cutting board and cut into bars.

Ideally, leave the Lebkuchen in an airtight container at room temperature for at least one day before serving to let the flavors meld. It will keep up to two weeks.

Quinn's Vánočka (Czech Christmas Bread)

1 package of yeast
1/4 cup warm water
1/2 cup sugar
1/4 cup butter
2 teaspoons salt
2 eggs
5 1/2 – 6 cups all-purpose flour
1 cup warm milk
1 teaspoon lemon zest
1/4 teaspoon mace
1 cup light raisins
1/2 cup nuts (Quinn likes pecans), chopped
1 egg yolk, beaten

Dissolve yeast in warm water. While yeast is dissolving, cream sugar, butter, and salt in a large bowl. Beat in eggs, then one cup of flour. When the mixture is smooth, beat in milk, lemon zest, mace, and the yeast mixture, then stir in as much flour as you can with a spoon (you'll add the rest later). Stir in raisins and nuts and turn dough out onto a floured board.

Knead in enough of the remaining flour to make a fairly soft dough that is smooth and elastic: this should take 3 to 5 minutes. Place the dough in a lightly greased bowl, turning once to grease the entire surface of the dough, then cover and let rise in a warm place until doubled.

When dough is ready, divide the dough into two equal sections. Divide one section of the dough into fourths (this will be the bottom braid): cover and let rest 10 minutes. While the first section is resting, divide the remaining dough into five sections, then cover and set it aside.

On a lightly floured surface, form each of the first four sections into 16"-long ropes. On a greased baking sheet, arrange the four ropes 1" apart. Beginning in the middle of the ropes, braid the dough ropes toward each end (you'll braid first one half of the ropes, and then the other). To braid the four ropes, overlap the center two ropes to form an "X," then take the outside left rope and cross over the closest middle rope. Then, take the outside right rope and cross it under the closest middle rope. Repeat braiding until you reach the end, then pinch the ends together and tuck them under. Turn the baking sheet and repeat the process to braid the opposite end. When the dough is braided, gently pull the width of braid out slightly. Then, on a separate pan or board, form the remaining five sections into 16"-long ropes. Braid three of the ropes together, then brush the four-strand braid with water and center the second braid on top; gently pull the width of top braid outward. Twist the remaining two ropes of dough together and brush the top braid with water, then place the twist on top of the second braid.

Cover the shaped dough and let rise till nearly double. While dough is rising, preheat oven to 350 degrees F. When dough has almost doubled, brush surface of the shaped dough with egg yolk and bake in oven for 35 to 40 minutes.

Bubba Allen's Glühwein (Mulled Wine)

1 (750 ml) bottle of dry red wine
1 orange, sliced into rounds
1/4 cup brandy (optional)
1/4 cup honey or sugar
8 whole cloves
2 cinnamon sticks
2 star anise
3 cardamom pods
Optional garnish: citrus slices (orange, lemon, and/or lime), extra cinnamon sticks, or extra star anise

Combine all ingredients in a nonaluminum saucepan, and bring to a simmer (not a boil) over medium-high heat. Reduce heat to medium-low, and let the wine simmer for at least 15 minutes or up to 3 hours. Pour wine through a strainer and serve warm with garnishes as desired.

Spiced Pear Jam

8 cups chopped or coarsely ground peeled pears
(about 5 1/2 pounds)
4 cups sugar
1 teaspoon ground cinnamon
1/4 teaspoon ground cloves

Combine all ingredients in a large, thick saucepan or Dutch oven. Simmer, uncovered, for 1 1/2 to 2 hours until jam sets (see below), stirring occasionally. Stir more frequently as the mixture thickens.

When jam has set, remove from heat and skim off foam. Carefully ladle into sterilized, hot half-pint jars, leaving 1/4" headspace. Remove air bubbles with a sterilized knife or spatula, then wipe rims and adjust lids. Process jars for 10 minutes in a boiling-water canner (Lucy uses a rack placed in a big stock pot). Yield: 6 half-pints.

How to tell if jam is set:

Put a plate in the freezer for about fifteen minutes. When jam has thickened and seems like it might be ready, put a spoonful of hot jam on the plate, then push your finger through it. If the surface wrinkles and the jam doesn't flood back in to fill the gap, the jam has set. If it's not ready, turn the burner under the pan back on, simmer for five minutes, and test again.

Brown Sugar Fudge Balls

2 tablespoons softened unsalted butter
2 cups light brown sugar
1 cup sugar
1 cup half-and-half
1 pinch salt
1 teaspoon vanilla extract
1 cup chopped pecans
32 ounces bittersweet chocolate or 32 ounces
    semisweet chocolate, chopped
3/4 cup chocolate sprinkles or finely chopped
    pecans

Coat inside of medium metal bowl with 1/2 teaspoon butter, then place remaining butter in the same bowl and set aside.

In a medium saucepan, combine sugars, half-and-half, and salt. Stir over medium-low heat until sugars are almost dissolved, frequently brushing down sides of pan with a wet pastry brush to capture sugar crystals (about 12 to 15 minutes). Increase heat to medium and continue to stir until it comes to boil, occasionally brushing down sides of pan (about 10 minutes). Attach candy thermometer and boil syrup without stirring until candy thermometer registers 234 degrees F (about 16 minutes); caramel will bubble vigorously in pan.

Move the thermometer to the bowl with the butter and pour caramel over butter (do not scrape pan). Add vanilla, but do not stir. Cool caramel until it reaches 112 degrees F (about 1 hour 30 minutes).

Using an electric mixer, beat caramel until sheen just begins to disappear and mixture thickens slightly, about 4 minutes. Stir in chopped pecans. Cool mixture until thick enough to roll into balls (about 2 hours).

When mixture is cool, line three baking sheets with waxed paper. Using about 1 tablespoon of mixture for each mound, spoon mixture into forty-eight mounds on one sheet. Press or roll each mound between palms of hands into a ball, then refrigerate 30 minutes.

When balls are cool, stir chocolate in medium bowl set over saucepan of barely simmering water until smooth and candy thermometer registers 115 degrees F (do not allow bottom of bowl to touch water). Remove bowl from saucepan and drop one ball into chocolate, using a fork to turn it and coat all sides. When ball is coated, lift ball from chocolate, allowing excess to drip into bowl, and slide ball off fork onto second waxed-paper-covered sheet. Repeat with fifteen balls, rewarming chocolate as needed to maintain temperature of 115 degrees F. While chocolate is still wet, sprinkle with 1/4 cup sprinkles or chopped pecans.

Repeat with remaining fudge balls and sprinkles/nuts in two more batches, placing sixteen balls on each of remaining two unused sheets. Chill balls until coating is firm (about 30 minutes).

Can be made two weeks ahead. Refrigerate in covered containers and let stand 20 minutes at room temperature before serving.

Mary Jane's Lavender Goat Milk Soap

13 ounces goat milk, frozen for at least 24 hours
6 ounces lye
12 ounces coconut oil
15 ounces olive oil
13 ounces palm oil or vegetable shortening
1 ounce essential oil (Lucy likes lavender)
pH strips for testing

Break up frozen goat milk into chunks and pour into a large glass or stainless steel bowl. Then put the bowl in a sink that is half-full with cold water and ice (it is important that the milk remains very cold).

Very slowly, add lye and "mash" it into the milk with a fork or stainless steel potato masher. Keep adding the lye until it is all incorporated, replacing the ice in the sink if it melts so that milk/lye solution stays very cold. The milk may turn orange or even tan to light brown, but if it turns dark brown, you will have to discard it and start over.

When the mixture is ready, keep it on ice while you heat the coconut, olive, and palm oils (or vegetable shortening). Measure them on a kitchen scale, then heat them slightly, until they are about 110 to 125 degrees F.

When the oils are ready, slowly pour the lye/

milk mixture into them. Mix by hand for the first 5 minutes, then use an immersion blender until the consistency is like cake batter or pudding. When it comes to a trace (when everything has emulsified and there aren't any streaks), add your essential oils and any additives and pour it into molds.

Wait 24 hours or more, then remove from molds and cut if desired. Let it cure for 3 to 4 weeks, turning the soap every so often so all sides have been exposed to air. The pH needs to drop to 8 to 10 so that it is gentle on skin. You can test the pH with test strips. Wrap soap when completely cured.

Notes:

Always keep goat milk frozen and the lye/milk mixture cold to keep it from scorching (turning dark brown).

Lye is caustic and can burn your skin. Wear long sleeves, gloves, and goggles (if you have them), and keep a bit of white vinegar handy in case you get any on your skin (the vinegar will neutralize the lye).

Use only stainless steel or glass bowls as plastic can pick up smells.

Acknowledgments

Thank you, as always, to my family (Helpful Spouse, Child #1, and Child #2, a.k.a. Eric, Abby, and Ian) for putting up with me (particularly during the grouchy bits), and the MacInerney Mystery Mavens for their support and suggestions! Thanks also to the amazing team at Thomas & Mercer for getting Lucy and Dewberry Farm out into the world and into readers' hands; I am so thankful for all you do! Thanks are always due to Maryann and Clovis Heimsath for getting all of this started, and to Jason Brenizer for pounding the keyboard with me so many mornings at Trianon Coffee. Speaking of Trianon, I'm thankful every day for the wonderful coffeehouse community that keeps me supplied with coffee, community, conversations, and interesting ideas. Thank you to Dr. John Unflat of Barton Creek Animal Clinic for answering my questions regarding veterinary care—any errors are mine, not his—and to Amelia Sweethardt at Pure Luck Dairy for letting me tour the farm and fielding all of my questions. And most of all, thank you to my amazing readers, especially my incredibly supportive, witty, and fun Facebook community. I couldn't do any of this without you.

About the Author

Karen MacInerney is the author of numerous popular mystery novels, including the Agatha Award–nominated series The Gray Whale Inn Mysteries and the trilogy Tales of an Urban Werewolf, which was nominated for a P.E.A.R.L. award by her readers. When she's not working on her novels, she teaches writing workshops in Austin, Texas, where she lives with her husband and two children. To receive subscriber-only free books, bonus stories, recipes, and deleted scenes—and to find out when new books are available—sign up for Karen's newsletter at www.karenmacinerney.com.

Center Point Large Print
600 Brooks Road / PO Box 1
Thorndike, ME 04986-0001 USA

(207) 568-3717

US & Canada:
1 800 929-9108
www.centerpointlargeprint.com